IRISH *Breath*

IRISH WOLVES LEGACY

ANNE GREGOR

OLIVERHEBERBOOKS

one

GRAY

"HOW CRAZY HAS THIS DAY BEEN?" Gray asked Mags and Blair as she fell onto the sectional where her friends were currently lounging. It wasn't as comfy as the girls' couch, but since they'd been asked to vacate their townhouse next door for the night, the slightly odiferous sofa would have to do.

Since finding out that their best friend, Bébhinn O'Faolain, had been stalked for almost two years, and that the freaky bastard had hidden a camera in the home they shared, specifically in Bébhinn's bedroom, Gray and her roommates were staying with their guy friends until Gray and Blair's fathers had their security company go through the whole house.

Gray shivered at the trauma her friend had been put through. The invasion of Bébhinn's privacy was horrifying.

The stalker, a teacher from TU of all things, had been arrested. At least Bébhinn would have peace knowing the wacko was behind bars. Still, they were all feeling uneasy that he'd been in their house. Gray had even met him. He was a member of Bébhinn's hiking club there in Dublin.

Her dad, Thomas MacGregor, and Blair's dad, Coll Barr, owned the security company that had installed their own system in their old townhouse. The two fathers were pissed that someone had been able to plant a separate camera inside the house without their knowledge.

So, it was no surprise to her or her friends that they were getting a newer, much more elaborate system installed in the morning, which was why they were forced to sleep at their next-door neighbor's place. Not Bébhinn, of course, her new man—an older, very hot new man—got them a room at the Fitzwilliam while they were stuck having a stinky sleepover with Bébhinn's cousins, Daniel and Jonathan O'Faolain, and Ciar Murphy, the third roommate and family friend. She honestly didn't mind. Bébhinn needed privacy and time away to heal.

All three of them were playboys, out with different women every other night. Still, the seven of them managed to be best friends. Their Irish, and American cultures blending seamlessly, and Russian on Ciar's part.

Mags and Blair, being much shorter than Gray's five-foot-nine, took the living room couches as their bed—the lucky bitches—but she was given Ciar's room while he would sleep on Jonathan's couch. Ciar was in his room now "tidying up," but the Lord knows what that entailed.

She was prepared to wrap a bath towel around her body if the sheets didn't look fresh. A shiver of disgust raced down her spine as pictures of cum stains peppering the bedding danced before her eyes.

Blair was lounging by her feet, so Gray nudged her with her toe to get her attention. Blair was deaf, and it was second nature to let her know by touch if she was about to speak. They all learned sign language as small children, and even though Blair was an excellent lip reader, it was dark outside, and the living room lights were low.

Gray signed, "Do you think Bébhinn is going to be okay?"

Blair sighed and rubbed her eyes. They were all exhausted. "It might take her a while, but she's strong. I know the camera," she winced, "was such a violation, but I think Dagr will help her move past it faster than anything else can."

"Blair's right," Mags joined the conversation, stretched out on the longer of the couch sections. "As crazy as today's revelations have been, I imagine Dagr's giant dick will make everything feel better."

"Jesus, Mags," Daniel growled as he walked into the living room. "Please keep my aunt's name and dick out of the same sentence."

The O'Faolains were a convoluted mess of family tree branches. Daniel swiped Mags' legs from the couch and sat down with a sigh. Jonathan joined soon after and sat by Gray, scooching Blair's feet over and dropping an armload of sheets, pillows, and blankets for the girls to make up the couch.

Last to join the tired group was Ciar. "I've pulled an extra blanket from the cupboard. We tend to keep the house freezing at night."

"And are the sheets questionable?" Mags questioned.

Gray swore that Ciar's cheeks pinkened at the razzing. Daniel spoke up then. "Ciar's never had a woman home. Isn't that right, Murphy?"

Gray felt her brows raise in disbelief. All three guys were serious whores, so this news came as a surprise.

"Fuck off, Dan," Ciar cursed. "I've an early morning meeting, so I'm off to bed. You better have cleaned off the shit covering your couch, Jon."

"I did, ye grouchy bastard," Jonathan mouthed back.

Had Gray not been watching, she would have missed Ciar's

wince. It was there and gone so quickly, she might have thought it was a trick of the shadows. Sad to admit, but she'd watched Ciar enough over the years that she'd learned his tells, and he didn't care for Jonathan's comment. At all.

Gray stood and thanked Ciar for lending her his room. "I'm to bed as well. Thanks for giving up your bed to me, Ciar. Night, everyone." The girls hopped up and called dibs on Daniel's bathroom, and with goodnights all around, Gray pressed down the handle of Ciar's bedroom door and entered his space for the first time ever.

It was tidy but definitely rocked his laid-back vibe. From the abstract, modern paintings to the plush wool rug covering most of the refinished wood floor, the black and cream theme screamed Ciar. He had a small painting on a stand on his desk that was different than the other art hanging on the walls.

It was a six-by-six oil painting, in grayscale, of a landscape. She bent forward, trying to decipher the location. "Russia," Gray muttered, which made sense. Ciar's mother was Russian, though he had never spoken of her.

Gray used his en-suite bathroom before climbing into the crisp white sheets covering the massive, extra-large king-sized bed. Ciar was tall like Daniel and Jonathan but more heavily muscled. The guys were always razzing him for how many hours he spent in the gym.

Muscled and tattooed head to toe...delicious. She shook her head at where her thoughts had wandered. Yes, Ciar was handsome. His dark hair and darker eyes had mesmerized many a woman. Gray refused to be one of them.

Ciar could afford to live anywhere, with anyone, but the man was nothing but loyal to his childhood friends. He was a few years older than Daniel, but according to Bébhinn, who had always lived in Dublin, Ciar and her cousins had been running rampant in the foggy streets of Dublin since they were children.

Gray might have grown up in Scotland, but her family was close to the O'Faolains and had attended all the same parties. Ciar and his father were considered family and had always been around.

She took a deep breath and stretched her arms above her head, trying to get comfortable. Mistake. Ciar's unique scent filled her nose as soon as her chin dipped close to the pillowcase. That man smelled like, well, he smelled like a dirty dream.

It was some combination of spice and tobacco. The Dunhills that she had occasionally caught him smoking smelled good enough that she'd almost considered trying them herself. Of course, she didn't, as she cared about her health, and her dad would kill her, but damn, they smelled good on that man.

She tossed and turned for what felt like days, but a glance at her phone revealed she'd only been rolling around Ciar's bed for just under two hours. It was close to two in the morning, but sleep seemed as impossible as it had when she'd first lain down.

Kicking off the covers, she decided to go in search of water. The boys' townhouse was the mirror of the girls', and she was able to traverse the layout without light.

Finding the cabinet that held the glasses, she grabbed one, filled it with plain tap and leaned back against the sink and sipped the room temperature water. It was much quieter than their house ever was in the evening. The four girls either played music, ran box fans, or had a television's drone for background noise. Even Blair, whose life was silent, preferred music. She said the low bass was soothing against her skin.

Gray was about to rinse her glass and put it in the sink when her ears picked up the soft shuffle of feet. Her skin instantly prickled in alarm, having just found out that a stalker had targeted one of her best friends, so when Ciar filled the doorway, her body tensed for a whole other reason.

"Christ, Gray. You scared the shit out of me," Ciar

announced once he cleared the threshold and noticed her presence.

She swallowed the moan swimming in her throat at the sight of Ciar dressed in tight, black boxer briefs. His heavily muscled chest and tattooed body, highlighted by the moonlight, had her heart pounding.

"I couldn't sleep. You?" Gray asked with what she hoped was a casual tone.

"Jonathan is a snoring prick, and that couch may have cost a mint, but the bloody thing is shit to sleep on."

She couldn't help but laugh. "Damn, I feel even worse for taking your bed. Here I was, thinking about how quiet it was. Your bed is lovely, though," she managed to tease without sounding flirty. She hoped. Ciar never needed to know she held even the slightest flame for him.

"I'll trade you bunks," he offered teasingly. "You done?" he asked, pointing at the half-empty glass of water in her hand.

At her nod, he took it and shot back the rest of the water. For some reason, that move felt awfully familiar and had her stomach clenching.

He was standing close enough to feel the warmth of his skin grazing hers. Up until this moment, she'd ignored that she was only wearing a thin, white sleep tank and barely there matching shorts, but when his eyes dipped to her chest, Gray's body involuntarily arched toward his gaze.

She felt her nipples harden under his stare, which instantly flicked to her eyes. His black gaze skimmed to her tongue as she licked her suddenly dry lips.

He took a cautious step to the side, putting his chest parallel to hers. One of his tattooed hands gripped the sink's edge at her back. She fisted her hands to stop from placing them against his sculpted chest, but as he moved infinitesimally closer to her lips, she gave in.

Without warning, she dragged her fingers over his hardened nipples, lightly scratching her nails against the raised bumps. His moan emboldened her exploration. He never moved, only his muscles, which jumped wherever her hands traced.

"Gray," he breathed her name against her mouth. "Can I—"

She didn't let him finish asking before closing the gap and licking into his mouth...and that was all it took. He took her mouth the way she's never had it taken—deep, dirty, needing air but not caring.

He grabbed her ass and lifted her against him so she could wrap her legs around his waist. She whimpered at the pressure and heat between her thighs where his sex was hard, hot, and insistent.

"Ciar," she moaned as he ground his hips against her.

"Christ, Gray, Christ." His moan and raspy words were loud in the quiet house.

He bit her lip before licking back into her mouth. The fingers gripping and kneading her ass were slowly getting closer to where she needed them.

"Jesus, Ciar, are you watching porn in the fucking kitchen?" Daniel asked from the living room, startling the would-be porn stars a part.

Daniel must have given up his room for Mags and Blair. She felt her face burn hot at what they'd almost been caught doing and how close she'd been to letting it go way further. Ciar let her slide down his body but kept a firm grip on her hips.

"Fuck off," Ciar barked. "Just getting some water and watching a video my buddy from the States sent. I'm back to bed."

Daniel's light snores were his only response. Gray's shoulders sagged in relief. She wouldn't have minded getting caught so much as she would have regretted it had they gone any further. She needed to know where Ciar's head was first—the one above his shoulders.

Sensing the moment was over, he brushed his thumb over her bottom lip and whispered, "I'll walk you back to my room."

At her nod, they walked as quietly as possible to his door, both of them hesitating at the threshold.

Feeling out of her element and unsure of what to say with a man she'd known most of her life, she settled for, "Goodnight, Ciar."

He didn't answer until he'd tucked her long, wavy golden hair behind her ear. "I'll be back in two days. Will you text me while I'm away?"

"Yes."

"I...I," he stuttered, "have a dinner meeting the night I get back, but the day after...will you meet me?"

"Where?"

"Anywhere."

"Yes."

two

CIAR

"WHAT THE FUCK?"

"What the fuck?"

"What the fuck?"

Ciar repeated the same thought quietly to himself while traveling to the airport, during the car ride to his boss's office, and while standing in the gold and black bathroom of the office high-rise, observing his reflection in the mirror.

He'd managed to get less than an hour of sleep after going back to Jonathan's room. His body flashed hot, then cold, then hot again. It sounded grossly similar to what his granny called "The Menopause." Clearly, not just for women.

He'd kissed Gray. "You did more than that, boyo," he muttered, instantly regretting the memory of how it'd felt rubbing his dick between her thighs. He clenched his jaw when he felt himself getting hard at the thought. Walking into an important team meeting with a boner wouldn't win him any favor from his humorless boss.

He still wasn't sure how the kiss had even started.

That was a bald-faced lie. The moment he'd walked into the kitchen and seen Gray's rocking body in those small bits of white cotton, he'd salivated at the thought of tasting her. He'd wanted her for so long that he'd become an expert at hiding his thoughts.

She never showed him special attention or treated him differently from Dan and Jon. But last night her eyes had naked want in them, and he purposely crowded her, forcing her to make the first move if she wanted.

And she had. If Daniel hadn't interrupted him, he had no doubt that he would have ripped the tiny shorts down her long-ass legs and slid inside her without thought of right, wrong, or consequences of taking her bare.

He'd never taken a woman without a condom in his life. He was only twenty-six. Kids were not in his ten-year life plan. But he would have done it. In his desperate excitement that she finally noticed him, he would have taken her in any way possible.

He was driving himself crazy about whether or not she would regret what happened. Regret him. She hadn't texted even though he knew she would have already gone on her morning run. Plus, her father was in town overseeing her town-house's new security system, so she would be meeting MacGregor for sure.

That shit that went down with Bébhinn's stalker was difficult to comprehend. He hated that the stalker had been near any of the girls, especially Gray. Ciar was sure MacGregor would hang around another day or two to ensure his daughter's safety.

He washed his hands after taking a piss and was about to leave the bathroom when his phone dinged. He would never admit it, but a small—very small—gasp left his lips as her name came across his screen.

Gray: Good morning.

His heart was thumping out of his chest. It's not like she said, "Good morning. I masturbated in your bed last night." He needed to calm down, but as his thumb hovered over the keyboard, he wondered if he should play it cool or talk about what happened.

Ciar: Good morning to you. How was your run?

There. Simple but shows interest.

Gray: Great. I really love the new shoes Bébhinn got me started on. Blair and I are going to breakfast with our dads in thirty. What's up with you?

Ciar: I have a meeting in ten.

Gray: Oh, well, I'd better let you go. Have a good day.

"Shit!" There's a vast difference between playing it cool and disinterest. He typed and deleted a few times, sweat beading his brow from stress.

Ciar: I wish I were home to take you to breakfast.

Gray: When you get back, I'll let you. Bye, Ciar.

Ciar: Bye, Gray.

He felt a smile tug at his lips as he pocketed his phone and headed to the conference room. He tended to be quiet by nature, not standoffish, really, just not as quick to laugh as someone like his father. His dad always teased that he got his stiff upper lip from his Russian ancestors.

He hoped that was the only thing he got from his maternal side. His mother's cruel indifference was record-setting. His father had a one-night stand with the exotic Russian bartender, which resulted in his conception. She'd managed to care for Ciar for eight years. Though "caring" for him was a stretch, as Ciar could still vividly remember the gnawing hunger of starvation. He'd lived with that feeling long enough never to forget.

His mother dumped him off in the middle of Murphy's Pub on a swinging Saturday night with a note pinned to his shirt that Ciaran was his father, and her name, Anna Morozova.

He'd never been to school and spoke only Russian. Needless to say, his father had been a saint to take him on. Ciar had always felt, if not different, then a bit of an outsider, but he had a good life, and the best father a man could ask for.

The Garda came round a month later to inform his father that Ciar's mother had been found dead. She'd finally overdosed.

He'd learned as a young boy to stuff the anxiety that threatened to smother him at unexpected moments into a mental box. He was good at compartmentalizing. He learned to enjoy the moment, to be proud of his grades in school, his milestones and success in business, and with women, of course. All of which kept his mind sharp and free of that pesky voice that tried every so often to tell him he wasn't worth the effort.

The day crept by in excruciating increments. His boss was a prick with the personality of drying paint, but the sonofabitch turned water into wine and real estate deals into gold. Ciar had managed an internship the summer before his last year of uni.

Mr. Anders looked like an old-school American mobster and acted in a similar Godfather fashion. Still, amazingly, he took a shine to Ciar and offered him a position on his personal team. He was given a year to prove his worth, or he could "Fuck off," as Anders so eloquently put it.

Now here he was, at the top of his game. A cutthroat shark that people feared when they saw him coming after their property or business.

And what was that cutthroat beast currently doing? Checking his texts like a teen who'd just grown his first chin hair. He was currently sitting at a luxe booth in one of Anders' newest swanky pubs in London, waiting for Mr. Dagr Griffiths.

He wanted to dislike the man on principle, simply because he dared touch the late, great Hugh O'Faolain's baby girl. Reality was that Dagr was sharp, successful, wealthy, and loved his best friends' cousin, or aunt as the case may be in that convoluted family.

He was in town sorting out his London firm before they went to Colorado. The man was making moves, buying out a law firm in Dublin, and purchasing enough property for him and Bébhinn to live. Griffiths was at the top of his game, and Ciar appreciated the man's single-minded focus and prowess.

The O'Faolains' possible newest long-lost family member had arrived and was cutting his way through powerful men and elegant women, lifting a hand to Ciar in greeting, who lifted his glass of vodka in return.

Ciar stood as a matter of respect and shook Dagr's hand. "Griffiths."

"Murphy," he smirked, slapping him on the back.

"Glenmorangie 18, neat," he told the bartender, making himself comfortable on the swivel barstool next to Ciar.

"I expected to see your new girlfriend at your side."

"Bébhinn wanted to spend time with her friends after

everything." Everything being the arrest of his girlfriend's stalker. "As soon as we checked out of our room at the Fitzwilliam, she asked to spend time with her friends. They were all eating dinner tonight with the family and MacGregor and Barr. She's protected," he added grimly.

"Hugh O'Faolain didn't raise a weak daughter, and for that, I'm thankful as I'm sure you are. She'll come out of this stalker shit stronger than ever."

Dagr took a long pull on his drink before setting the glass down, twisting the crystal this way and that before responding. "She is strong. Still, I would kill that man for watching her. Us."

Ciar didn't respond. There was nothing to say because he would feel the same. "I fly out late tomorrow afternoon. You?"

"First thing in the morning. I'm showing Bébhinn the law firm property I've bought. It has two full floors that she can renovate into living quarters if she wishes."

"You move fast," Ciar noted.

Dagr shrugged. "When you know, you know. The only hurdle was her family, and they've accepted us. I would have taken her as mine regardless, but for her sake, I'm glad it didn't come to that."

Ciar's phone beeped. *Oh, Christ.* Gray.

Gray: The new security is installed. I hope you don't plan on walking around our properties naked because Dad has every angle covered.

Ciar: I'll keep my nakedness confined to my bedroom…and yours.

Fuck. Fuck. Fuck. Why had he sent that?

"Do you normally blush when you text?" Dagr said, smirking like he was the funniest man alive.

"You can fuck right off, Griffiths."

Gray: I wouldn't kick you out.

Oh damn. Ciar had to shift on his seat to put his semi in a more comfortable position, all the while keeping a running dialogue with Dagr while staring at his phone wearing a perma-grin.

Ciar: I'm out with Dagr for drinks. You're making my trousers uncomfortably tight.

He was escalating their conversation quickly, but he couldn't make himself stop. Switching his attention back to the man sitting in front of him, who was wearing a knowing smile, Ciar said, "I appreciate the invite to Colorado. I haven't taken a real holiday in years, and I've never been there."

"Dad's folks left us several properties around the world. We sold most of them, but Colorado has always been one of our favorite places to visit," Dagr explained.

Gray: And you make my panties uncomfortably wet.

Jesus Christ and all His Saints. "I...I...yes. Nice," was all Ciar could manage as he stared at his phone screen.

Ciar: Gray. You're killing me.

"How long have you had a thing for Gray?" Dagr asked.

Ciar fumbled his phone like a comedian on stage, barely catching the damn thing before it crashed at his feet. "I'm sorry. What did you say?"

"You heard me."

> Ciar: I have to go. You are so going to regret teasing me, little girl. I bet you'd enjoy receiving a nude courtesy of me.

Ciar sighed and set his phone down—with difficulty—before giving his full attention to Dagr. "What would you know of it?"

"Only what Bébhinn has told me."

His smug look said he knew Ciar wouldn't be able to let that comment go. He was right. "What did she say?"

"That you and Gray stare at each other whenever the other isn't aware of the attention. That you aren't as promiscuous, her words, not mine, as the others think. That you secretly moon—again, her word choice, not mine—over her best friend."

Beep.

> Gray: I bet you'd like one of me more.

"No comment." *So many, many comments.*

"Well," Dagr held up his tumbler of whisky between them and tapped the rim with his finger before swallowing down the rest, "Colorado should be interesting then."

> Ciar: Please.

"We'll see."

Ciar could barely fit his large body and even larger hard-on in the backseat of the Uber after his drink with Dagr. *I bet you'd like one of me more.* Her words cramped his body with need. Surely, she was only teasing him. Was he teasing her, though?

It was eleven by the time he stepped out of his shower. His eyes met the foggy mirror, taking in his body, slick and damp from the shower. Just in case she was serious about this sharing shit, he quickly snapped a picture with the black marble countertop, cropping just enough of his junk for modesty.

He'd never sent the equivalent of a "dick pic" in his life. The fact that he was considering sending one now to one of his best friends was a second level of screwed up.

"Fuck it." He pressed send before he could talk himself out of it. It wasn't like it was a true dick pic. He saw waving dots immediately. "Oh, Christ." He quickly dried his body and slipped on boxers, all the while eyeing his phone like his life depended on it.

Waving dots.

Nothing.

Waving dots.

Nothing.

Waving dots... "Fuck me," he groaned.

Leaning against his headboard, he touched the photo so it filled his screen...and there she was. Fresh from the shower, dripping water with steam wrapping her body.

"Gray," he moaned. His obsession was naked with a perfectly placed arm crossing her full breasts, and the other cupping her sex.

His mouth was dry. His heart was about to explode. He needed more.

three

GRAY

"WHO IN THE hell are you, and what have you done with my best friend? You sent a man a nude. Have you lost your mind, Gray?" Blair was so worked up that she was signing and speaking some of the words. "And if your dad found out. I shudder to think."

Gray could only sit on the bench next to Blair's back garden oasis with her shoulders slumped in mortification. Sending the picture had made her feel powerful last night, but with the morning sun came a boatload of regret.

She had to tell someone, and Blair was the likeliest candidate. She refused to tell Mags because she would have kicked Gray's butt after what happened to her in high school. Mags had sent a picture to her boyfriend of her in a sexy bra and panty set. The boy had shown his friends. Jonathan and Daniel kicked his ass.

Mags was so embarrassed because the whole family found out. Gray and Blair's dads had explained that they should never put anything out in the world that could ever be used against them. A picture may start on your phone and end up on every social media site around the world.

Not that she was in any way worried about that happening. This was Ciar they were discussing, not that Blair knew that. Gray only said she'd been seeing the guy and that their back-and-forth messages had gotten carried away.

"I know, Blair. I trust him completely, though."

"How can that be if your best friends haven't met him?"

She should never have started this conversation. If Gray explained who it was, Blair would be surprised but excited for her, the picture forgotten. However, she wasn't ready to say anything because Gray didn't even know if Ciar was serious about seeing her or if she was just another woman in a long line.

"You'll have to trust my judgment." At Blair's raised brows. "I had one lapse! Let it go. I wanted to tell you, not because I don't really like the guy, I'm just...I can't believe I did it. I did cover all the bits. Kind of."

Gray felt her face blaze once again. Never had she ever sent a guy a nude, but after Ciar sent his, she wasn't exactly thinking clearly.

His body was a work of art and not because he was covered in ink. The night in the kitchen, she caught glimpses, but nothing like his bright bathroom lights had shown. Just thinking about his ridged abdomen and sharp V-line had her panting.

She'd gotten a peek of trimmed, dark hair and the base of his penis above the marble countertop. She'd stared at that counter for hours, wishing it away.

Blair touched her leg to get her attention, leaving behind her calling card, a smudge of soil. "You're right. Sorry, I freaked out. If you trust him, then there's nothing to worry about. This isn't high school. We are adults," she grinned and patted my leg, leaving another trail of brown before kneeling between her plants again.

The reminder that Gray was, in fact, an adult did make her feel better. She could own her sexuality and not feel silly or guilty over it.

Blair twisted enough to ask, "Well?"

"Well, what?"

"Did he send you one back?"

Gray grinned. "He sent one first."

***

Gray finished tying the bow on her favorite cream-colored wrap dress. She kept her hair long and wavy, with minimal makeup and jewelry, and a killer pair of nude heels.

Her mom surprised her dad this morning, flying in from Scotland. They were taking Gray out to dinner at a swanky steak restaurant that a friend of Bran's owned. It was a good thing they had the connection. Otherwise, she and her parents would never have been able to get in at such short notice.

She was able to shake off her embarrassment about sending the sexy picture after Ciar messaged her before lunch. He'd told her that he'd dreamed about her. When she asked what he dreamed, he said that it was too X-rated to text a woman he hadn't even taken out on a first date.

She'd been walking around with a stupid grin for hours now. Her parents should be here any minute. Picking up her phone and clutch, she went to the front of the house to wait. She had worked on a plan for opening Ciar's new high-end pub. He'd purchased the property a year ago and hired O'Connor Hospitality to help make his dream a reality.

It was an exciting project and one that she'd already spent countless hours on. Her mom had given her the project, of course, as she and Ciar lived next door to one another. They planned on finalizing a schedule over the Colorado holiday.

She received a text notification and assumed it was her folks. Her stomach flipped when it was from the man she couldn't stop thinking about.

> Ciar: I wish I could take you to dinner.

> Gray: Me too, but it'll be nice to spend time with my parents. I bet I'll have a better time than your stuffy business meeting.

> Ciar: Oh, you will. Can I call you tonight?

> Gray: I'd like that. My parents are pulling up. Don't have too much fun without me. x

She grabbed her purse and ran outside.

four

CIAR

CIAR WAS PISSED. Furious that he hadn't insisted to his boss that he needed to cancel tonight's dinner. He might have touted the evening to Gray as a business meeting, but the spoiled princess from Saudi Arabia on his arm would call it something else.

Anders, the sonofabitch, had ordered him weeks ago to make sure Daria Khan enjoyed the evening. Her father was a wealthy royal who made his money in technology. He planned on buying up as much of Old Oak & Park Royal in West London as possible. Old Oak & Park Royal was one of three of London's largest industrial boroughs.

If his boss landed that account, the entire firm could retire filthy rich in a few years. So, he understood why the "date" was important. Usually, he wouldn't even blink at the ask, but sitting next to a woman in a romantically lit dining room when that woman wasn't Gray was incredibly distasteful and felt like cheating even though he and Gray weren't dating. Not exactly.

He was only required to chat her up, feed her ego, ply her

with drinks, and make her believe he worshiped every insipid word that puked from her mouth.

He didn't have to touch her, but she seemed eager and willing to touch him. From the moment his car had picked her up from the Fitzwilliam, she had treated him like a paid escort instead of the highly sought-after real estate mogul he was.

At least he'd made her fly to Dublin instead of taking her out in London, which is what she'd wanted. He'd done his research on her socials. She would have tried to drag him to one of London's notorious after-hours clubs, where drugs and public sex were encouraged.

He didn't do drugs, and though he'd been relatively open to sexual encounters where maybe a few wandering eyes might have watched, he was not interested in exploring any kink with the self-absorbed woman doing her damnedest to get her long-nailed, spindly fingers as close to his flaccid dick as possible.

He'd been sick for two days over tonight, and every time he'd texted Gray about his "boring" dinner meeting, he felt worse. He'd dreamed of her for two years, and to suddenly have the chance of having her for himself—he didn't want to screw it up.

While Daria was ordering another disgustingly sweet mixed drink, he slipped his phone from his pocket and quickly texted Anders. **Never again.** Then he texted Gray.

> Ciar: How's dinner going? I can't wait for you to call me later.

While he watched the waving dots for her response, Daria slid her hand once again over his thigh. Her hand felt like a crab's pincer.

"I need to take some pics for IG. Here and in the back of the car. My assistant will meet us after dinner. She's much better at getting the lighting right."

He was about to tell her he wasn't interested while watching the waving dots still wave on Gray's end. When he pulled his eyes from the screen to ask Daria to fuck off in as PG a way as he could manage, he instead watched in frozen horror as a smiling Josephine MacGregor and her scowling husband stopped beside his table.

The married couple parted...Gray. *Oh Christ, Gray.* She was holding her phone, her eyes riveted to Daria's hand, practically molesting his crotch with a look of utter devastation on her beautiful face.

"Ciar, what a surprise. Gray was just telling her dad and me about your Colorado trip. How fun for everyone." And then, because Josephine unfortunately had manners, she turned to Daria, whose fake nails were still in ball tickling distance, stuck her hand out, and said, "I'm Josephine O'Connor," then looked at MacGregor, "this is my husband, Thomas, and my daughter Gray," she added, tugging Gray forward.

Daria, true to her nature, said, "A pleasure, but I'm sure I've never heard of you."

MacGregor was not a man to take someone insulting his wife and daughter lightly. The look he was throwing at Ciar was brutal and promised consequences. He couldn't even care, so sick about Gray witnessing the travesty at his table, he couldn't think.

He finally blurted out, "It's very good to see you. Josephine. MacGregor." He nodded to them both before meeting the steely gray eyes of Gray. "Gray."

Where her face, a moment ago, had exposed her hurt, it was now blank. No emotion. No anything.

MacGregor glanced at his wife's confused face and then at his daughter, who had yet to respond. The giant Scotsman's body stiffened further if that was even possible.

"We'll take our leave, Murphy." Gathering his women, he

gave Daria a cursory glance, barely containing an impressive sneer of dislike, before leading them away.

Finally pulling his head from his ass, Ciar pulled Daria's claw from his thigh and placed it on her own. "No pictures. I can suggest a few places you and your assistant might like to check out later that are sure to get you thousands of likes."

Her unintelligent eyes lit up like a Christmas tree, all the awkwardness of the past three minutes forgotten with the promise of gaining new IG followers.

Seventy-two minutes had passed since he'd quite possibly screwed up every chance he'd had with Gray.

He kicked Daria to the curb, literally, at Fitzwilliam's posh entrance and had the driver take him directly home.

He'd been tight fisting his phone since the moment Gray had stood over his table. The situation was bad, dire, absolutely catastrophic. He wasn't an ignorant man. He lied. She caught him. Even though he had no plans further than dinner, she would never believe him after what she saw.

He realized he was sawing in breaths, the closest he'd ever come to what must be a panic attack.

He ripped the front door open and stormed through the living room where Daniel and Jonathan were watching a rugby match on television. He ignored their questions and went straight to his bedroom, shutting and locking the door behind him in case his two roommates decided they wanted to come in for a chat.

Shedding his dinner jacket and unbuttoning his dress shirt at the neck so he could breathe, he sat on his bed and stared at his phone.

She wouldn't answer. He knew she wouldn't.

He'd never felt frantic over a woman. Panicked. But Jesus, the look in her eyes flayed him. She had the ability to hurt him, physically and mentally. She just didn't know it.

His hands shook as he brought up their text thread.

> Ciar: I know it looked bad, Gray. Meet me. Let me come over. Let me explain. I promise what you saw isn't what it really was. Please.

He watched his screen until the sun brightened the sky. Silence, the most damning of replies, met his plea.

GRAY

A WEEK after Ciar ripped her heart out, Gray was hunkered over a toilet seat, puking her guts out and wishing she could die right alongside him.

She'd caught some horrific bug that, unfortunately, had her spewing from both ends. Her mom sent a doctor round to give her enough nausea meds to keep shit in, literally, so Gray could hop on a plane and fly to Scotland and let her mom take care of her.

Moms knew just how to rub a sick child's back or scratch their scalp. Gray didn't care that she was twenty—a month from twenty-one—Moms could fix everything.

She was snuggled up in her childhood bedroom on the second day of her convalescence, when her mom came in with a tray of Lipton's unsweetened iced tea. A beverage her Oklahoma-born mother refused to give up when she moved to Scotland.

She tossed a few decorative pillows from the chair next to the bed and made herself comfortable.

"Thanks, Mom," she said as she took the proffered red Solo cup of tea—another favored Oklahoma thing.

Her mom propped her feet on Gray's bed before asking, "Are you and Ciar a thing?"

Gray decorated her nutmeg and cream-colored bedspread with Lipton's best thanks to her mom's zinger of a question.

"What the hell?" She asked while using an embroidered tea towel to dab up the mess. "Why would you ask me that?"

"Are you under the impression that your mother is ignorant, young lady, because I can assure you that I am not. You've had a crush on that boy forever, and yes, I'm aware Ciar Murphy is far from a boy, but still, he's the only man you've ever made moon eyes over, and he did something that night at dinner to hurt you.

"Your father saw it, and trust me when I say, I've had to distract him with a lot of sexual favors so that he didn't fly back to Dublin and beat the shit out of Ciar."

Gray felt her gorge rise even though she was well past whatever flu had ravaged her body. "Never. Never, never, never, speak to me of sexual favors and Dad again."

Her mom snorted in amusement. "Fine, Miss Priss, but the fact remains, Ciar did something to hurt you. I don't like it, and your father wants to burn Dublin to the ground to fix it. Please give me something."

Gray aggressively rubbed her eyes, ending with her fingertips pressing her lids together. Her parents were two of the best people she'd ever known. She hated that she was causing them concern. She and her friends were meant to fly to Colorado tomorrow morning. Gray was flying back to Dublin that afternoon, or she'd never have time to pack, and she didn't want to leave with her folks worrying.

"Ciar didn't do anything wrong. Not really."

"I'm going to need more than that, sweetheart," her mom urged.

"I thought he and I...Jesus, I thought he and I might make a go of...something. He texted me. I texted him. We kissed. One night." Gray glanced at her mother's face to see how she took that news. She only found her nodding in understanding.

Gray felt her body relax, and the rest poured out like water. "He told me he had a business meeting. He asked me to go out the following day. He texted me while I was eating with you and Dad. And then...well, you saw that part."

Her mom didn't speak for a moment, not a woman to react without processing. "My first reaction is to say, fuck him and the dumb bitch he was with. My more analytical side forces me to admit that Ciar looked miserable. He was not reciprocating that snotty woman's advances. I guess the big question is, did he explain himself? Did he ask to explain himself?"

Gray took a deep breath, not wanting to discuss Ciar but needing her mother's opinion more. "He's asked. Multiple times."

"And," she started hesitantly, "you chose not to let him?"

Her mom didn't take an accusatory tone, but Gray's hackles went up. "Like you did when you found out Dad was married to Aileen while he dated you?" The minute the words left her mouth, she regretted them.

"I'm sorry, Mom. Nothing about your situation was similar to mine."

When her parents started dating, her dad hadn't divulged that he had a wife and child at home. It appeared much worse than it was. Her dad had married Aileen to help her out of a tough situation because her brother was his best friend, and Coll and Aileen's folks were assholes, and their unmarried daughter turning up pregnant wasn't something they would tolerate.

He raised Mirren as his own, but he and Aileen never had a true relationship. They lived as a family only. Her mom hadn't known the backstory and didn't let him explain. She refused to speak to him for months.

Even though she knew her mother wasn't pointing fingers at Gray's decisions, her feelings were raw, and she lashed out thoughtlessly.

"You don't need to apologize. Who better to help you through this than a woman who wasted months away from the love of her life because she was too pigheaded to listen?" She chuckled and patted Gray's foot to let her know she truly wasn't put out.

"Fine," Gray sighed, "you may be right about the pigheaded part, but Ciar and I aren't you and Dad. We aren't in love. We shared one kiss. I thought from his texts...no," she cut herself off.

"I read more into his interest than I should have. I'm angrier at myself than him. Embarrassed, if I'm honest.

"He's not even six years older than me, and yet he seems so much wiser, successful, and just more, I guess. I have a year left of uni, and I'm just getting started at O'Connor." She shrugged, having nothing more to add.

"First thing, you aren't just starting out," she air-quoted the last. "You've been working your tail off for the company. Your Uncle James is impressed, as are your grandparents. *I'm* impressed.

"But more importantly, you should never be embarrassed for how you feel. Ciar was one hundred percent in the wrong for not explaining what that dinner was about. I don't think you mistook anything he said, did, or texted.

"I've known Ciar since he was a little boy. His life was not always good."

That got Gray's attention. She knew his mother wasn't in

the picture, but little else except that his dad and uncle were amazing, and Ciar clearly loved them both.

"I won't discuss that. However, he has never struck me as the type of man who wouldn't honor his word."

Gray raised her hands in a pleading gesture. "I know that, and that's why I believe he was never serious in the first place. I need to let it go. I will try to speak to him as I normally do. Try being the operative word. I don't want to make our trip uncomfortable.

"Rowan is having a breakfast the morning we leave for everyone before we head out, I can say hello to him there. I know I need to fix it. Plus, I've put too many hours into his new business plan to turn it over to someone else."

"I think that's a very good start, but I still think you might consider that you won't know his true feelings until you let him tell you." She chuckled, saying, "I spoke to River about the big breakfast reveal. I can't believe they think Dagr and his father might be related to the O'Faolains. I bet Bran and Patrick are shitting bricks."

"Oh, they are. Bébhinn told me that all four of the boys have been out of sorts and that her aunts keep teasing them about their long-lost brother."

"The odds are strongly in their favor, however improbable it might sound. It was good to see Raven, River, and Rowan when I was in town last. Especially Row. I told your dad that I would like to visit more often and invite them here again."

"I think that Bébhinn falling in love with Dagr has given Rowan something positive to think about. Well," Gray said as she threw the bedcovers back, "I'd better get my lazy ass out of this bed and pack up.

"Thanks for taking care of me, Mom," she stood and hugged her, "and for talking through the other. Oh, and you can tell Dad to chill out."

"How about you tell me to chill out yourself," her dad growled. He stood in the doorway, his big frame shrinking the area. His arms were crossed, and he was scowling.

Gray hugged him next, wrapping her arms tight around his much larger frame. He reciprocated, wrapping his arms around her back and squeezing the breath from her.

"Chill out, Dad," she grinned when he finally let her go.

He looked toward her mom and asked, "Did she tell you what that cocky fuck did to make her cry?"

"Dad! For crying out loud, I just told you to chill out."

"The fuck I will," he replied obstinately.

Her mom walked over and gave her dad a side hug, to which he instantly snuggled her in. He was still not happy, though.

"Thomas," her mom said in a warning tone. "Gray and I spoke. It was a misunderstanding."

"A misunderstanding," he huffed. "You cried on the drive home. I didn't misunderstand that."

Gray loved how much her father loved her, but he could be relentless if he knew someone was keeping something from him. "I love you, Dad, but you need to trust me. Ciar and I were only sideways with each other. Everything is fine. You like Ciar. Let it be."

"I used to like Ciar," he corrected, "but I do trust you. I don't like it, but I have to believe Daniel and Jonathan will keep me updated if the need arises."

"Babe," her mom started, "you are not giving off 'I trust you' vibes. If you ask those boys to spy on Gray, so help me God, you won't like the consequences." Her mom turned to Gray and winked. "No favors."

"I'm so out of this conversation. Get out of my room, Dad." When he looked like he might want to argue, she added, "I need to talk to Mom about my period cramps."

He threw his hands up in a stop gesture. "Enough. Christ,

lass," he sputtered before pivoting on a heel and speeding in the opposite direction.

"Cruel, but effective. Good call," her mom praised.

After her mom left her alone to pack, her phone chimed. Her friends had been texting her well-wishes and keeping her up to date on the goings-on at home. The text wasn't from the girls.

Ciar: I'm not taking no for an answer. Blair said you would be home tonight. You will see me.

six

CIAR

CIAR STOOD PANTING in sweaty exhaustion in the gym's mammoth showers. He and Jonathan had just finished a sparring session with the owner's brother, who was a retired boxer that still trained a few clients.

The brutal workout was just the mind-numbing activity to force his brain from the message he'd received earlier from Gray. The first one she'd sent him since that dinner travesty almost two weeks ago.

He still wanted to slam his head against the cool tile over and over so his outside looked as screwed up as the inside of his head felt.

His life had become nothing but work and working out, with a side obsession of texting a woman who didn't return any of them, until now.

Silence would have been preferable.

> Ciar: I'm not taking no for an answer. Blair said you would be home tonight. You will see me.

> Gray: I have plans when I get back to town, but I will see you at breakfast at the O'Faolains' tomorrow morning. I don't need your apologies. I assumed something that wasn't, and that's on me. I have made some changes to the pub's business plan and have some final questions for you while we're on holiday. I can finish a plan easily after that. See you tomorrow.

She had shut him out completely with five sentences. Screw that. He wasn't letting her walk away without a fight.

He would see her.

He would make her listen.

"Jesus, Ciar," Jonathan groused, "what the hell has been up your ass lately?" Jonathan asked as he stripped out of his clothes and walked into the multi-headed steam shower where Ciar currently leaned, arms crossed and brooding.

"Work." It was his go-to answer for any bad mood his friends had called him out on over the last week.

"Bullshit. You don't have to tell me or Dan, but Christ man, you know we'd listen to you and do whatever to help."

Ciar felt his face heat, which was a rarity for him. He was as close as brothers with Daniel and Jonathan, but for some reason, it still took him by surprise how open they were with their feelings. They weren't all hugs and kisses, but they were solid, real friends, and they didn't mind letting him know.

"Thank you, but I'll figure my shit out." At Jon's steady stare, he added, "If I can't, I'll let you know."

That seemed to satisfy his friend, and he moved on to talk of the upcoming trip and the fact that everyone decided to go out for a drink together later since Gray was back in town.

"Say what now?" Ciar asked as he swiped shampoo bubbles from his face.

"Yeah, Mags told Daniel. Well, she said to meet them or not. She didn't give a shit. Typical of the wee shite."

It had always amused Ciar as a kid that Daniel, Jonathan, and Bébhinn said just as many Irish sayings as American since their parents were a mix of both.

Without letting on to too much interest, he said, "Mags is something else. So, is Gray going? I wondered if she was fully recovered."

"She's right as rain now. The girls said she looked pale on their video chat, but she said she felt great. Everyone's packing tonight and then meeting at your da's."

"I'm down for a pint." And cornering a stubborn, gray-eyed girl.

Ciar was at the bar bullshitting with his old man while keeping one eye firmly on the front doors. Blair and Mags already had a table, and Daniel and Jonathan walked in not two minutes ago, nodding in his direction.

Dagr and Bébhinn were stepping through, and Ciar felt his body stiffen as Bébhinn said something over her shoulder, laughing at whatever the person behind her said.

There she was, golden waves, gray eyes, and the most stunning pair of long legs he'd ever seen on a woman. Gray MacGregor.

"Christ, boy, you've got it bad," his dad said, punching him in the shoulder.

Ciar rubbed his offended appendage, already sore from boxing. "What are you going on about?" he asked, never taking his eyes from Gray.

He'd never seen a more beautiful woman. Never. Not to mention she was kind and crazy smart. She was way too good for him, but he was still going to try for her. She hadn't let him explain about that damned dinner yet, where he was entirely in the wrong, but she would.

"Don't start with me, Dad," he warned.

"Gray...well, your uncle and I always wondered. She giving you the runaround?"

He had too much respect for his father to lie. "She has her reasons. I fucked up."

Mags must have said something funny, and the table erupted in laughter. Gray laughed, her eyes were twinkling, but damn if she didn't look tired. He wished he could have taken care of her while she battled her sickness.

"Well then," his father said grimly, "I expect you'll make it right."

"Count on it." Ciar pushed off from the bar and headed in the table's direction. There was only one spot left on the long bench, which happened to be next to his obsession.

Her eyes caught his, her mouth rounded in a silent O before smoothing into indifference. She was as indifferent to him as he was to her.

He slid into the empty spot, making sure to take up all the remaining room so that their thighs were fused. He set his iced vodka on the smooth hardwood top.

"Fancy finding you rabble here. How goes the buyout, Griffiths?"

"I'm satisfied with the progress. The London office will take a bit of sorting, but my partner is more than capable. We plan to take on cases in both cities that align with our specialties. Our teams love a good challenge."

"Did you fire the crazy cunt you screwed in the office?" Mags asked all innocent inquiry.

"Mags, you bitch. I told you that in confidence," Bébhinn hissed.

"Sure, but I like to keep things real, and you're my best friend and shouldn't have to wonder."

Face flaming, Dagr admitted, "Another law firm found her an acceptable position."

Bébhinn looked surprised by the news. "Really," she whispered, even though the table heard.

"Nothing and no one comes before your happiness, baby." Dagr was smooth. Ciar would give him that.

"How are you feeling, Gray?" Ciar turned his attention to the woman doing her level best not to move. "I texted you while you were in Scotland. Did you not get them?" He knew he was playing with fire, but with Gray, he couldn't help himself.

Under the table, Gray pinched the top of this leg. Before she could pull away, he flattened her hand on his thigh and held on tight enough that she couldn't yank free without making a scene.

"I'm much better," she gritted out. "I did get your messages. Thank you for your concern. Today is the first day I've felt well enough to respond to everyone. I'm starving after days of puking my guts up. Who wants a starter?"

Conversation started again, but as he scanned the table, Blair, who was sitting in the corner of the booth, had her eyes trained on him. She propped her menu against the napkin dispenser and quickly signed, "So, you're the naked selfie guy."

Oh shit. Gray told Blair about the pictures. Not who it was, though, but Blair was one of the cleverest people he'd ever met. She kept his attention another moment, long enough to sign, "Be careful."

Ciar gave the tiny redhead a slight nod. He had no doubt that she would call in the big guns if he hurt her friend, and the big gun would be strapped to Thomas MacGregor's thigh.

"Let me out, Ciar. I need to use the restroom," Gray whispered and gave his side a small poke with her elbow.

Loudly, he replied, "Me too. I'll walk with you." To the table, he said, "Order me and Gray the crab cake bites." It was a test of his acting skills not to smile at the fuming woman shoving him out of her way as she exited the booth.

They walked in silence to the back, but instead of letting her go into the women's room, he grasped her upper arm and propelled her to the door just past the restrooms. Punching in the security code, he pulled her in behind him and shut the door fast.

Swinging her around until her back was pressed to the wooden storage door, he growled, "Now, Miss MacGregor, you're going to listen to what I have to say whether you want to or not."

Her "I want to" threw off the righteous anger he'd been building.

"Well, good then." *Real cool, Murphy.*

"That dinner was business." At her disbelieving snort, he added, "It was business to me. My boss set it up weeks ago. The office is about to land one of the biggest, most lucrative clients we've ever had. Daria was the client's daughter. Anders leaves nothing to chance, and if he thought me wining and dining that idiot woman would give us a leg up in negotiations, he wasn't above taking it.

"Or at least having me take it. It was business, Gray. Damn it," his palms slapped the door on each side of her body, "I fucked up. I should have told you I had to take a woman out. I should have told you that I would never touch another woman as long as I thought I had even the barest chance of having you."

When he finished his speech, they were both breathing heavy, their lips almost touching, their heaving chests brushing.

He let his hands slide down the door until he had her hips in his grasp. She placed her hands on his chest and leaned forward until her breath tickled his ear.

"I believe you, but business or pleasure, no woman would ever touch what is mine. I stood there and watched her lay a possessive hand on you, and you did nothing to stop her.

"I'm worth more than that. I'm a MacGregor, Ciar. I'm no one's second best."

With that shocking announcement, she shoved his chest. The unexpected move caused him to stumble back, allowing her to open the door behind her and escape.

"Well, fuck me."

seven

PRESENT—FLIGHT TO COLORADO

GRAY

STOP LOOKING AT HIM, *you idiot.* No matter how many times Gray berated herself, her eyes kept finding Ciar's over and over.

She had every right to put him in his place the night before and refused to feel guilty. Over breakfast with the O'Faolains that morning, she spoke to Ciar as she always had, as friends and now as a client.

While the group chatted, waiting for Dagr's father, Ulf, to arrive, Gray approached Ciar and went over some of the details she hoped they could finalize for his high-end pub while they were in Colorado.

He hadn't liked her no-nonsense, we're back to being friends, approach. When he responded, it was low enough that no one could overhear. "Cut the shit, Gray. Don't treat me like you haven't had my hard dick rubbing between your legs, and my tongue as deep in your throat as it could go."

She'd felt her face flush in embarrassment. Her body, on the other hand, had warmed for a wholly different reason.

She couldn't let him break the carefully constructed act she'd decided to play. "Let it go, Ciar. I have. Have you ever heard any stories about me sleeping around?" He shook his head negatively. "One-night stands?" Again, no. "Because I don't.

"Seeing you with that woman all over you helped me remember that I don't want to be just another number to you. I'm trying to save us both regrets." Blair caught her eye. She quickly signed that they were going to draw attention. Gray nodded once and stepped away from Ciar.

He clasped her arm, stopping her long enough to growl, "You aren't a one-time anything to me, Gray. I would never—"

Jonathan cut off whatever he was about to say. "Save business talk for later, you two. My long-lost uncle might be about to walk through the door," Jonathan joked, thankfully not catching on that she and Ciar were fighting.

Gray laughed as she was meant to and, without glancing at Ciar, moved to stand next to Blair and Mags.

Now, Gray was on a beautifully appointed jet and instead of enjoying her celebratory shot of Glenmorangie—she may currently live in Ireland, but her dad would never forgive her for drinking anything but good, Scottish whisky—her whole body was attuned to Ciar.

Aside from their earlier argument, she couldn't help but notice that Ciar was brooding about something. He had gotten a message or email before they took off and had been silent ever since. And even though they had Wi-Fi, he hadn't done anything but glare at his phone. *Stop, Gray!*

While trying to get back into the conversation with her friends, she noticed that Bébhinn was wearing new jewelry. "That's a gorgeous locket, Bébhinn. It looks antique. Did you recently buy it?"

Bébhinn clasped the piece, briefly glancing at Dagr, who

nodded encouragement, which was all kinds of odd. She glanced at Mags, who shrugged and shook her head.

"Dad left me some things with our solicitor. I just opened it a few days ago. Here," she said, scooting forward in her seat and flipping the clasp to open the locket, "he commissioned Fiona, Mirren's sister-in-law, to paint a miniature of him and Mom on their wedding day."

She swallowed deeply before continuing. The others on the plane were silent. "Dad left a note that said the other side was for my husband and me." Closing the piece, she shook her head, attempting to dispel the tears that wanted to fall.

"He also left a bunch of his mother's jewelry to me. I treasure them all because I saw Gran wearing them on occasion when I was little, or in pictures. Dagr put them in a safe at the bank until our place is ready and we're settled."

"It's stunning, Bébhinn, and unsurprisingly so thoughtful. Hugh loved your mom something fierce. I love that he gifted you with something that you can always carry with you and remember them together."

Blair touched Bébhinn's leg to get her attention. "It's beautiful."

"I mean, seriously, how will Blair, Gray, and I ever find a man who loves his wife and children even half so much as Hugh O'Faolain. Talk about standards. You don't have to worry now that you've found your version of Hugh, or rather your brothers, as the case may be," Mags laughed and gently elbowed Bébhinn in the side, "but we still have to."

Mags could always be counted on to lighten a mood, and it worked because Bébhinn laughed and looked over her shoulder at Dagr. "I did, didn't I?"

As if she had no will of her own, Gray's eyes found Ciar. He was gazing off at nothing, tapping his fingers repetitively over his knee. She was getting worried that something besides their own squabbles was stressing him. Could it be his father? Surely, he would have said. Their friend group all loved Ciaran Murphy.

She sipped her whisky while casually pulling her messages up.

Gray: You seem stressed. Is everything okay?

She pushed send, and ten seconds later, his phone pinged. He flipped his phone over, and as soon as he saw it was her name, his gaze flicked to her. Looking back at his phone, he opened the message and started typing, a deep frown pulling at his eyes and mouth.

Ciar: It's nothing.

After all that time typing, and two words come through. He was lying.

Gray: You're lying to me again.

Low blow, but needs must. Gray watched his shoulders stiffen.

Ciar: My boss messaged me. He needs to see me as soon as I'm back from this trip.

Gray: Why does that bother you?

Ciar: It's strange. He didn't tell me what it's about.

Gray: Either let it go for a week or call him when we get to Dagr's.

Ciar took a deep breath as he read her last message. He put

his phone down and looked at her, giving her the barest nod. She didn't know what option he would choose, if either, but she hoped he would relax and enjoy the time off work.

Gray might be disappointed in Ciar's behavior lately, but he was still a close friend, and seeing one of her friends stressed wasn't something she could easily allow without trying to help.

Forcing herself to once again focus on something besides Ciar, she joined Mags in making a list of Colorado activities that everyone might be interested in.

After two hours chatting with her friends, she yawned and stretched, ready for a nap. She signed to Blair that she was going to use the restroom. Mags and Bébhinn just got back. Blair nodded and followed her to the back of the plane.

There was only one enclosed toilet, and Gray told Blair to go first, as she splashed water on her face and fluffed her waves. Blair came out and washed her hands. Gray signed in the mirror.

"I'm so ready to get there."

"Me too. How are you and Ciar?"

Gray's face was instantly on fire. She couldn't believe her friend figured out the man she was exchanging nudes with was Ciar.

"We're friends. Nothing more. I'm going to try and forget my lapse."

Blair only raised her brows and made a humming noise, a sound completely unique to her, before giving her a wink and leaving the restroom.

Gray finished going to the bathroom and was washing her hands when the door opened. "What the hell, Ciar. You could have waited."

He came closer until they stood inches apart. "I want you to tell me that you'll give me a second chance." He took her hands that were hanging limply by her sides and placed them on his chest, crowding her between his big body and the sink at her back.

"I care about you. You know that," he demanded, leaning closer to her mouth. "You have to care about me even a little. You proved it out there by asking after me."

She should be shoving him away, but when his hands smoothed up the sides of her ribs, and his thumbs lightly massaged under her breasts, she was helpless to do anything but whimper.

"Ciar, I do care. You're my friend. Of course, I care, but that isn't enough for me to take that chance. You haven't even told me how you feel."

He cut off anything else she wanted to say when he slowly licked into her mouth. They both moaned. She was thankful he kept it slow and soft. Her poor mind would click offline if he kissed her like he had that one night in his kitchen.

"Why do we have to talk about feelings? This feels good. What else matters?"

He might as well have dumped ice-cold water over her head. *This feels good. What else matters?*

With her hands on his chest, she pushed him away. He looked surprised but complied. "You just solidified my fears." She walked past him to the door, and before she turned the handle, she added, "Leave me alone, Ciar. Keep having meaningless relationships if you want, but I won't be one of them."

eight

CIAR

CIAR CURSED himself through the rest of the flight, ignoring the quiet conversations and Daniel and Dagr's snoring. Jonathan made sure to video the two men, asleep and sitting side by side.

He sent it to the family's group chat, which he normally would have enjoyed getting one over on Daniel, but he had been too deep in misery for mirth of any kind.

Once they'd landed, he tried to enjoy the Colorado countryside through the windows of the SUV, but even that was spoiled when Gray chose to ride in the second vehicle. The one he wasn't in.

They'd reached the cabin, which didn't meet his expectations. To him, cabin spoke of rustic accommodation and outdoor adventures.

The Griffiths' "cabin" was a sprawling wonder, secluded and surrounded by giant spruce, fir, and pine trees, and who knew what else. He wasn't a dendrologist after all—a term he'd learned from Blair.

For all the home's seclusion, there were well-tended roads leading into the town of Telluride. The girls said it was one of the poshest towns in Colorado. As long as they had steak and vodka, he didn't care much about any other details.

The cabin itself had ten bedrooms sprawling over one open level that still had stairs to climb here and there. Dagr said the architect wanted some of the natural landscape to dictate the floor plan.

Ciar tracked Gray, who was studiously ignoring his presence, to discover which bedroom she chose so that he could secretly get one near her.

He didn't know why he told her that feelings don't matter. He had her back in his arms, her tongue sliding so perfectly against his own, and he went brain dead.

Did he like speaking about his feelings? Not particularly. Until he'd begun to verbally kick his ass over the idiotic statement, he hadn't realized that he'd never spoken to a woman about feelings. He'd never had any to speak about, honestly.

He did have them for Gray. "You're an idiot," he murmured as he slipped into his chosen room after Gray went into hers. He dropped his bags quickly and made his way back to the enormous kitchen and bar area so she would be none the wiser about who her next-door neighbor was.

Blair was there with an excited Bébhinn, who was describing how stunning Dagr's rooms were. The grandness of American homes never ceased to amaze him. Even simple, working-class family homes had quadruple the garden area for kids to play and for get-togethers.

When Bébhinn turned to speak with Daniel, who was getting everyone drinks, Blair glared at him and signed, "Stop being a dumbass."

He didn't know if it was because of her deafness, but Blair

saw more than most. Combine that with her big brain, and people weren't able to get away with shit.

"I'm trying," he grimaced. He didn't sign, so no one would notice. She was highly adept at reading lips.

"Unsuccessfully," was her response.

"Help me then." Even mouthing the words sounded whiny.

"I'll give you one thing, Ciar. Gray has mooned over you for years." After that explosive intel, she turned back to Daniel and placed her drink order.

Ciar felt heat rip through his body and a shuddering thump in the vicinity of his heart. He hadn't known. She never gave him more or less attention than the other guys.

If what Blair said was true, and she would never lie, he felt something akin to hope for the first time since his dinner with Daria.

Gray, Mags, Dagr, and Jonathan joined the group, and he couldn't take his eyes off Gray. She wore a simple white button-up tucked into slim, straight-legged jeans, with simple sandals. He'd always thought her style was beautiful and classic.

She glanced his way and quickly moved on. He decided then that he wouldn't give her space. She could like it, love it, or hate it, but he was going to be her new shadow.

Implementing his newest plan, Ciar casually moved, finding a place to lean against the bar behind Gray's back. He watched her shoulders stiffen as Daniel handed him a drink, and Ciar let his arm graze her own as he reached.

"Thank you again for the invite, Dagr. This place is incredible." Ciar took a sip of his vodka and was pleasantly surprised.

Dagr noticed and said, "I'm happy to have you. What do you think of the Aspen Vodka, then?"

"It's no Absolut, but consider me impressed." While everyone discussed their plans for the rest of the day, which included scouting around the property and ending with a cookout and relaxing in a hot tub, Ciar moved closer to Gray's back.

He leaned in so he could speak quietly in her ear. "I'm sorry for being an idiot on the plane. I lied." Her head swiveled enough for her to see his face before quickly turning to the front again.

"Feelings are important. The truth is, I've never had feelings before," he hesitated, "you. Consider this your warning. I'm not giving up."

Where no one could see, he slid his knuckles down her spine. He didn't care whether their friends knew he was into Gray or not, but he wanted her ready. She needed to admit to her feelings too.

nine

GRAY

CIAR WAS NOT PLAYING FAIR. His little performance earlier had wrecked Gray's concentration for the rest of the day. She half-heartedly explored, stumbling around after her friends, all the while reliving the feeling of Ciar's knuckles running down her back.

Dagr hired a chef for the days they were staying and made sure the evening's dinner was finished early since they were all a bit jet lagged. Better to push through a few more hours to get on track.

She was in her room changing into a swimsuit when a knock sounded on her door. She assumed it was one of the girls and yelled, "Come in."

She was about to put her matching red cover-up on over her tiny, red bikini when her door opened and there stood Ciar in short, tight black swim trunks showing off his gorgeous body covered head to toe in ink—literally, head to toe.

His eyes widened at her standing in the middle of her assigned bedroom wearing skimpy attire. "Ciar. What are you doing?" she asked when he stayed standing in the doorway. She tried not to notice the slight tightening of his trunks, but inside, she was thrilled that he liked what he saw.

"Christ, Gray." He whispered something that was definitely in Russian, though it was too low for her to catch. She'd been taking lessons on and off for two and a half years. She could speak and understand the language, but her writing was still middle-of-the-road.

There was an older Russian woman who lived above her favorite coffee shop near Trinity. They met by chance one day and struck up a friendship. Gray promised to redecorate her tiny flat over time if she taught her the language. She never told anyone because it might reveal her obsession with a certain man.

He didn't move from the doorway, but his eyes swept her body in slow perusal, finally coming back to her face. "Sit by me in the hot tub, or I will make a point of moving by you." He unashamedly adjusted his dick. Gray tracked each movement of his hand. "Do you understand?"

Gray swallowed thickly. "Yes."

He left as quickly as he'd come, leaving her with noodle legs. She sat on the end of her bed contemplating how he'd turned the tables so easily on their non-relationship.

Fifteen minutes later, and with only the slightest hesitation, Gray made sure to sit on the bench closest to Ciar. The jets were bubbling the water enough that, with only the darkness and stars surrounding them, seeing below the surface was impossible. A good thing since he had his big man paw draped possessively over her thigh within seconds.

Ignoring the man staking a claim on her body, she threw herself into making plans for the next couple of days. They were hiking tomorrow, Dagr practically vibrating with excitement at showing Bébhinn his favorite scenic trails. Tomorrow night, they were going to some trendy club in downtown Telluride.

For almost an hour, she'd been overwhelmed with the feelings that Ciar was swamping her body with, but she wasn't a meek woman...normally. She didn't want to be now.

She raised her Scottish whisky on the rocks to sip while her free hand slid a path from the back of his hand stationed on her thigh, to his own, trailing her fingers across his leg. He jumped so high, it was a wonder no one noticed.

She made sure her fingers dug into the space between his leg and groin. "Gray," his rumbling voice warned.

All innocence, she asked Ciar, "Before we hike tomorrow, do you want to spend some time on the proposals? If we give my plans some attention, by the time we get home, I can start hiring contractors."

While she was speaking, she barely moved her fingertips back and forth. His sex was slowly hardening with the slight attention, causing her breath to hitch, but she wasn't backing down now.

"Fine," he gritted.

She was feeling mighty smug until his fingers dipped deeper between her own thighs, where her body was currently pulsing. He made a show of finishing off his drink and setting the glass behind on the railing circling the extra-large hot tub.

He answered a few questions about the new pub while casually using his now free hand to move her hidden hand over enough to cover his erection. He pressed her palm firmly against his sex causing him to groan, which he covered with a cough.

Blair signed, "It must be hard."

Ciar coughed for real with that comment, releasing her hand and placing it back firmly on his thigh.

"What?" he asked Blair, glancing at Gray with wide eyes.

"It must be hard to open a pub when your father and uncle already have a successful one," she explained.

Gray stared intensely at her friend, and at the little redhead's smirk, she knew Blair was aware of what they were up to, causing a blush to spread from her face to her neck and chest.

Ciar regained a semblance of calm before Gray could. "Not at all. Both Dad and Uncle Cormac have been beyond helpful. They have perfected a traditional Irish pub—good food, good service, and excellent live music.

"My place will be similar but focused on more business clientele versus families and students. My place won't have dancing. You girls will have to save your moves for Murphy's. I envision a quieter, more private experience—a high-end menu, card tables, smoking lounge—different, but still all about a pleasurable evening."

As he finished describing his new venture, his thumb brazenly caressed over her throbbing center. Her legs instantly clamped tight over his wandering hand. His wicked smile made her want to strangle him and straddle his lap at the same time.

"I'm sorry, everyone," Gray announced, with a fake yawn following. "I'm exhausted and going to head to bed." While everyone told her goodnight and that they would follow soon, she grasped his length and gave it a quick squeeze, whispering as she stood, "Enjoy the rest of your evening."

If she bent over to climb out where her ass was inches from his face, well, she wasn't going to apologize.

ten

CIAR

IT TOOK everything Ciar had to not grab Gray's hips and pull that stunning ass in for a bite. She was taunting him. Gray MacGregor might have thought she had the last word of the night, but she couldn't be further from the truth.

He adjusted his damn hard-on for the tenth time since she left, praying it would subside. She departed five minutes earlier and was likely now in the shower, which he intended to join her in shortly.

Dagr, who held Bébhinn in his arms across the tub, looked at him with raised, knowing brows. *Damn him.*

Needing something, anything to think about that would deflate the monster trying to escape his pants, he asked Bébhinn, "Has your mom said anything about how Ulf and his newfound brothers are getting on?"

Her face lit instantly. She would have moved closer to speak to Ciar, but he noticed Dagr placed a restraining hand on her stomach, which had Bébhinn smiling softly at her man.

"Oh God, even though Mom said she hadn't spent much

time with Dagr's dad, my aunts have kept her updated. The three of them seem to get along as though they've known each other their entire lives.

"It's like they didn't want it to, but DNA is apparently calling the shots. I can't wait to talk to my brothers in person," Bébhinn winced. "I don't think I like the idea of calling Ulf a brother, but technically, he is."

"I can't," Mags moaned.

Blair signed, "We should be taking our holiday in Arkansas for all the hillbilly shit the O'Faolains and Griffiths are subjecting us to."

Thankfully, things deflated in his nether region, and he was able to stand and say his goodbyes. Blair put her back to Jonathan and signed, "Last chance, dickhead."

He cupped one hand, so his one-finger salute wasn't visible except to her. Blair's low chuckle, which she verbalized, stopped the group, since it was such an anomaly for her to verbalize anything outside of her girlfriends. Blair's friendship made him smile. Ciar grinned back and winked at the ornery fairy.

Ciar went to his room and grabbed a clean shirt and boxers before sneaking into Gray's room, handily next door.

She left the door unlocked. "Good girl," he whispered.

The light was on in the bathroom, and he could hear the shower running. Perfect for his plans. He stripped before walking into the bathroom. She had her head tipped back, rinsing her hair, and didn't see him immediately, giving him a moment to study her body.

The picture she'd sent him alluded to her perfection. She was all smooth and pale gold. Her long legs and arms were strong and muscled, her stomach was fit yet feminine, her breasts and round, firm ass...he wanted his mouth on.

Water was sluicing down her curves and funneling between her thighs. He was back to being hard as stone. There was nothing for it. He certainly couldn't hide it.

He opened the glass door at the exact moment her eyes opened, a small shriek on her lips.

"What the hell are you doing, Ciar?" Her attempt to cover her body was cute.

"Don't bother, baby. I'm seconds away from licking my way from your toes to your mouth."

Her eyes widened further as they trailed over his naked flesh. The lingering stare focused on his groin made his dick twitch.

Honestly, he had debated with himself on whether or not to go in naked, but after her teasing and how she fondled his junk, he decided to go for it. He had no intention of having sex tonight, but every intention of them getting to know each other's bodies—hence the naked part.

Ciar took himself in hand and stroked, pinching the head to stave off some of his anatomy's excitement.

"Pass me the shampoo." She startled, still fixated on what he was doing to himself. He had to let go to grasp the bottle she handed him, making quick work of lathering his hair. He made sure to crowd her body while he rinsed.

"Have you washed your body yet?" She shook her head no. "Hand me the soap and sponge then, baby, and I'll do it for you." She obeyed, not speaking but definitely watching.

He stepped behind her and started with her arms and back, moving her golden waves to the side so that he could run the sponge down her spine.

"I've only touched your body through your clothes. The other times were only in my dreams. You were definitely naked, though." Dropping the sponge, he added more soap to his hands and slicked up her sides, hesitating a beat beneath her breasts before covering the full globes.

"Ciar," she moaned, as he squeezed and massaged, twisting her nipples into hardened peaks.

Her ass kept brushing his sex, driving him wild. Forcing himself to leave her breasts, he dropped to his knees, loving it when Gray groaned, "Don't stop."

He picked up each foot, washing them before sliding up the back of her calves, thighs, and finally her firm cheeks. Committed to being thorough, he slid his fingers between the cleft, making her moan louder.

"So beautiful." He told her while turning her body to face him. He ran his soapy hands up the fronts of her legs until his fingers gripped her upper thighs, loving that he could feel the tremor of her muscles beneath his palms.

"Only one place left to wash. Lean your back to the wall, Gray," he instructed. "Spread your legs for me." She obeyed. He looked up at her half-lidded eyes, observing his every move.

"You ready?"

"So ready," she said, breathless.

He kept watching her face as he brushed back and forth over her seam. Dipping his fingers past her lips had him groaning. Her mouth fell open as her hips bucked against his fingers, which had yet to penetrate.

When his tongue replaced his hand, it could have been one minute or thirty. Nothing mattered but her taste.

She stiffened beneath his mouth, her hips quivering until a keening wail escaped. "Ciar. Ciar. God, Ciar, don't stop."

"Never," he groaned against her slick folds. She erupted seconds later, screaming his name while her shaky limbs barely kept her standing.

Ciar bit her inner thigh, leaving an impressive souvenir, before standing and shutting off the water.

Towels were handily hanging on a warmer as soon as he opened the steam-filled shower. He wrapped Gray in the soft, white folds before quickly using one to furiously dry his body.

Seeing her drooping lids, he said, "You'd better get your second wind, Gray MacGregor. I'm not finished with you yet."

eleven

GRAY

BETWEEN A KILLER ORGASM and jet lag, Gray barely managed to stumble to the big bed that had been calling her name for hours. Falling onto the plush pillowtop and sleeping until morning sounded perfect.

However, the minute Ciar's towel dropped, and it was clear that he was far from sated, a shot of adrenaline catapulted through her body, knocking the drowsy right out of her.

They stood facing each other, him naked and wanting, her draped in a towel and wanting. "I thought we were taking things slowly."

"I still taste you on my lips, Gray. Slow went out the window the moment you didn't kick me out of your shower."

He wasn't wrong. "True. What now?" She had a comfort level after years of being friends, but she wasn't exactly some female lothario.

Ciar took over and walked her backwards until her legs hit the bed. With his fingers curled over the edge of her towel, he loomed over her. "Did you like my mouth on you?"

"You know I did," she answered truthfully. When Ciar crowded her, Gray's body shivered in anticipation, clearly loving his domineering side.

"How many men have you let do that to you?"

His question took her by surprise. Speaking of past conquests hardly seemed appropriate, but if he wanted to know, she wasn't ashamed.

"You're the second." She felt his grip on the plush cotton at her chest tighten.

"Who?"

"I'm not discussing him with you, Ciar."

"Did you fancy yourself in love?"

She refused to allow him to bully her about her past. "I didn't fancy anything. I did love him."

That took him back. He winced at her honesty. "Why wasn't he the man in your shower instead of me, then?" He tugged roughly at her towel until the tuck came free and fell to the floor.

He lifted her until her legs had little choice but to wrap around his waist. Gray moaned as his sex aligned with her incredibly sensitive one.

She tried to kiss him, but he pulled out of reach, not giving her what she wanted until she gave him what he wanted first. "We...we broke up because he moved to the States," she stuttered, because he might not have allowed the kiss, but he was slowly driving her mad below.

Truly, Cannon wasn't taking up even the slightest bit of her brain right now. She couldn't understand why Ciar was pushing the subject.

"Do you speak to him still?" He grasped her waist and lifted her, tossing her naked body on the bed before quickly covering her with his. His skin was hot as a furnace, and she groaned at how good he felt.

"Answer me," he demanded.

It took her a moment to remember the question. "Occasionally."

He pinned her head between his forearms, his fierce countenance hovering above her. "Lose his fucking number, Gray. Never again. You're mine, and I don't fucking share," he growled.

The spell his dick had put her under fizzled at his autocratic tone. "I suppose you'll promise me the same level of exclusivity?" She smirked, knowing he'd never been exclusive with anyone in his life.

"I swear it to you, Gray. I meant it when I said I wanted to make a go of us. I haven't been with another woman, sexually," he grumbled as though he was embarrassed to discuss his sexcapades, "for almost seven months, and even then, it was a meaningless one-night stand. Hell, the totality of my experiences has been meaningless.

"You're different, and I want to know that I'm different to you too." He nudged her entrance with his length, causing her to momentarily lose the train of her thought.

"Are you committed to me, Gray?" He sucked one of her nipples into his mouth, making her squeal as pure sensation flooded her body.

"I want to be," she said quietly, pulling his head more firmly into her chest.

"Not good enough." He followed that announcement with a long slide of himself through her slick folds.

Her mind was melting along with her inhibitions. "Please, Ciar. I want you." She actually whimpered when he pulled away again.

"Are you committed to me? Through thick and thin. Even when I do something to piss you off. I want to know that you are mine. Tell me, damnit!"

Who was she kidding? He wanted her. Therefore, she was his. "I'm yours, Ciar," she hissed before grabbing his ass and pulling him in tight. "Now make me yours. Now!"

"Of fuck, baby. Yes. You are so mine. I'm clean," he stuttered over the omission. "Are you on birth control? Have you seen a doctor?" He was panting as heavily as she was, rubbing himself back and forth over her center.

"Clean and pills," she panted. "Don't make me wai— Argh!" The sudden invasion was intense. Thankfully, he stopped halfway to let her adjust.

After a few deep breaths, Gray was able to relax around the intrusion. "I'm ready," she moaned, clenching her inner muscles around him.

He pulled out before sliding all the way in and going completely still. Her breath whooshed out, and she whispered his name at how good he felt. "Ciar."

"Christ, baby, you're tight." He kissed her deeply and slowly until her hips started to roll into his.

"Can I move?" His voice cracked with restraint.

"Yes. Kiss me again."

He was on her, taking her mouth in a parody of sexual pene-tration. Their tongues glided together, building a heat that overwhelmed.

She moaned, holding his nearly shaved head tight. Her hips undulated with increased force, causing his thick member to glide faster, his breaths to saw harder. Leaning on one arm, his free hand moved over her breasts until she was quaking.

"Yes, Ciar," she wailed. "Faster, baby. Harder!" Her demand made him frantic. He could do nothing but obey. His pace quickened, and a sheen of sweat covered their bodies, making the skin-on-skin friction almost unbearable.

He looked down at her with such a serious expression that

her heart stuttered. "I've dreamed of this for longer than I should have," he grunted as he kept pistoning in and out of her.

Leaning back to put space between their bodies, his fingers played her body perfectly. "Come for me, baby. I'm...oh Christ, I'm close."

She felt her body falling. "Ciar," she cried, "I'm there." And she was, her body already flexing and tightening.

"That's it, Gray. Yes, baby."

After three more pounding thrusts, he roared, and she felt his release pulse deep inside her. Although she had only had one lover before Ciar, she couldn't deny that this experience was on a whole new level of sin. She should have known that being intimate with Ciar would be nothing but raw sensation and passion.

Ciar stayed still in the cradle of her body as their breathing evened out. Ciar placed small kisses over her face and neck, thrilling her with his sweet side.

Gray was captivated by the intricate tattoos covering Ciar's body, wishing she could devote the next seventy-two hours to tracing every single one.

"Are we telling our friends about us?" Ciar asked.

Gray felt her body tense at the thought. Once they went public to their group, there was no going back—and if he hurt her, it would be that much worse.

Gray skimmed her fingertips over his back while she considered his question. "I want to claim you, Ciar, but only because I know my feelings. I'm not convinced you understand what I need from you."

"Gray," he started, his voice gruff, "if I wasn't into this one hundred percent, I would never have even laid my eyes on you."

"I've been into you for a while, which is why I only had one boyfriend. I always hoped you would find your way to me.

Instead, I had to watch you go out with women who weren't worth your time, over and over and over again.

"You say you've wanted me for some time, Ciar, then why all those women? I know we've just had sex, and honestly, I'm not happy with myself. Being with you was everything I hoped —more than everything. I never knew sex could be this way, not to mention you gave me the best orgasm of my life," she grinned and kissed his cheek.

"I want more, though. I want commitment, but I'm not sure I can trust you to give it to me."

He sighed and placed a lingering kiss to her throat. "I went out with other women because, honestly, I never thought you would look at me twice. I screwed up by lying to you because relationships, being in one, and with someone that I care about, is a learning curve, sure, but one I plan on giving my all to.

"I know you're scared that I'm not in this with you. I can only ask that you let me prove it. Will you?" He didn't admit it, but he was afraid too—afraid that if she ever found out who he really was, that she would turn her back on him and run far away.

"What choice do I have? You're a great lay," she giggled, kissing his strong jaw.

He chuckled with her, giving her side a tiny pinch before turning serious again. "Keeping us a secret is a big ask, Gray. I want everyone to know you're mine."

"Let's give it a few days, at least. Sneaking around might be kind of fun."

Gray might try to convince herself and him that hiding their relationship would be exciting, but he wasn't fooled. She didn't want their friends to know in case he hurt her. All he needed was time to prove himself.

With time, she would learn to trust him when he said he wasn't going to hurt her.

With time, she might not run away from his past.

twelve

CIAR

CIAR AND GRAY entered the kitchen at the same time. Everyone was there, helping themselves to a buffet-style breakfast. They would have been fifteen minutes earlier, but when Gray happened to bend over to pick her panties off the floor, his dick had other ideas despite how many times they'd come together last night.

He should be exhausted, but nothing but exhilaration coursed through his satisfied body. He glanced in Gray's direction, where she was pouring herself some tea. She must have felt his eyes, because hers tipped up, her cheeks flushing pink when he smiled.

Ciar loaded his plate full. The night's cardio had left him starved. He was about to sit by Dagr at the high bar when Mags announced, "I'm not surprised to see you eating enough for three, Ciar, after last night. The things I heard outside Gray's room made even me blush."

Ciar fumbled his plate, cursing under his breath before

zeroing in on a smirking Mags. Blair covered her mouth, but it was clear she was hiding a silent laugh.

"In the shit now," Dagr murmured at his side, not lifting his face from his plate.

"What the fuck are you on about, Mags?" Daniel asked.

"It's Mags," Jonathan chuckled. "The woman doesn't need a reason to be a nut."

"Fuck off, Jon. I'm only trying to help our friends come clean. I can reenact what I heard if everyone's game."

Bébhinn stepped beside Gray, bumping her side to see if her friend would shed light on Mags' allegations.

"Don't you dare," Gray hissed.

"What the hell is this about, Gray?" Daniel asked with a look of confusion, not yet connecting the dots.

Ciar had agreed with Gray to wait, but right then, he wanted to kiss Mags' shit-stirring little toes. Gray looked at him, her teacup frozen midair.

If she thought he could magically put the cows back in the barn, she had way too much faith in him.

Setting his plate down, he gave Gray a stern look before making his way toward her. Her panicked, silent "no" didn't stop him. He took her cup and set it on the counter while wrapping an arm around her waist and pulling her tightly into his body.

"Gray and I are together. Exclusively. I'm hers, and she's mine. Oh, and we also plan on having sex every chance we get." He grasped her chin and made her look up at his face before kissing her tenderly.

Background noise filtered through his haze of satisfaction at claiming her in front of their friends.

"The romance of it all," Mags sighed.

"I'll be damned," Daniel cursed. "I fucking knew it, you bastard. I swore the night I slept on the couch that I heard you talking to a woman in the kitchen. From the noises, I was forced to endure, more than talking. It was Gray."

Ciar could only smirk and shrug. "Guilty."

"I always knew you had a thing for Gray, Ciar. I'm only shocked she returns the sentiment," Bébhinn laughed. "I'm happy for both of you."

"Thomas MacGregor is going to break every bone in your body," Jonathan added cheerfully.

"Why don't you look surprised, Dag?" Bébhinn asked. "Sharing is caring, you ass."

When Ciar let Gray up for air, she was putty in his arms. He caught Blair's sparkling eyes first. She signed, "About time."

Mags grabbed Gray's shoulders and brought her into a hug. "Forgive me for outing you, but I know you well enough that you'd overthink your relationship until water turned to wine. At least I didn't truly reenact you screaming Ciar's name."

Turning to Ciar, Mags said, "Let me know at least three months before you propose, boyo. I've already envisioned the perfect embroidery for Gray's veil."

Ciar and Gray spent the next four days working on pub business in the morning. Their days were filled with white water rafting, hiking, trail riding on horses, ziplining, and checking out Telluride's nightlife.

Tonight was their final night in Colorado, and despite the nagging worry about what his boss needed to see him about, this had been one of the best holidays he'd ever taken.

Being inside Gray every chance he could, paired with the wild landscape around them, made this time together more special. It was going to be hard to leave tomorrow morning.

They were going out tonight, and from Dagr's frayed nerves

over the past five hours, Ciar had a feeling he knew what tonight's main event would be.

Ciar finished buttoning his dress shirt and smoothing his hands down the front of his dress pants when Gray walked into the bathroom.

Once the group knew they were a couple, he moved into her room immediately. He hadn't brought up how well they got along living in the same space, but he planned to make his case. Soon. That night.

He already knew the two-story, historic brick building close to his new pub was for sale, and it would make the perfect home for him and Gray. Her job would take her all over the world, but he knew that Gray and Bébhinn planned on making a name for themselves in Dublin. Mags and Blair had yet to commit to either Ireland or Scotland.

Tonight, he would tell her that he'd already made an offer on the property. By the time it was renovated, she would hopefully have come around to his high-handedness.

It had taken him almost two years to lock Gray MacGregor down, and he wasn't about to let her slip through his fingers.

"You look stunning," he said, leaning down to kiss her soft lips, "and you're all mine."

She ran her hands down his chest, kissing him back. "You're lucky I lo—" she cut herself off, "like you so much, Ciar Murphy, because my body hasn't been this sore since I did two hot spin classes in a row last year."

He pulled her against his chest. "Don't tell me about how sore your body is, baby," he groaned, "or we won't make it to dinner and miss Dag's big announcement."

She hummed against his lips, seemingly contemplating his offer, which had him fighting an instant hard-on. "Gray," he warned. She was wearing a black slip dress that showed her curves to perfection, and his unruly body was already wondering how long it would be before he could peel the material from her body.

"Tonight," she promised. "So, you've figured out what Dagr has in store for Bébhinn tonight, huh?"

"I'd have to be the King of Obliviousness not to know. It's taken everything Daniel, Jonathan, and I have to keep quiet. The man's blood is pumping through his veins at such a rate that his normally pale skin looks sunburned."

"It's romantic," she sighed. "The girls and I have had a damn hard time keeping Bébhinn in the dark."

He didn't want to bring up their living arrangements yet, but with Dagr's proposal, he was getting nervous that he wouldn't have his chance if he waited.

Grasping her silk-covered hips, he told her what he'd done without her permission. "I put an offer on the building near the new pub."

Gray's gray eyes widened in surprise. "Wow. Well, I suppose that makes sense. I grew up hearing that one could never own enough property. Good for you. It's a beautiful neighborhood. Maybe you could reno and lease."

"I plan on you and Bébhinn renovating the place."

"Oh, well...that's...well, of course."

She was flustered but still not grasping what he was saying. "I want the space for us, Gray. To make a home together."

Her sudden intake of breath had her choking. He never let her go, just watching her face for any indication that she might not hate the idea.

"You..." she paused, her gaze steady as she met his. "You purchased a home for us after only a few days of dating each other, and without consulting me?"

"Yes." He gave her lips a quick smacking kiss. "You are mine, right?"

She scowled at him but eventually rolled her eyes and admitted, "You know I am."

"Through good times and bad, baby. I just have to survive your dad, and we're golden," he teased.

"Christ, have mercy," she moaned. "Dad."

Her grimace said it all. Thomas MacGregor would be a tough sale. "Don't stress, baby. If my offer goes through, which it will, I want to be in by Christmas. Can you manage the new pub, our home, and school?"

Her head hit his chest, and her groan of exasperation vibrated his collarbone. "You're a shithead, Ciar Murphy."

"But you love me anyway?"

"I do, fool that I am."

thirteen

GRAY

AN HOUR LATER, and Gray was still kicking her ass over the love comment. Why had she said that? Why in the hell had she admitted that?

"Christ, Gray, you airheaded numpty." No amount of whisky shots could erase that she'd admitted her feelings to Ciar. Groaning in mortification, she leaned heavily against Blair's spare frame, wishing her friend could put a Harry Potter invisibility cloak over her shoulders to cover her shame.

Blair leaned into Gray and rasped "What?" in her ear.

She faced Blair, so signing wouldn't be necessary. "I may or may not have told Ciar that I love him."

Blair, bless her, faced Gray, turning her back on their friends so she could sign privately. "Do you?"

Gray covered her face with both hands, wishing she could bang her head against the bar top at her back. Facing her friend, she admitted, "Yes, but I hadn't planned on admitting it quite so soon, damn it."

Ciar never blinked an eye, but he also didn't reciprocate the sentiment. His attentiveness never wavered, and Gray could admit that she liked their relationship being open—but the not knowing how he truly felt about her sucked.

Despite not loving her back, she had made a commitment to their relationship, and because of that, she called her parents earlier to break the news, not willing to chance Daniel or Jonathan telling one of their parents and it getting back to Scotland.

She phoned her mom earlier, knowing it was a weekend and that her dad would be close. Her mom answered, "Gray, sweetheart, I've been thinking of you. Isn't Colorado crazy amazing?"

"I love it here. I'm not ready to come home. It's been so much fun. Is Dad around?"

Her mom hollered for her dad to come to the kitchen. "Okay. You're on speaker. It's Gray," her mom told her dad, who must have joined her.

"Hey, Dad." She made sure her tone was upbeat and confident.

"Gray. What's wrong?"

Of course. There was no faking anything with that man.

Mom chided, "Thomas. Lay off, will you?"

"Nothing's wrong, I just wanted to tell you both some exciting news."

"Oh?" her mom asked, starting to sound nervous.

"What the fuck is going on, Gray?"

Dad never did well with his youngest daughter coloring outside the lines. She decided to just come out with it and deal with the fallout from a continent away.

"Ciar and I are...we're dating. He's my boyfriend," she winced at how juvenile that sounded. Her mom oohed and aahed. She'd always had a soft spot for Ciar. Her father didn't take the news the same way.

"Tell that tattooed bastard that I'll be expecting him on my doorstep sooner than later."

"Mom, Jesus," Gray whined, "make him stop. I called to tell you before you heard it from someone else. Don't treat me like a child, Dad. I mean it."

"That boy made you cry not two weeks ago, and you somehow believe I'm going to think he's the love of your life? Not likely." There was grumbling and cabinet slamming, which was impressive, considering her parents' kitchen had soft-close hinges. After a few more drawer slams, he asked her mom, "Is she serious?"

"Very," Gray replied before her mom could intervene. "Ciar is it for me. He bought us a place to live. As soon as it's renovated, I'm moving in with him.

"I want my parents' blessing. Won't you be happy for me?"

"I'm very happy for you, sweetheart. Very happy. Never think I'm not. It is a lot to take in. You must see that," her mom spoke carefully. "It's sudden for me, and I've known since you were eighteen that you were in love with Ciar. Your dad, however, is only learning about it. Don't get angry, Gray, have patience instead, and trust that we only want what's best for you."

She sighed, knowing her mom was right. She shouldn't have expected a parade of hearts and roses immediately. Since her dad had already stormed off, she told her mom she would be patient and ended the call.

Now, here she was begging Blair with her sad eyes to tell her something that would make her feel better. No one was better at reading a situation or people than Blair.

"I told Mom and Dad this morning." At Blair's wide eyes, Gray threw her hands up in an "I know" gesture. "Did I tell you that Ciar bought us a house?" Gray moaned as the admission slipped from her lips.

Gray didn't dare look at Blair for a moment, afraid to see shock and censure at how fast she was allowing Ciar to move, but once her mini panic attack was over, she opened her eyes to find Blair patiently waiting to sign.

"Get a grip on yourself, Gray. I imagine your dad was a trial. Whatever. So, you love Ciar. Great. A relationship needs love to be real. As for Ciar, he's a virgin to feelings, or at least talking about them.

"Give him grace. I believe men need grace at least once a day." That made Gray smile. "I think he loves you too. You don't see how he looks at you, but I have." Blair squeezed Gray's hand briefly. "Grace and time. That's my advice."

"You two look serious," Bébhinn said as she and Mags joined them.

Everyone sat on barstools putting them closer in height to Gray in her heels. "Ciar already do something to piss you off? You know, men can't help their asinine tendencies," Mags chirped.

Blair told the newcomers, "Gray told Josephine and Thomas about Ciar."

Mags and Bébhinn looked as shocked as Blair had.

"And?" Mags asked slowly, not sure which direction the announcement had taken.

Before she could answer, strong arms wrapped around her waist from behind, and Ciar's spicy scent filled her nose. He placed a lingering kiss at the crook of her neck.

"And MacGregor, and probably Blair's father, will take their pound of flesh from me. I'm to report to Scotland immediately."

Gray was glad Ciar didn't seem particularly worried about her father's temper. She, however, was shitting bricks.

"Do you know how weird it is to see you and Ciar kissing," Bébhinn said wistfully. "Beautiful but weird."

"Try watching you and Dagr, Bébé," she mock shuddered. "Now that is weird."

"Sorry, Bébhinn, but I have to agree with Mags. The first time I saw you two sitting together at that bar, I liked to shit when I finally realized it wasn't one of your brothers."

"You lot are a pack of jackasses," Bébhinn declared before spinning on her heel and walking into Dagr's arms. "Let's blow this joint, Mr. Griffiths."

Dagr's face pinkened and he swallowed nervously. Either love had blinded Bébhinn to Dagr's distress, or she was one hell of an actress.

Gray wondered if love truly made one blind. That was a scary thought.

Bébhinn was officially an engaged woman. Shots were flowing, and the newly engaged couple hadn't stopped staring into each other's eyes all evening.

At Bébhinn's request, Gray had taken their picture, the ginormous diamond on her ring finger sparkling like a thousand suns, and sent it to her mother.

It was four in the morning in Ireland, but Gray's phone started ringing. Bébhinn had left hers on the bar, so naturally, Gray knew why her phone was lighting up. Rowan insisted on speaking to her daughter.

Gray watched her friend laugh and cry on the phone with her mother and felt her eyes grow misty with happiness.

"You've been quiet tonight, Gray," Ciar whispered against her ear before spinning her in his arms and hugging her tightly to his body.

"I haven't," she denied. "Dagr's proposal was perfect. When

he asked for the band's microphone, I literally died. What a great night, huh?" she asked, kissing the side of his mouth.

"It has," he agreed, "but you haven't told me why you've been quiet."

Damn, stubborn men. The truth was she was quiet because her mind was too busy exploding with the newness of...them.

He forced her chin up so that, with her heels, he was only a few inches taller, and their eyes met easily. "I know I made light of your father's approval. Believe me when I tell you it is very much a priority. I want your family happy, but I want you happy more.

"If there is something that I've done, or not done, Gray, I want to know. I need to know. Okay?"

She nodded her head, feeling some relief at his heartfelt words, and they were sincere. She knew Ciar, and artifice wasn't in his makeup. She had to trust and stop getting hung up on the details.

"No, Ciar. You've done everything right," Gray said as she wrapped her arms around his neck and pulled him closer. "Kiss me and all will be right in my world."

And God, when his lips touched hers, it felt like it.

"Yes, Ciar," Gray moaned. They'd made it past her bedroom's threshold, barely, before he had her pressed against a wall, her panties stripped, and his hard length out and gliding through her slick folds.

"Wanted you all night. Fuck, baby, I want you day and night."

Her legs barely managed to gain traction around his hips when he began thrusting hard and fast. Even against a wall, he managed to hit her G-spot, hammering the sensitive flesh until she started begging him not to stop.

"There, baby, there," she panted. Gray was seconds from shattering, her back bowed from the wall, and her heels digging into his ass.

"Gray. Gray. Gray," Ciar chanted. "Before I fill you up, swear you'll never leave me. Swear it!" he roared as her body flexed around his jerking shaft.

As he came deep in her body, she swore. "Never, never, never…"

fourteen

GRAY

GRAY MISSED Ciar like a woman with severe arrhythmia missed heartbeats. She craved him, needed him. He had become a life-supporting function as crucial as breathing.

He'd slept over at her place the night before, leaving early in the morning for London to meet his boss.

While they were in Colorado, Ciar had done a fantastic job of pretending he had no worries, but the moment his feet touched Irish soil, a tenseness had taken up residence under his skin.

He promised to call the moment he walked out of his boss's office, which should have been by eleven that morning.

It was currently six in the evening.

He wasn't responding to texts or calls, and not even to the stupid email she had succumbed to sending.

She'd spent the early morning doing their laundry, having lunch with the girls, and the past five hours contacting contractors for his new pub. Ciar had given the real estate agent her number to handle their new "house," which was really a two-flat monstrosity, less than three blocks from the pub, in a stunningly posh district of downtown Dublin.

His offer had been accepted—of course it had—and she made arrangements to see the property so that, fingers crossed, she could convince the same contractors working on the pub to remodel the two-story.

She was working, doing her job at O'Connor Hospitality with all due diligence. Ciar had one job in her eyes today.

To call.

And he hadn't.

fifteen

CIAR

CIAR WAS a good Catholic boy at heart, but in that moment, his imagination of what hell must be was realized.

He stepped into his boss's spectacular, flat-sized office at eight-thirty-one, dread leaching from his limbs.

"Boss," Ciar spoke with authority, swallowing his discomfort.

"Murphy. Have a seat."

Anders finished sending an email on one of the four screens in front of him, buzzed in his assistant for coffee, and while Cinde was filling their mugs, he straightened the eight different piles of correspondence awaiting his attention.

"Close the door on your way out, Ms. Shields."

Alone once more, Anders took a sip of his scorching hot sugared coffee before leaning back and steepling his fingers below his chin.

Ciar was too old to squirm, but clearly, the powers that be didn't give his body that memo. "What's happening, Boss?"

Better to get whatever shitstorm necessitated this tête-à-tête out in the open.

"You fucked one of my client's wives. A Mrs. Agapov. Eight and a half months ago."

Ciar felt his gut plummet to his toes. Why in the hell was his boss calling him out for screwing a willing woman?

"I did," he admitted immediately. "After she signed off on her husband's contracts with us, she asked me to have a drink."

"Chris Agapov contacted me the day you left for the States. He will stop using our firm unless you fix his wife's problem."

"What problem? Christ, Anders. The woman told me that her husband was elderly, and he gave her permission years ago to take pleasure where she would. I had no reason to doubt her.

"If I need to personally apologize for...disrespecting the man, though unintentionally, I will."

"Oh, they do have such an agreement. Last year, Chris encouraged me to take care of his wife. I hired Marie an escort for the evening. I don't mix business with pleasure. I assume that is a lesson you're learning as we speak."

Ciar winced at how unprofessional he appeared at that moment, when the whole of his career had been above reproach. "Of course. My apologies, sir. Marie is Russian, and I enjoyed speaking to her in my first language. Clearly, a mistake.

"Like I said, I'll do whatever it takes to appease Mr. Agapov, but if he allows his wife certain liberties, why has he taken offense now?"

"None of the other men left her pregnant."

Ciar barely made it to his small flat. As the door clicked open, he fell to his knees. He felt as though a vise was pressing against his neck, making his breathing so labored that he grew dizzy.

Before he'd stumbled from Anders' office, his boss informed him that Marie's husband forced her to stay in London until she had the baby.

His baby? "Fuck," he groaned, peeling himself from the hardwood floor to make his way to his kitchen and the bottle of vodka that awaited him.

According to her husband, Marie didn't tell him about the pregnancy until it was too late to do anything about it. Supposedly, he loved his wife, but he would not let her return to Moscow and embarrass the family.

Remembering the last of their conversation gave Ciar some hope.

"Marie told Chris that the baby is for sure yours, but you've admitted that you used a condom, and we know she wasn't a woman to go without male company for long.

"You will have to wait it out until the child is born and force a DNA test. Marie has avoided all overtures from me to set up paternity testing. For your part, only a swab of the inside of your cheek is necessary."

Anders stood and walked around his desk, placing a hand on Ciar's shoulder. "Don't let this derail you, son. No matter the results, your life is far from over. You are the brightest person I've ever had on my team, and I don't plan on seeing you go anywhere but up.

"Now, take yourself home for now. We have important clients coming in the morning, and I expect you here and ready to work."

Ciar had done nothing but mumble a thank you and goodbye. He watched as the vodka filled the glass, wondering how his life could have imploded to such a degree.

"Gray," he groaned, taking his phone and bottle to the living room, falling onto the plush, leather sofa.

What was he supposed to do now? He and Gray were so

new, and he'd already screwed up once for lying. She'd forgiven him. Would she forgive him again?

She said she loved him. Did she really? Did he love her?

He'd never said those words to anyone but his father. How was he supposed to know? The thought of losing her physically pained him and telling her what was going on was a sure way of losing her.

If he could wait out any big decisions until after Marie had the baby, then things between him and Gray might still work.

The baby was due in a few weeks, four at the most. The one time Marie had responded to Anders, she at least gave him that much. Marie said she would call the moment she went into labor.

She expected Ciar to be at the hospital to meet her solicitor, where she would legally sign all her rights over to Ciar.

The only way he would agree to that was if Marie agreed to a DNA test before the birth. According to Google, it could take one to two weeks to get the results, so he needed to speak to her as soon as possible. Hence, the vodka.

He needed liquid courage to meet the possible mother of his child.

Before he could think of how to handle Gray, he needed to speak to Marie. Anders gave him her number, and he dialed it quickly, knowing the longer he waited, the less likely he would do it.

She answered on the fourth ring. "Who is this?" she asked in her thick Russian accent.

"Ciar Murphy." Silence met him. "Meet me for lunch," he demanded, rattling off the name and directions of a café not far from the city's center.

"Ciar," she pleaded.

"No, Marie. You will meet me. You brought my name into this. The least you can do is speak to me face to face."

Her sigh had the barest of hitches. She wasn't as unaffected by the circumstances as she might wish him to think.

"I'll be there."

sixteen

CIAR

HE WAS early and asked the waitress for a table in a secluded corner. He also ordered most of the brunch menu for Marie, not willing to have food ordering interrupt them.

He saw her before she noticed him. Her blonde bob was sleek and stylish. Marie was pushing forty but still stunning. Her makeup, clothes, and attitude screamed "affluent woman."

He got to his feet when she noticed him. He wasn't happy with the situation, but he was raised to be a gentleman, and this pregnancy took two people to create, and whether he was the father or not, he would respect her as a woman.

"Marie," he said solemnly as she approached. She didn't respond except to dip her head. When she undid the tie to her Burberry raincoat, he helped slip it from her shoulders and laid it over one of the four chairs at the table where water and juice awaited. His eyes couldn't help but rudely stare at the large bump her coat had hidden.

The waitress approached bearing a full tray, unloading the fare at their silent table. "We won't need anything else. Thank you," he tipped his head to the graying waitress who had probably served enough patrons to recognize when they needed less service. She finished unloading the tray of food without fanfare, nodded, and left them to it.

At Marie's hesitancy, Ciar said, "Please, fill your plate. I might not have any experience with pregnant women myself, but I've heard stories about not letting one go hungry."

She actually snorted in amusement and relaxed enough to smile before taking his advice and picking through the offerings while he poured them both glasses of orange juice and ice water.

After she'd taken several bites, he decided it was best to speak plainly. "We both know the likelihood of my being this child's father is small." He'd used a condom and to his knowledge, it hadn't been torn when he took it off. Always a chance of course, but the probability...

Heat flared across her cheeks, and the slightest bit of sweat beaded her brow, but still she didn't speak.

"Marie, please," he said in Russian, "tell me what this is about."

She choked and pressed her fist to her mouth, shaking her head in denial.

"You have to know that I won't sign any papers when this child is born unless you agree to a DNA test immediately. Now. When we leave here," he added, wanting no misunderstanding of his intention.

Her shoulders slumped in defeat. "This child belongs to you or...oh Jesus, or to a man from an underground sex club three weeks after us. My due date may not be accurate because I didn't have my first ultrasound until the second trimester, and because I suffer from polycystic ovary syndrome, both of which can alter the date.

"If I go a full forty-two weeks and it's the other man's, it can be weeks more," she moaned in despair, "and I already miss Chris desperately.

"The man from the club was fair and beautiful. I don't even know his name," she whispered, shame scorching her admission.

Ciar couldn't bear to see a woman appear so broken and reached across the table and grasped her hand.

"Marie, I will help you even if I'm not the father, but I need to know what it is you truly want. Anders said you wanted to sign away your rights. Why? You could have ended this pregnancy at any time. You chose not to. Why?"

She placed one of her delicate hands over her stomach, the first sign that she had any connection with the child she was growing. Soon enough, she let her hands rest on the table and sat up, facing him with more determination than she'd shown since entering the diner.

"I grew up attending the Russian Orthodox Church. My parents and their parents and their parents and so on held true to the church's ban on abortion.

"I may have strayed outside the tenets of marriage, but I would not, could not take the life of a child if someone else would give it a home. It was a step too far outside my family's beliefs. My beliefs," she grimaced.

"Chris wanted a young, trophy wife. Before we married, he explained he had limitations in the intimacy department. No one would ever believe me if I told them that I do love my husband. He is my best friend, and he trusted me to live a discreet life.

"It killed me to disappoint him. I never wanted a child. I still don't, but that doesn't mean I don't want this child to be loved. I knew you would be that person, whether it was yours or not. I'll take the test and gladly, but I'm still asking you to put your name on the child's birth certificate.

"Chris and I will place five million pounds directly in your account and twenty million in an account for the child to be used at your discretion.

"I know you didn't ask for this, Ciar. I know Chris and I are asking the world. There is a chance this child is yours, but I agree, it is unlikely. That night at the club," she grimaced, "I wasn't just drinking alcohol. I don't know if protection was used or compromised.

"I've made a commitment to Chris to change the trajectory of the path I've been taking. I'm finished catting around. I will devote myself to Chris for the years he has left and strive to be a better woman, a person who leaves this world better than it found me.

"You are a good person, Ciar. No matter what, I believe there is something inside you that this child will heal."

Ciar stiffened, not liking the direction the conversation was veering. Some things that were dead and buried needed to stay that way.

"I think you would make an amazing mother, and Chris an amazing father. You're quitting before you try."

"No. I'm giving this child a chance at family. I've done too many things in my past that are so shameful," she shook her head and clenched her eyes before focusing on him again and continuing. "This child deserves everything. Give it to her. Please."

If he did this, he could see the life he's been envisioning with Gray slip through his fingers, but if he didn't, he could never live with himself. Children were meant to be loved, never abandoned to chance. Marie would be going back to Russia. She would never know whether her child was being properly cared for. He'd lived a childhood of chance. Could he let Marie's? "Let's go to the hospital for testing. That's all I'll commit to now."

Three hours later, Ciar's hired car was outside Marie's leased home. "We'll discuss the test results when they come in."

"Fine." She was staring out the car window, pleating her skirt between her fingers over and over.

"I will consider this...the child, the future, while I wait to hear from you."

"Okay. Thank you," she said quietly.

Marie was clearly flagging. "Do you want me to be there? Not after, or in the waiting room, but," he stuttered, not believing what he was about to say, "with you?"

A lone tear tracked down her pale cheek and rested above her red-stained lips. She wrapped her hand around the door's handle, about to let herself out, but turned to face him at the last second. "Yes. Please."

seventeen

GRAY

SOMETHING WAS WRONG. Something had been wrong since coming home from Colorado weeks ago. Gray just couldn't put her finger on what was setting her off.

Ciar was attentive physically, not so much in the communication department. He worked nonstop, almost maniacally. He slept at her place when he was in Dublin, even though his home was twelve steps away, but he spent even more time at his London flat.

He explained that he had several difficult deals he was juggling at once, and since he was his boss's top broker, there was no shirking his duty to the company.

Gray did understand work. Her father had always taken MacGregor Security seriously, and the Royal Marines before that. Her mother was also a role model. Josephine O'Connor was a badass in the hospitality world, and even though she kept her schedule lighter over the past few years to spend more time at home with her husband and Gray's brother, her days were always full and fulfilling.

Her mom even worked closely with a charity that helped people who have been rescued from trafficking. She was the one who set up the training workshops that taught job skills for the survivors. So yeah, Gray very much understood a devotion to work.

It made sense on paper, but living it, seeing how different he'd become from the man she'd grown up with, or the man she'd fallen in love with, was making her feel crazy.

Despite her misgivings, her life was also quite hectic, which thankfully kept her from dwelling on Ciar to an unhealthy extent. She was simultaneously working on the pub's hospitality side, renovating and remodeling the two-story building Ciar had purchased for their new home, while still maintaining top grades at university.

She'd always been a diligent student, and since graduation was getting closer, she was able to spend less time on campus.

The pub renovations were moving along, partly because the interior had been in excellent condition, leaving the contractors to focus on the bar installations, liquor shelving, a sound system, a specialized cigar lounge, and Ciar's favorite, a high-end poker room in the back for special event nights.

Most of the original blackened beams and worn hardwood floors were intact and gorgeous. The decorating and décor were left to Raven, River, Rowan, and Bébhinn. Between the four women who ran Triskelion Territory Design, the pub was ahead of schedule. Gray's real work at the pub would be ramping up the following week.

The chef and kitchen staff had already been hired. Gray planned to meet with Chef Teddy Dean to give final approval of the menu and to ensure that the extensive list of kitchen appliances and equipment were checked off and ordered. Some larger appliances had already been delivered and installed.

A local job agency had overseen the hiring of the majority of the waitstaff, but it was Gray's job to set up training meetings. Her mother helped her finalize those.

For a few more days, Gray's primary focus could stay on their new home, which was only a short walk through a posh part of town away from the pub.

Gray was obsessed with creating the perfect home for them. Even better, Ciar had given her free rein and a freer budget to see it done quickly. He was excited about their new place. Or he was a great actor. She was beginning to question a lot of things.

Hopefully, the evening would ease some of her anxiousness.

It had been a while since she and her friends had all gotten together, and the group decided to meet at Ciar's dad and uncle's pub to enjoy the best crab cake bites in the world and to hear some hot new Irish band debuting their talents.

She hoped Ciar would relax enough to set work and worries aside for one evening. They toured his new pub before meeting everyone. Ciar was pleased with the progress and made many suggestions for next week's training that she planned to implement.

He refused to tell her the name of the place, which was causing quite a bit of strife between them. She needed the name to create graphics for the staff, menus, and signage. He was beyond stubborn, saying it was a "Surprise," and he was taking care of it. Not what a person in hospitality wanted to hear.

All was well until they stepped through their home's front door. She felt him pull away, sending a barrage of red flags through the space.

He thanked her several times for putting in so much effort, complimented her color choices, kitchen appliances, flooring, and paint, but it felt forced. The weirdest part of the walk-through was that he seemed concerned about the bedrooms. Specifically, how many guest rooms Gray had planned.

When she jokingly asked if he was planning to have

overnight company as soon as they moved in, he huffed out a laugh, but it was strained.

When they were about to lock up and meet their Uber, Gray placed a hand on Ciar's chest to stop him. "Can you tell me what's bothering you? Please tell me." The guilty look that flashed across his face had her extremities turning cold.

"You've been different for weeks, Ciar. It's making me nervous about," she spread her arms wide, encompassing the flat's renovations, "all of this. The contractors will be starting here soon, and if you've changed your mind…"

He gathered her in his arms and held her tight. "Of course, I haven't changed my mind. Work is stressing me, babe. I'm sorry if I've made you feel any type of way but cared for."

Gray wasn't convinced. "I don't want to scare you, but I'm all in with you. I love you, you know that. If something is going on, something big, promise to tell me."

His arms tightened around her, scaring her further. In that moment, she was less concerned about him not confessing his feelings for her. The biggest worry was what had him so unsettled that he couldn't or wouldn't share it.

"You are the most important person in the world to me, Gray. Never doubt that. Trust me to sort some things out. Okay?"

As they walked hand in hand into Murphy's, she realized he never promised to tell her anything.

It felt good to sit comfortably between her friends again and laugh and forget the shit with Ciar for a time. When he laughed at something Daniel said and glanced her way, his eyes sparkled like they used to, she felt her shoulders relax—infinitesimally but enough to take a deeper breath.

Since walking into Murphy's, she'd made up her mind to force the truth out of him when they got home. He might not want to share what was bothering him, but he would or suffer the consequences—withholding sex and ear-twisting came to mind. Breaking up...

"Have you spoken with Ulf about the internship in Wales for next spring, Blair?" Gray asked.

Blair's face lit up like an American Fourth of July ad. She quickly signed, but then glanced in Dagr's direction, who'd joined them not long ago, and slowed her response as he was new to BSL. Bébhinn watched the intensity with which he watched every move of Blair's hands and grinned, winking at Blair.

"Ulf said they had to wait to make their decision until the cutoff date for applications. As if there will be someone more qualified than me," she signed, rolling her eyes at the rule. "I've already asked my instructors for distance learning next semester. They'll want me longer than the internship intends."

No one laughed or teased Blair for her confidence. She wasn't wrong.

"Of course," Gray said. "It's smart to be proactive, for sure."

"I told Dagr months ago that the INCS nature reserve was wasting their time with the selection process," Bébhinn added, "but rules, I guess."

"Speaking of upcoming events, Bébhinn, just because you work for our moms and are engaged to some wealthy snob, no offense, cousin," Jonathan smirked at Dagr, "you still need to take your place at the O'Faolain board of directors' table. Dan and I aren't going to be the only young guns our dads get to yell at."

Bébhinn threw her hands up in surrender. "I know. I know. Dad wanted me to get more involved in the Three Wolves Distillery. I have ideas for some of the unused property that I plan to discuss at the next board meeting. It will require all my roommates' input and help."

"Consider us intrigued, though I'm awfully tied up at the moment with the Prime Minister's wife's birthday present."

"How is the piece coming, Mags? You haven't shown me your progress for weeks." She was trying to pay attention to Mags, but Ciar's phone kept vibrating the hand that she had resting on his thigh, where his phone sat.

Gray waited for him to pick it up and at least look at who was trying to get hold of him, but he stoically ignored it until she leaned over and said, "Are you not going to check your phone?"

"No." He was curt to the point of rudeness.

Gray forced her attention from Ciar and back to Mags. "I know she'll love it, and I'll become modestly famous from that alone, but I'm Scottish and want to get back to my roots. I've been toying with setting up a shop in Inverness once I graduate."

"I know from Mom and my aunts and Gray's mom that your work would smash the décor world, Mags," Bébhinn assured.

Gray tried not to stare as Ciar flipped his phone over on his lap, which was still under the table, and she certainly didn't miss how his muscled body touching her from shoulder to thigh stiffened.

When he didn't move or say anything, Gray couldn't take it. She leaned over and whispered, "What is going on?"

He looked at her then and swallowed thickly, causing Gray's stomach to turn over, the crab cake bites she'd eaten threatening to make a second appearance.

He shifted in his seat, sliding closer to the edge of the booth as if he meant to stand. "I'm sorry, Gray. There's an emergency at work."

He stood suddenly, and Gray stood right after. "Let's go to

my house. Maybe it's something you can deal with over the phone."

"I'm sorry, Gray. I'll make it up to you, but I'd better just go home and pack a bag. Get to the airport," his voice tapered off when he noticed how badly he was crushing her.

"You can pack a bag and leave, but I'm coming. Before you walk out my door, you will tell me what's going on, or—" Gray stopped mid-threat, not wanting to say something that she couldn't take back.

He looked like he was in pain when he nodded in agreement. He took her hand and said to the table, "Sorry, guys, work emergency. Gray and I have to head out."

eighteen

CIAR

CIAR HAD to swallow bile that threatened to spew from his throat during the taxi ride home to Gray's townhouse. He held her hand, but she was stiff and refused to look at him.

He could feel her body shaking. He had hurt her. Actually, he'd been hurting her since the day he'd found out about Marie and the baby.

All these weeks, and he'd never discovered a way to explain that would allow him to keep Gray and the child. A girl.

A daughter. His daughter.

Day after day, he'd prayed for a miracle. He feared nothing so much as losing Gray, and he would lose her.

Time was almost up, the constriction of loss closing his throat, worsening his nausea. The cabbie called out that they'd arrived. He paid and exited the car, helping Gray pull free after him.

He let them into the darkened house, his feet leading them to Gray's bedroom, where an open duffel awaited him on the floor. He'd stopped unpacking weeks ago as Marie's doctor's appointments had become more frequent.

Once he'd agreed to allow his name to be put on the child's birth certificate, an instinct to protect the unborn bundle kicked in, and leaving his daughter for longer than forty-eight hours was intolerable.

Leaving Gray was equally as debilitating. Yet here he was.

A liar living two lives.

A coward.

He only told his dad two weeks ago when he'd ambushed Ciar outside Gray's house and threatened his health and manhood if he didn't come clean. Gray hadn't been the only one to notice his odd behavior.

Ciar told him everything while his dad drove him to the airport. His dad was furious that he hadn't explained what was happening to Gray, but finally agreed to let him handle it in his own time.

Now here he was, two weeks later, and still lying to Gray. Marie texted to let him know that she thought she was having contractions and was going to the hospital to get checked out.

She had gotten checked, and she was in labor.

He knew from the doctor visits that he took Marie to, that first-time moms could be in labor for many hours. He had a window of time to try to patch the hemorrhage in his and Gray's relationship.

Gray walked in behind him a moment later, her accusing silence pummeling his back. He could at least be man enough to look at her. To see what his decisions had cost him and what they were costing her.

He approached where she was leaning against the door-frame. Her face was white, and her pale gray eyes were nothing more than pools of pain.

He didn't speak. There was nothing to say. He did touch her.

There was nothing in that moment more necessary than feeling her against him—perhaps for the last time.

He dipped his mouth and firmly pressed their lips together, not seeking entrance but begging for it with every ounce of his being.

Gray's shaking hands fisted his t-shirt in what might have been equal parts anger and wanting.

Her mouth opened, and Ciar fell into her body. His tongue and hands were frantic and needful. While their tongues dueled and breath became less of a necessity, he worked at stripping their clothes.

He lifted her in his arms until the bed was close enough to drop her on the edge, his body already stepping between her legs. Her body hadn't finished a single bounce before he'd grasped her hips and lifted her high enough to watch his sex push into her tightness.

"Fuck," he groaned, "nothing is better than being inside you, Gray."

He pulled her long legs over his shoulders to switch up where he struck inside her body. Her keening whine let him know she was close.

"Come for me, baby, Christ, come now," he panted, before pinching the bundle of nerves crowning her sex.

She set off like dynamite, causing a chain reaction. The second he felt her body tighten and pulse around him, Ciar's own release roared up his legs, tightening his balls until there was nothing left but to fill her body with everything he had.

Other than sucking in a deep, shaky breath, she didn't change her position or speak. Her gray eyes watched him intently. Her quiet was unsettling.

He pulled free, groaning again at the sensitive glide of separation. She looked like a goddess stretched out before him, her lips swollen from his kiss, her body glittering with a sheen of sweat, and her golden waves standing out proudly against the white of her bedsheets.

Time was ticking by. No matter how badly he wanted to stop the clock or how badly he needed to be in London watching his daughter be born, there was no turning back the minutes and hours.

Time. He'd fucked it off, and it was fucking him.

She carefully sat up, crossing her legs before pulling a rumpled sheet under her arms to cover herself.

Gritting his teeth at her silence, half wishing she would scream at him, he pulled on his discarded clothing and began repacking his bag.

When he stood at the door, bag in hand, he watched as Gray stood from the bed in all her breathtaking, wounded glory. She watched him. Waiting.

And waiting.

Waiting for him to be a man.

Waiting for him to be a man who didn't hurt women—that didn't hurt her.

He watched as his body's essence slipped from between her thighs, slowly trekking down her leg.

Gray was gloriously heartrending.

"You promised in Colorado to stick by me in the good and the bad. It won't be bad forever. Will you stay by my side?

"I will never leave yours, Gray." He hated himself for asking, but he was too desperate not to.

She briefly glanced at the bag clutched in his hand before finally dropping her eyes to walk to the bathroom across the room.

Her heart-shaped ass, lean back, long legs, and all that wavy hair moving like ocean waves with every sway of her hips. A siren who stopped singing.

"Gray," he barked.

She stopped and grasped the door's frame without turning around, the lowering of her head the only indication that he was crushing her.

He acted monstrously but saw no way to explain his actions or their reason without causing the same outcome.

Losing her.

She never said a word before softly shutting the door behind her.

nineteen

JOSEPHINE

JOSEPHINE WAS HAVING lunch with Thomas's sister, Catriona, and his ex-wife, Aileen, at a pretty sidewalk café in Inverness.

Looking at each of her friends, it amused her to no end that the three of them had daughters who were the spitting image of their mothers, while she and Cat's sons were the image of their fathers.

Her friends ordered hot, herbal tea, of course, while Jo sipped on ice water. She wasn't a fan of their gross, sweet milky concoction, still preferring, even after all the years she'd lived in Scotland, the good old unsweetened iced tea that she grew up drinking in Oklahoma.

"You're such a tea prude, Jo," Catriona smirked, adding a second teaspoon of sugar.

Aileen splashed more heavy cream in hers, saying, "Your tea is so bitter."

"I don't think it tastes bitter, but it certainly doesn't taste like I've blended iced doughnuts up and dumped them in my glass."

Once they ordered, Josephine decided to just come out and ask what was on her mind. "Have Blair or Mags mentioned anything about Gray?" When the women looked at each other before quickly glancing away, Jo felt her pulse rise.

"So, there is something." She felt deflated because she and Gray were normally very close. "I was planning on calling the Byrne sisters after our lunch to see if the boys had mentioned anything, but they're thick as thieves with Ciar, and I thought maybe Daniel and Jonathan hadn't, but maybe Bébhinn mentioned something to Rowan."

"All the kids are busy, so maybe that's why we didn't hear anything before now, but Margaret let slip a few days ago that she was worried about Gray," Aileen offered. "She didn't want me to say anything to you yet until she cornered Gray herself, because she didn't want her to think that everyone was talking behind her back.

"I said she could have a few days before I went to you. She told me that Gray is keeping up with school and work. I hope I haven't hurt you, Jo, by keeping this to myself."

Jo grasped one of Aileen's hands, sitting on the table, and assured her that, "No, if Gray is safe, then I don't need to know everything. You and Mags were right to wait. It's just that I've felt that something was off with her for a while.

"Even during the employee training for Ciar's place a few weeks ago, I felt she was hiding from me in particular, not physically, of course, but it was like she was wearing a mask. And you both know, if she's trying to hide something from me, that means she wants something hidden from her dad.

"I also noticed that all of Gray's correspondence related to the pub's schedule has been CCed to me, Cormac, and Ciaran. Never Ciar.

"Gray said it wasn't a big deal, that Ciar was flying all over for work and had handed over all of the day-to-day responsibility to Gray to do as she saw fit, and to Triskelion for the decorating.

"It would make sense because his father and uncle are going to be smaller partners in the place, except Gray tried way too hard to convince me of how excited she was to have the responsibility of the place. She said she couldn't wait to surprise him."

Josephine turned to Catriona, who had yet to join the conversation. "Has Blair mentioned anything? Cat?"

Catriona sighed before clasping her tiny hand around Jo's. "I asked her last week if she was getting tired of having a man always underfoot at the house, and she said no because unless he snuck in late at night and left before it was light out, she didn't think Ciar had stayed over for weeks.

"I asked her if everything was okay between them, and I could tell Blair felt terrible that she didn't know. She said with their schedules, her and Gray's paths rarely crossed, but that she would ask."

"Now that I think about it, Jo," Aileen mused, "Mags did mention in passing, oh, it must have been at least three weeks now, that when she'd asked Gray how the new home renovations were going, Gray said that they were putting that on hold until the pub was finished and running. She said it would be easier to finish one job at a time.

"But I remember you telling Cat and me that Ciar was determined to work the projects simultaneously so they could be moved in by Christmas. Right?"

Josephine felt her stomach plummet. Looking at her friends, she sighed, chewing her bottom lip in unease. Her mom had always told Jo to trust her gut. She said that it was preferable for her instincts to be mistaken and act, rather than be correct and do nothing.

Jo already knew she wasn't going to do nothing.

"He did say that. Odd to change his mind partway through. My daughter is definitely hiding something, and Lord help Ciar Murphy if it's his fault. I can only talk Thomas down for so long.

"I don't want to jump off the deep end of what ifs. I did warn Gray that Ciar might have trouble sharing his feelings. He didn't grow up with any women in his family home, and the mother that raised him until he was seven or eight wasn't... good.

"This could be just one of many growing curves for them. I don't want to jump in all mother bear to save the day, but I would appreciate it if you could see what your girls find out. I'll call Rowan this afternoon. I doubt Raven and River know anything unless Row shared something with them."

"We've got your back with this, Jo," Catriona said.

"And we'll keep it from our husbands, because those bromancers will spill to Thomas first thing," Aileen huffed, shaking her head in exasperation, even though the three women loved that the men were so close.

"Thanks, you guys. I know Gray needs her privacy, but I think we can all agree from our past mistakes, that it might not be the best thing."

twenty

TWO MONTHS AFTER COLORADO

CIAR

IMOGEN ALYA MURPHY. That was the name of Ciar's two-month-old daughter sleeping soundly in his arms. Alya was his aunt's name from Russia, and Imogen was Gray's middle name.

He hated his mother most days, but she did give him away when times got too tough. His Aunt Alya dredged up many unhappy memories of his mother, but it was also a name that represented some happy times, too, and he wanted something good from his first life to touch his daughter.

His father had been a new beginning for him when he needed it most.

He wanted to be that type of safe haven to the sleeping child happily nuzzling his chest. As much as he wanted to break and run back to his family and friends—to Gray—he would take any and every punishment for Imogen.

Except he felt like he was slowly dying. His paternity leave ended in two weeks, and then the grumpy, silver-haired nanny he'd hired would be Imogen's primary caregiver during the day.

Tina already lived with them, making his transition from man to father bearable.

She was a ball-busting hellion where he was concerned, but an absolute angel to his daughter, so she stayed.

He hadn't seen Gray for four weeks. One month had passed since his heart was ripped to shreds. He'd been placing plasters on his lacerated chest for weeks in the hopes of surviving another day.

Gray had refused to respond to all personal or impersonal communication since the day he left her bedroom to fly to London for Imogen's birth. Not that any of the messages contained any truths.

Marie had taken two days to recover in the hospital before booking a flight to Russia to see her husband. They had been separated for almost a year. Marie and Ciar had signed the solicitor's documents twenty minutes after Imogen had made her screaming way into the world.

Marie's stated that she had given up all rights to her child. His said that he was the father and sole caretaker.

He'd tried to get Marie to look upon her child even for a moment. She refused. It killed him to imagine what this conversation might look like when his daughter was older, but knowing his own past and how it had colored his decisions, he couldn't fault Marie for her stance.

Everyone grieved differently.

He was euphoric each time his eyes met his daughter's dark ones, so much like his own. He was equally despondent over the loss of Gray.

His best friends, Daniel and Jonathan, didn't know what was going on. They offered him support, but Ciar knew they were disappointed his actions had caused Gray such grief.

He didn't blame them. They didn't ask for an explanation

for why his relationship with Gray had fallen apart, and he didn't offer one.

The only news he had of Gray and the pub was through his father and uncle. He knew that she had stopped all construction on the home he'd bought them, but he had rehired all the contractors to finish the work.

Hope was an emotion he clung to for dear life.

He missed Gray MacGregor. He missed everything from her sharp wit to her smile, her soft lips, and her arms wrapped around him. She gave the best hugs.

He missed how she looked at him, as if he were her world.

He missed her love.

And she did love him. She'd told him several times, and she wouldn't lie. He was the liar.

Gray thought the worst of him. He thought the worst of himself, but Christ, he wanted her back.

He wasn't sure if what he felt for her was love, but it sure as hell was destroying him.

twenty-one

THREE MONTHS AFTER COLORADO

GRAY

CIAR'S PUB was ready to open its doors. The staff was trained, the kitchen was fully staffed, and the provisions for opening week were purchased. Liquor bottles shone, and the stunning chandeliers that Bébhinn insisted would be perfect, sparkled.

Weeks ago, O'Connor Hospitality had sent out numerous coveted invitations for the pub's grand opening, where Dublin's elite would be treated to the best of the best.

Special menus, rare wines, old whiskeys, and high-stakes poker were some of the treats guests could expect. Gray's family's business specialized in not only opening a business but doing it with smashing success, and this opening was going to be one that the O'Connors could be proud of.

If only Gray could find a modicum of joy in a job well done. Instead, she went to bed each night with a ferocious headache and woke with pounding temples and swollen eyes.

The latter was likely caused by her never-ending tears. She'd believed that time and distance would cure her broken heart. It had been two months since she'd seen or spoken to Ciar—three months since he'd begun to pull away.

She wished they'd never kissed in his kitchen that first time. She wished they'd never been anything other than friends... better to have never known.

His father had been kind during their update meetings. He never broached the subject of his son, but from his sad eyes and worried frowns, Gray could tell he was well aware that his son had walked away from their relationship.

She'd thought about the why of it all thousands of times, finally landing on a girlfriend. Perhaps they had been broken up when he hooked up with Gray, she'd give him that much at least, but no matter his status in Colorado, it changed the moment he took that first trip back to London.

The worst, above having her love thrown aside as though it meant nothing, was that he never looked back besides a few half-hearted apologies. He never spoke to her again, not even a text to say it was over or that he was sorry. There had been... nothing.

Silence and complete rejection.

Her friends and her mother had been breathing down her neck for weeks about what had happened between her and Ciar.

She couldn't tell them since she was in the dark as much as they were. Welcome to the Cold-Blooded Bastard's Club—Gray wasn't the founder, but she certainly was a VIP member. She'd finally relented and let those closest to her know that she and Ciar had broken up, but that she wasn't prepared to speak about that yet.

She'd hated not confiding in her mother, but she'd needed the time to reflect on her own thoughts. Her mom and friends would mean well, but she didn't need any voices in her head besides her own, and even her voice sucked to listen to.

The wallowing had to end. She couldn't continue the self-pitying journey she'd been rocking. It took realizing that the only way to survive her heart's wounds was to own that she allowed herself to stand in the conflagration's epicenter, and the only one who could walk out of it was herself.

She was intelligent, kind, loyal, a good friend, and great at her job. Ciar might have changed her—he had changed her—but he wouldn't break her. Thinking those words was empowering.

Her job for Ciar Murphy was done and dusted. The media outlets had been tipped off about the opening, and hints of a few bigwigs attending were dropped. Her mom had kindly sent two O'Connor employees, Jess and Derek, to work the event and make sure it was a success.

Because he would be there. Millionaire Broker Heartthrob, Ciar Murphy.

The opening was tomorrow night. She planned to visit her folks, stay well away from Dublin, and stay off social media. She didn't want to read or see anything about it. Jess and Derek would give her and her mom the rundown after.

The thought of seeing the name of that damn pub—a name that she'd only learned before the invitations went out—splashed all over the internet had her grinding her poor teeth.

Gray Eyes. Why would he name his passion project after her? It had to be a play on her name and the color of her eyes. There had been plenty of time over the past few months to have changed it.

It felt like he ended up thinking the name was cool, and since she didn't mean shit to him, he decided to keep it. No matter how it would make her feel.

The logo for the menus, napkins, coasters, and all other paraphernalia was a black and white drawing of two large eyes, with the iris shaded gray.

As if he hadn't stabbed her hemorrhaging body repeatedly for months, keeping her weak and confused, he pulled that kind of bullshit.

Her mother had seen the mockup of the name and logo and clenched her jaw, thankfully not saying anything.

Now here she was, about to sneak out of town with more than a weekend bag packed. She'd asked for the Zurich job and got it. Her grandmother, Mary O'Connor, helped start what had become one of the most sought-after spas in Switzerland, and the owners were adding on.

Gray scheduled schoolwork and exams to be done online for the next month.

Four weeks away. She planned on cleansing Ciar from her system in one of the most beautiful countries in the world.

twenty-two

CIAR

CIAR LEFT Imogen with Tina at his flat in London. He would only be gone one night, but it killed him to leave his sweet girl. Nothing, however, would keep him from seeing Gray.

He'd practiced his speech for days. He'd made up his mind he was going to tell her everything. Even the parts that he'd rather stay unknown forever.

He was wearing a sharp, black Armani suit, diamond-crusted cufflinks, and his favorite Blancpain Villeret keeping time on his wrist.

He'd gotten dressed in his old room at Daniel and Jonathan's townhouse, half hoping he might catch a glimpse of Gray next door.

He never saw her.

His best friends were unusually quiet. Courteous but distant. Nothing of their years-old camaraderie was present.

They were having a drink in the kitchen before their car picked them up to take them to Gray Eyes.

Not willing to allow the uncomfortable silence to last, he cleared his throat to get their attention. "Things have been difficult. I apologize for keeping quiet."

They didn't respond, just continued to take nips of their whiskey. Clearing his throat yet again and tugging at his shirt cuffs, he tried again.

"I plan on explaining everything to Gray first. Then I'll tell you, I promise."

"Do you know how many times we've spoken to Gray in over two months?" Daniel asked harshly.

"Once," Jonathan growled. "Your business is your business, Ciar, but those four girls are our best friends, and you've mistreated one of them."

"How are we supposed to be okay with that?" Daniel finished.

"Damn it," he rubbed his hand roughly over his face, "you're not. I'm ashamed, okay?" Finishing off his Absolut and lime, he slammed the glass tumbler to the bar. "I never meant for it to go on this long.

"I know you all think I'm some sort of cheater, but that isn't true. I've just been a fucking liar because I've been afraid to lose her."

"You already lost her, bro. She blocked our numbers weeks ago, and the girls refuse to give us access to Gray because we're friends with you," Daniel explained, finishing his own two fingers of Three Wolves.

"I'm glad to hear you didn't disrespect her like it seemed you had, but brother, seriously, clean up your shit." Jonathan finished his drink and announced their car was pulling up.

"Listen, Ciar," Daniel started, "despite your personal shit-show of a life, I'm proud of you. Gray Eyes looks to be a success. Let's go and enjoy the night."

"The success is Gray's."

As they moved out of the kitchen, Jonathan stopped abruptly and placed his hand on Ciar's chest, halting him as well.

"Nice ink, dickhead."

Daniel flipped an overhead light on, his eyes widening at the new tattoo taking up the remaining real estate on Ciar's neck.

"Jesus, dude. You never stopped caring about her, did you?"

Ciar shoved by both of them. "Let's go." Two weeks after Imogen was born, he'd gotten the new ink. Gray Imogen. The two loves of his life.

A doorman opened the massive wooden and steel door for the three men. The door sported an impressive carving of the Murphy crest. He never okayed the expense, but it had Gray's attention to detail all over it.

Being cut out of her life, her thoughts, had been hell, but he supposed it must feel the same on her end. She had loved him. *Jesus, please* let her still.

His whole body felt like he'd rolled in stinging nettles. His suit felt restrictive, as if his chest were in a vise.

He was going to come face-to-face with Gray tonight. Ciar smiled and took pictures with several of the evening's guests, who kept approaching him to congratulate the pub's success. He ordered drinks, shook hands, and watched his dream coming to fruition in real time.

His father and Uncle Cormac were in attendance and looking sharp. They commandeered a table in the cigar room, and Ciar imagined they'd be there until closing.

He gripped his vodka and orange on the rocks so tightly he

hoped Gray had chosen sturdy glassware. He couldn't help but ask his friends, "When are the girls to be here?"

Daniel gave him a sharp look but answered, "Anytime."

As if his query called them, Mags walked through the door, beautiful with her "Don't mess with me" expression, her brunette hair swinging with every sway of her hips. Blair was next, brilliant red hair tamed in one thick, puffy braid down her slim back, and then Bébhinn, the dark-haired O'Faolain princess on the arm of her fiancé, Dagr Griffiths.

All eyes seemed to focus on the parade of gorgeous women. Ciar took a deep breath, realizing if he held it any longer, he would pass out.

Any second, a leggy, golden-haired bombshell would enter the new pub that she'd had a hand in creating.

Ten seconds.

Thirty seconds.

One minute.

Two.

Four.

"Mr. Murphy. Mr. Murphy," someone at his side interrupted his vigil again. He focused on the man and woman who were trying to get his attention. Swallowing his anger at the interruption, he said, "I am."

The woman, dressed in a sharp business suit, stuck out her hand, which he took. "I'm Jess Rathers, and this is," she nodded to her companion, "Derek Banner. We wanted to introduce ourselves before the evening went on any longer. We work for O'Connor Hospitality. If there is anything you see tonight that doesn't please you, we ask that you let us know immediately."

Ciar's confusion must have shown on his face because the woman, Jess, added, "Josephine and Gray O'Connor hired us to oversee that the evening goes smoothly."

He felt a man come in close and whisper, "Breathe. The show must go on, so just fucking breathe." Jonathan.

He managed to nod at the O'Connor representatives. "Appreciated. Enjoy the evening." And then, once they moved on, he looked at his best friends. "She isn't coming."

"We heard. I would have been surprised if she'd been willing to see you. She'll need a lot more from you than a chance meeting at your own fucking pub."

He felt his head nod in understanding when, in reality, he no longer understood anything. He was about to flag a waiter down to order another drink when the girls and Dagr joined them.

The absence of smiles was the only clue he needed that the next conversation wouldn't be pleasurable either.

He nodded to the new arrivals. Dagr shook his hand. "I'm impressed, Murphy. Gray Eyes looks to be a raging success. Congrats, man."

Ciar finally flagged down a waiter and ordered a round of drinks for him and his friends. Though if the girls' faces were anything to go by, adversaries were a better fit.

Once the drinks were delivered, Ciar faced the angry lineup of femme fatales. "Gray is out of town?" He didn't mean to word that as a question.

No one responded.

He barely stopped himself from frantically looking around for his father. His dad was not happy with his decisions and wouldn't have saved him from this torture even if he could.

He was reaping the rewards of his closed mouth. Gray had been, no, she was the end-all woman for him. When he told her that, he'd meant it.

He still meant it. He just didn't know how to explain his actions, or explain that his past affected his present, or how he hoped it wouldn't affect the future.

His phone buzzed with a text from Tina. She sent the third picture of the evening. This one was of Imogen snuggled in her crib with her favorite lop-eared bunny he'd gotten from the hospital's gift shop the day she was born.

He liked the photo before putting the phone back in his pocket. His life had become a mockery of what he'd envisioned only short months ago.

He would never change the fact that Imogen was his daughter, but his treatment of Gray...he had nothing but regrets.

"Do you remember that night you three brought those horrible dates to our house party?" At his confirming nod, Bébhinn continued. "Do you remember how they hurt one of your friends?" She was speaking of Blair. Of course, he remembered.

"Do you remember how I forgot my dad was dead?"

He bowed his head in shame, as did Daniel and Jonathan standing at his shoulders. "I do. Yes."

"I would rather that night on replay than watch the results of what you've done to Gray. We don't even know what that is," Bébhinn sneered, slapping the table between them, her anger palpable to anyone close, "because she refuses to speak about it."

Mags stood on Bébhinn's right side. For once, there was no amusement to be found skating over her features. "Fuck you and fuck your new pub. I only came tonight to make sure you know that none of us has any plans on speaking to you again. Anyone who shits on one of my friends is an enemy."

And then Blair. Christ, when her lip quivered, he almost broke. She held up shaking hands and signed, "I'm ashamed that I encouraged your relationship. I asked Dad to revoke your access to our home. The girls are telling the truth. She's never spoken your name even though you hurt her. You don't have to be a couple, Ciar, but you at least owed her respect."

twenty-three

BÉBHINN

"SCREW HIM," Mags fumed as the girls left Gray Eyes. "He didn't even try to give some lame excuse."

Bébhinn thanked the doorman who held the door open for their Uber, which was waiting at the curb. Once they were settled and on their way back to their townhouse, she couldn't help but worry that Gray would be so pissed if she knew they'd gone to the opening with the sole intention of telling her ex off.

Bébhinn glanced at Blair. She was looking outside the car window, effectively cutting herself off from the conversation. The confrontation had upset her. It upset them all.

Touching Blair's shoulder to bring her back into the conversation, she asked, "I'm so angry at Ciar, but don't you guys think it's odd that he's never admitted the why of it all?" Dagr had walked her to the door, deciding to stay and enjoy the night with his cousins and Ciar, or at least enjoy what they could after the girls went in on Ciar.

"When Dagr was walking us out, he told me that he believes Ciar must have a good reason for his behavior and wanted us to try and remember that he's always been a good friend up until a few months ago."

Blair sighed, "I agree. I'm so upset with him, though, because even if something terrible was going on in his life that he didn't want to tell us, he could have told Gray. He knows very well he could trust her to keep it to herself."

"Gray hasn't come out and said, but I think she believes there's a girl in London. I just," Mags started, "can't believe it of him, no matter how mad I am."

They sat in silence, contemplating the matter. Bébhinn spoke first. "Ciar didn't tell Gray that he loved her when they were in Colorado, but during the holiday, I would have sworn he did. Didn't you?"

Blair shook her head yes. Mags admitted, "Absolutely. The way he watched her...if that wasn't love, it was damn close. Looking back, everything changed once he went back to London. He stopped coming back home."

"And he's always said he prefers to live with his friends in Dublin because they're his best friends but also because his father is here," Bébhinn reasoned.

The Uber driver stopped outside their townhouse. They all said thank you, and as they went for the door handles, the driver, a middle-aged man, surprised them by asking, "A bit of advice, ladies?"

At their nods of agreement, the driver said, "You three should take a trip to London. Stalk the man who hurt your friend. It's what my blasted, nosy sisters would have done back in the day."

Bébhinn looked at her friends, who stared back with wide eyes. "You're brilliant," she told the driver. I'm going to write you the best damn review of your life."

As soon as the three women reached the living room, they

kicked off their heels and fell onto the comfy couches, ruminating over the driver's suggestion.

Mags hummed as she took off her jewelry.

Blair unbraided her hair, letting loose the thousands of loops and curls.

Bébhinn sat up straight, gaining their attention. "Gray is out of town for four weeks. Would you guys mind helping me pack up the last of Dagr's belongings from his London flat if your schedules allow? He's swamped and could really use our help."

By the grins she received, she knew they were in.

"Anything for Dagr," Blair signed, her eyes twinkling.

"What she said," Mags crooked her thumb toward Blair.

FOUR MONTHS AND TWO WEEKS AFTER COLORADO

GRAY

"MISS YOU, TOO, MOM," Gray smiled at her laptop screen since her mom insisted on video chatting to make sure her daughter wasn't lying about being fine.

She'd been in Zurich for six weeks and was flying home tomorrow. The spa that her Grandma Mary had helped launch years ago had built several small villas dotted around the property for guests who wanted more privacy and treatments in the comfort of a home away from home.

Gray's job had been to market the new additions, throw parties, and lead walkthroughs for potential clients. Many wanted to lease or buy the villas. The spa hadn't been prepared for the level of interest they received, and Gray encouraged them to quickly pivot in their marketing.

Once she'd revised her original proposal, the owners asked her to stay on an extra two weeks. They were convinced she was their lucky charm—they may have been right. She'd helped convince six singles and couples to purchase a villa, as well as got a few more on the line for the remaining three units.

She may have worked her tail off, but there was plenty of pleasure too. The owners had given her carte blanche for all of the spa's services. She'd never looked or felt better.

"It's going to be tough to pull myself away from this place, but I think I've pushed my professors enough." Online school sucked, but it had kept her evenings busy and her thoughts away from a certain man.

"I can't believe you've never brought Dad here. Amra said that any member of our family is always welcome. She remembers Grandma Mary working with her mother-in-law all that time ago."

"You know, maybe I should plan an anniversary getaway for Mom and Dad," her mom mused. "We could make it a family trip."

"I'd be down but give me some time to drop the four pounds I've put on since I got here," she chuckled, sighing when she released the button of her slacks. "I swear, Mom, I've eaten Caramalklöpfli twice a day since I got here."

Her mom laughed. "I doubt you've been that bad."

"Caramalklöpfli is flan topped with caramel sauce. It's to die for, and yes, I have been that bad."

"Besides getting fat," she joked, "has the time away done you good?"

"It has," Gray admitted, "I've thought about what moving forward looks like, and I think it has me confronting Ciar. I deserve answers, and then maybe we can eventually be friends again or at least not avoid each other for the next fifty years."

"That sounds like a wise decision. I hear Gray Eyes is smashing it." Laughing, she added, "River told me that Ciaran and his brother Cormac told Patrick that they finally told Ciar that they were, and I quote, 'Bloody well done with wearing suits.'"

"That sounds like those two," Gray sighed, missing the

thought of hanging out at Murphy's Pub. She was being a big talker to her mother, but she wasn't ready to run into Ciar at his father's pub quite yet. Or anywhere, really.

"They told him to hire some 'posh lad,'" she air-quoted, "to fiddle with the place."

"Ciar should have seen that one coming. I left a list of potential managers with Jess and Derek. Did they remember to show him?"

"They did, and he chose your top recommendation without interviews."

She swallowed whatever snarky comment that wanted to sneak out, choosing to change the subject. "How are Dad and Loch?" Her brother was fifteen and the spitting image of their dad. He was the best brother, though, and Gray couldn't wait to force him to give her a hug when she flew home tomorrow.

For her parents' sake, she'd agreed to fly to Inverness to have a day and night with the family before facing real life in Dublin.

"They miss you. I miss you, Gray. I know you've been going through it, and damn if you haven't taken after me in wanting to suffer alone, but I don't think I can take much more," she admitted.

"I'll see you in the morning, Mom. I land at nine, and I expect chocolate scones at Mindy's Bakery before facing the men."

"From Swiss flan to good old-fashioned Scottish biscuits and jam. I like how you roll. It's a deal. They sound yummy."

Her mom still insisted on calling a scone a biscuit. However, Gray admitted that Scottish scones had nothing on American biscuits. Talk about drool-worthy. Everyone should have an Oklahoma diner on their bucket list, even if it was only for biscuits and sausage gravy.

They said their goodbyes, and Gray promised to text before

she boarded in the morning. "Mom," she hesitated briefly, "thanks for giving me the time away."

"Anything Gray. I'd do anything. Let's be honest, though, sweetheart, you made O'Connor Hospitality a pretty penny in Zurich. Grandma saw the numbers and hasn't stopped crowing that you take after her."

That made them both laugh. "We both know I'm all yours, though."

"We do," her mom agreed.

twenty-five

BLAIR

"HOW IN THE hell have I let myself get talked into this 007 bullshit?" Blair signed her two best friends, who were currently hunkered down under a covered transit shelter across from Ciar's flat.

If Bébhinn and Mags thought their hoodies and umbrellas made them inconspicuous, they were sorely mistaken.

"We have been sitting here for three hours, Bébhinn. Maybe we should pack it in and find a pub and some dinner where it isn't pissing down rain," Mags urged.

"Not yet. I called his work this morning," Bébhinn insisted, "and he is out today. So, unless he left before the butt-crack of dawn, that man is in his flat and eventually has to come out for food or something." She threw her hands up, as exasperated as the rest of them.

"Let's agree. One more hour and then we take a break and assess our plan over a pint," Blair bargained.

"Fine," Bébhinn agreed, though her downturned mouth showed her irritation at the compromise.

"Who knew staking out a criminal could be so wet and boring?" Mags shook the rain droplets from her slicker, where the pelting rain had splashed inside the bus shelter, which they technically shouldn't be resting in as if they were actually trying to catch a bus.

They'd waved on five buses already. Fifteen minutes later, the rain petered off. Fifteen more, and the sun began to shine.

"Thank Christ," Mags muttered.

Sitting between her and Mags, Bébhinn gasped, "Oh God," and grasped their upper arms in a fierce grip, "there he is."

As if the sodden trio were witnessing the eighth wonder of the world unfold before their eyes, they watched as Ciar spoke to a gray-haired woman manning a pram. He was in a suit and clearly dressed for work. They didn't stand, not wanting to draw attention, but they did gather up their surveillance para-phernalia—i.e., cell phones, snacks, and water—ready to follow their mark if necessary.

Blair wanted to touch her friends to get their attention and ask questions, but she didn't want any of them to miss a clue about what Ciar's London life was like.

The three women gasped when Ciar bent and lifted a baby from the pram. He held it close to his chest and peppered its downy head with kisses before gently placing it back in the waiting buggy.

"Oh, fuck no," Bébhinn moaned.

"He is dead to me," Mags hissed.

Blair felt shock sting every part of her body. She was sitting, but felt as if she were falling, as if a centrifugal force were bowing her spine.

"That sonofabitch," Blair croaked out loud in what she knew was her odd-sounding "deaf" speech.

He had a child.

He was a father.

"What do we do?" Bébhinn practically whimpered.

"I think Gray is better off not knowing. This will kill her and rightly so," Mags sniffed back tears. Her sassy temperament was abandoned.

Blair reached over and touched them both to get their attention as they watched Ciar hail a cab. "The only question is, would you want to know? Would you be hurt if your best friends hid this type of truth from you?"

twenty-six

JONATHAN

"I NEED to speak to you. Privately," Blair pointedly stared at his date, who was wide-eyed at the petite, red-headed devil standing next to their table, signing BSL—a table that had cost him a grand to secure.

The only reason he hadn't told the fairy to screw off was the fact that she was sporting reddened eyes. Blair had been crying, and nothing short of his dying would allow him to brush off one of his best friends.

"Now?" he signed back.

Blair nodded while sucking in a shuddering breath. Blair would never interrupt one of his dates if it wasn't important, unlike her brunette banshee friend. Mags interrupted life simply by breathing.

"I didn't know you sponsored special kids, Jonathan. That's so nice, but why is she here? Where are the girl's parents?"

Not again. *Not. Fucking. Again.* Was it so much to ask that a woman be beautiful, intelligent, and not a discriminatory bigot?

"Our date is over, Samantha." He waved to the waiter who had been taking care of their table. "Marty, would you mind showing her," he nodded toward his date, currently sporting a shocked face, "to the cloak room to gather her belongings?"

Focusing his attention back to one of Europe's hottest international models, he said, "Educate yourself before setting foot out of your flat. Never call me again."

Samantha finally stumbled to her feet, glaring between himself and Blair before finally, thankfully, walking away.

"Sit, Blair." He didn't bother to sign, as she was an expert lip reader. Once she sat in his date's vacated chair, he did sign, "I'm sorry." She brushed her hand in front of her body like it wasn't a big deal.

Blair wore a simple navy dress, capped sleeves, belted at the waist, and paired with navy ballet-style slippers. She did look like a fourteen-year-old and not the brilliant adult scientist that she was.

He wasn't sure how she'd made it this far into the restaurant without a reservation. "How'd you get in?"

"The hostess asked me if I was meeting anyone? She specifically wanted to know if I was meeting my parents." She grimaced and shook her head. She hated that she looked so young. "The outfit didn't help. I had to give a speech in front of several visiting botanists.

"Anyway, once she realized that I'm deaf, she got flustered and instead of offering to write it down, I pointed toward your name on the computer screen, and voila, they led me here. No one wants to be mean to a deaf child," she smirked.

"And you decided to interrupt my date because?" True to Blair's personality, she wasn't remotely embarrassed or apologetic.

"I was late leaving school because I had to endure dinner

and cocktails with the visiting scientists. I needed to speak to you, and I didn't want Daniel to know. Not yet anyway. I found out you were here from Mags."

"You couldn't have waited until after the date?" It was clearly no loss, but the principle of it rankled.

"Mags knew who your date was. I looked her up. Her personality on social media is about as pleasing as a puppy kicker, so I knew I was doing you a favor. Anyway, make sure they still bring Samantha's dinner, I'm starved. The food at my event sucked. I'll take a Guinness, as well, please."

Whoever thought Blair Barr was a sweet, softly spoken sort, didn't know her at all. Knowing when he was beaten, he called Marty over with Blair's instructions. When he asked for Blair's identification, she rolled her eyes and handed it over.

"What? You don't look drinking age, especially in that dumpy frock." He laughed at her outraged gasp.

"Fine. It isn't a good look for me. If my tits were bigger, it would be a different story."

When he choked on his whiskey, she made the BSL sign for laughter. Blair never laughed out loud in public. He'd heard her laugh twice in his life. She saved her voice for her girlfriends.

"Jesus. Do you kiss your mother with that dirty mouth?"

Marty brought their meals and new drinks to the table. Once they were alone again, she took a sip of her Guinness and tucked into the salad and grilled salmon Samantha had ordered. Halfway through, she set her utensils down to sign, "At least that woman can order a decent meal."

Jonathan let dinner play out, not bothering to ask what Blair needed to speak with him about. She'd get there. Once her plate was clean, which he was quite sure his date would never have done even if she were hungry, she focused her attention on him.

"Mags, Bébhinn, and I went to London yesterday."

"I know. Daniel mentioned you were packing up the rest of Dagr's flat."

"That's not why we went."

Blair tapped the table linens, a frown marring her expressive face. Whatever was going on, she wasn't happy to discuss it.

"Why then?" And then his chest squeezed tight. "Is something the matter with one of you girls? And why don't you want Daniel to know?"

"We went to spy on Ciar."

"Jesus, Blair. Are you serious? I know he's been different, and the Gray thing isn't good," his jaw clenched at the reminder, "but don't you think spying is a step too far?"

"He has a baby."

Jonathan could only blink, blink, blink. "Wha, wha, what now?"

"A baby. We saw him step from his building with an older woman, probably the nanny, and a pram."

"And you jumped to the conclusion that it was his?"

"He picked the child up and cuddled it, kissing its head. He had the look of a man attached. He handled the infant with confidence. Have you ever known him to pick up other people's babies for cuddles?"

"But...I don't know what to say or think, really."

"The girls and I are undecided as to what to do. Should we tell Gray or not? Should we confront Ciar? There's a chance, but given his bizarre behavior recently, the chance is slim that it wasn't his child.

"His best friends live in Dublin. His father and uncle live in Dublin. He's opened up that swanky pub, and it's in Dublin.

"He won't be able to keep himself permanently in London.

Gray will have to see him again, and if the baby is his, he won't be able to hide its existence forever."

"Why didn't you want Daniel to know?" he asked again.

"Both of you are compassionate and fiercely loyal, but where you might sit on this information for a few days, dissecting the best course of action, Daniel would immediately fly to London to beat the shit out of Ciar and immediately thereafter, call Gray. His conscience wouldn't allow him not to."

Her assessment wasn't wrong.

However, he didn't need days to figure out what to do. He knew exactly what needed to happen. He swallowed the last of his shot and sighed, watching Blair finish off her Guinness—how someone so tiny could handle the boldness of that black tar was a mystery.

"I'll call Ciar tomorrow morning. I'll tell him he was seen with a baby. He doesn't have to know it was you three. If I ask him pointblank, he won't lie."

"And if he has a baby?" Blair asked.

"I will give him an ultimatum. He can tell Gray, or I will."

He and Blair took an Uber back to their townhouses, and unfortunately, Daniel was sitting on their front steps smoking a cigar. Blair stiffened next to him. She hated cigars. Passionately.

"He'll have questions. You go on inside as if you've not a care in the world. I'll handle Nancy Daniel Drew's inquiries."

Blair waved to Daniel as she climbed her own stairs. Jonathan leaned against the balustrade close to Daniel. "Nice night for a smoke, huh?"

"Why is Blair with you? Thought you had a date with that smoking hot model."

"She was terrible. I knew Blair was at school late. Trinity is close to the restaurant, and I asked if she wanted a free meal.

"Food was excellent by the way. Blair loved her salad and

salmon. I'm off. I have several reports to go over before I speak to Dad tomorrow. We still meeting for lunch?"

Daniel was silent for a beat. "Yes."

His cousin was definitely suspicious. By tomorrow, the whole Ciar scandal would hopefully be proved wrong, and he could tell Daniel.

twenty-seven

CIAR

CIAR LET his head fall back against the car's headrest and groaned. He'd gotten a lift to work and for once was on time.

Imogen had gone through weeks of night screaming, which Tina assured him was colic and very normal. Imogen's doctor confirmed. Last night was perfect silence. He'd even gone in to check, fearing the quiet, but his sweet girl was sound asleep and breathing normally.

Thank God he hadn't woken Tina. He learned the hard way that waking her up was a no-no. Tina shared the small bedroom with his daughter's crib and had assured him, multiple times, that she didn't need his assistance taking care of a child.

He groaned at the reminder that he needed to source a larger flat, but London wasn't where he wanted to raise his child. His family and friends were in Dublin, and he was desperate for them to meet her.

Before she was born, he'd hoped that he, Gray, and Imogen

"

would move into the home he bought when they were in Colorado.

It was absurd for him to expect that outcome, considering he never explained anything about Marie or Imogen to Gray, nor the reasons behind his actions.

He didn't even know if Gray was back from Zurich. No one mentioned her to him, and he was too ashamed to ask after her.

His phone began to ring, and he answered it as the driver pulled up outside work. "Hey, Jon. I'm just walking in to work. What's up?"

"I'm at work."

Jonathan's typical banter was nonexistent, instantly alerting him to a problem. "Is something going on?"

"Listen, Ciar. I hate asking you this, but if it's true, and you played Gray, I'm not sure how we'll move past it."

Ciar lost all mobility in his limbs. Thankfully, outside Anders' office stood several metal benches, and he dropped onto one.

"You were seen by someone in London with a baby. Did you have a baby with a woman and not bother to tell Gray? I'm trusting you, Ciar, to tell me true."

His heart pumped so ferociously that he feared a heart attack. His guts were cramping, and bile rose to his throat.

What the hell did he expect? Secrets never stay secret.

Had he still been holding out hope for a happily ever after with Gray? Yes. Every time he had mentally walked through "the talk" with Gray, laid himself bare, there had only been one outcome in his mind. Total rejection.

Not hearing her tell him she was through was better than hearing it, and so he lived in limbo and forced Gray into the same.

The time for hiding was over.

Jonathan knew Ciar wouldn't lie to one of his oldest friends.

Omitting the truth for months was bullshit enough. Outright lying wasn't who he was.

"I do. A daughter. I found out after Colorado."

"Fuck, man. What the actual fuck?" Jonathan was pissed.

"Why didn't you tell Daniel and me? Why the fuck didn't you tell Gray?" Before he could answer either of those questions, he said, "Wait. Are you with the mom?"

"No. We were never together. And I didn't tell anyone because I'm a fucking idiot coward," he growled.

"I didn't want to lose Gray, but I lost her anyway. I've messed up, Jon, in every which way that I can. I miss my friends, especially you and Daniel, but I don't know how to breathe without Gray."

Ciar heard Jonathan cursing in the background, like he'd taken his phone from his ear. "Talk to me, Jon. I'm sorry. For all of it. Not for my daughter, but the rest..."

"Listen," Jonathan finally started, "I'm happy for you. Happy about the baby. Gray though. You hurt her, Ciar, and no matter what you say, what your reasons are, you hurt one of our best friends.

"She left her friends and family for six weeks because of you, and if we're being completely honest, it wasn't only the past three and a half months. It was four and a half. You pulled away from her, from all of us, the day after Colorado.

"We've always been more family than friends, but Christ, Ciar. What now?"

Ciar felt tears prick his eyes and pressed his fingers into them, hoping physical pain would counteract the emotional kind.

"I've asked myself every day how I saw all this going. I've had months of could-haves and should-haves. I've become a man I don't even recognize.

"There isn't anyone I've not disappointed. Everything

snowballed into the shitstorm that I live in every day. I used to believe I could fix things. Now, I don't know.

"The house I bought for Gray and me sits finished and waiting, and yet we haven't laid eyes on each other for months."

"I thought Gray halted work on the place. At least that's what Mags said."

"She did. I rehired everyone. It's done."

"And yet, you're living a secret life in London. Why couldn't you have told Gray? You weren't with the baby's mother. You didn't cheat on her. She would have understood."

To make Gray understand, he would have to talk about things that he never had. Or wanted to. That he refused to do even now, though it was costing him everything.

"She's home. Tell her, or I will."

"Understood."

twenty-eight

GRAY

GETTING a hug from her mom felt so good after six weeks of not feeling her arms wrapped around her back. Gray wasn't a child, but there was nothing like walking into the familiar safety of your parent's embrace.

Her mom kept her promise and took her for a full breakfast. Now they were lounging in a hammock, side by side under her dad's outdoor kitchen's pergola, sipping unsweetened Lipton's iced tea.

Her dad was working on a late lunch feast with her brother. It was comforting to be surrounded by her family. She'd needed the healing of being far away from everyone, but her family had always centered her.

Gray mused, "I shouldn't be so hungry, but dang, Dad, that smells good. I swear, Mom, when I get home, I'm going on a cleanse."

Her mom turned on her side and wrapped her arm around Gray's waist, snuggling against her back. Gray felt her stomach rumble and hoped the gas turning over in her stomach didn't slip. Her brother would tease her for ten years if she farted on their mom.

Had they not been so close, Gray would have missed her mother stiffening into a statue, but she felt it clearly and was about to ask if she was okay when her mom caught her eye and shook her head no.

She whispered, "If I had to pass gas, I would have moved. Geesh."

"I know. Drop it."

Unsettled by her mother's tense mood all of a sudden, Gray started to say, "But—" except her mom cut her off.

"Later, Gray, please."

That evening, Gray excused herself to go to her room and pack. She was flying back to Dublin first thing. She wasn't the best packer, so when her mom knocked on the frame of the open door, it was to find Gray bouncing her ass on the stuffed suitcase trying to get the zipper to close.

"Jesus, Gray," her mom sighed, getting on her knees to help with the zipper. "You are so neat and tidy in every other aspect of your life. Why can't some of those organizational skills spill over into packing?"

"If there's a master class on packing, sign me up," Gray quipped. "I'm not above learning a new skill."

Her mom stood and went over to close the bedroom door before turning and leaning against it. The sad look on her face had the hair on the back of Gray's neck standing.

"You're freaking me out. What the hell is going on with you?"

Her mom lifted her oversized t-shirt from her jeans and pulled out a box, which was weird as all hell, but when she said, "Baby, I think you might be pregnant. I ran uptown and bought you a test," Gray felt time stop.

She looked at the box, looked at her mother's worried face,

and then back to the box. She grappled with getting off the suit-case and pressed shaky hands to her bed until she sat heavily on the comforter.

"What is this? Why would you say something like that? I told you I've put on a few pounds. Jesus, Mom, I hardly think that necessitated buying a...a pregnancy test. Plus, I haven't had sex since...since him."

Her mom sat next to her on the bed and laid the test between them. "When I had my arm around you earlier in the hammock, I felt something nudge me."

"I was gassy! For the love of God!"

"I know it's a lot to take in, but when I was pregnant with you, I was exactly the same. I gained a few pounds. I thought it was water retention, or that I was eating too much, or some dire gastrointestinal disease.

"I was almost five months pregnant when I got the news. I've thought about this all afternoon. Do you remember when you got that horrible flu, and you came home to recover? The diarrhea, the vomiting—"

"I certainly don't need reminding. Nightmare."

"You would have puked up your birth control pills for at least three days. You went to Colorado right after you recovered."

Those words settled as comfortably as a pinless grenade. "But," Gray paused, placing a hand on her stomach, "I'm not pregnant. No way. I think I would know."

"Have you had a period during the placebo pill weeks?"

Gray blanched, trying to remember. "The first month or two after Colorado, I did have slight spotting, but I've never had heavy periods," she defended.

"The last two months, I assumed it was my stress changing things," she ended lamely.

"One thing at a time. Take the test."

In a state of shock, Gray grabbed the test box and trudged to her bathroom. She read the instructions, peed on the stick, and then carefully placed it on the counter while she righted her clothes and washed her hands.

If she was pregnant, she clenched her eyes tight in denial, but if she were, the test advertised that it would tell you how many weeks along she was.

Let it be negative. Let it be Negative. Let it be negative.

Positive. "Fuck." Very positive.

"Mom. Come here, please."

She must have been waiting on the other side because the door opened before she finished asking.

"Oh fuck," her mom whispered, as she looked at the test.

"Yeah. Pretty much. And look at the weeks. I'm practically halfway done. How could I not have known?" Gray wailed. Fat, ugly tears started to drip down her cheeks.

Her mom hugged her tight, letting Gray soak her shoulder, and grabbed several tissues from the box and gently placed them by her hand.

Gray pulled away and dried her face and blew her nose. She sat on the counter, still staring at the test in disbelief.

"It must have happened our first time. How in the hell am I this unlucky?"

"I have a feeling you'll change your mind on that pretty quickly." Her mom placed a hand over Gray's mostly flat stomach. "You have a son or a daughter in there that's going to think you are their sun, moon, and stars, and you'll think the same of your child."

That was sobering. Gray took a deep breath and squared her shoulders. She could do this. She would do this. She had no choice.

"Now what? I've school, and if that test is accurate, this little one will come before I graduate."

"That's easy," her mom waved off the worry. "You sit down with your instructors and explain the situation, and ask them if they would mind giving you the rest of the year's big projects early, and then you work your butt off. You've done online school before, so if needs must, I imagine they will work with your new mommy schedule."

"Oh, God. And Ciar?"

"That," she hesitated, "is not so simple. I think you should fly to London instead of flying home tomorrow. Corner him until he tells you what in the hell is going on, and once he does, because that man loves you, you surprise him with the baby news."

"That sounds terrifying."

"It does, doesn't it? Better you than me."

"Asshole," Gray laughed, tapping her foot against her mom's thigh. "Dad and Lochlann?"

Her mom took both of her daughter's hands. "We tell them now. Together. I won't keep something like this from your father, and it would hurt Loch's feelings terribly if he were left out of such a huge family event.

"Your dad will love you no differently than he does right now. Of that you can be assured. The hardest part will be convincing him not to go to London and strangle Ciar before you have a chance to speak to him."

"I feel like I could vomit."

"Come on then, better to get it over with, and then we can change your flight."

It turned out to be an hour of torturous waiting. Her mom decided to hide all the car keys so the boys "can't rush off like chickens with their heads cut off." Then she decided to call in her dad's best friend, Coll, his sister, Aunt Cat, and their son, and Lochlann's best friend, Laith.

Her mom wouldn't tell them why and made them promise

that what they were about to find out couldn't leave the house —Gray would want to tell her friends first. Her mom felt that Coll and Laith would help keep their boys in line, and Catriona would bust her brother's balls if he got unruly.

Now here they were, standing awkwardly around the kitchen's massive island. The men were shifting restlessly, shrugging, and exchanging confused looks. The moment her Aunt Cat walked in, her eyes went to Gray's middle, and a small smile played across her lips, quickly extinguished before anyone else could see.

Not much could get past Cat. She was Blair's mother after all.

Gray knew she couldn't stay quiet much longer, and with a last look at her mother, who nodded in encouragement, she said, "I'm pregnant."

twenty-nine

GRAY

SILENCE TRULY WAS DEAFENING. Gray could only hear her heart beating in her ears—until she couldn't.

All hell broke loose when her dad's water glass shattered in his hand, and blood started leaking over the counter and floor.

"Thomas," her mom shrieked, "don't move, baby." She started throwing everything out of the kitchen medicine cabinet until she found the kit she was looking for. "Get to the sink. Now."

Not the response Gray was hoping for. She glanced at Lochlann. His cheeks were seared red, and his fists were clenched. His eyes, though... *Oh, God.* His eyes were glassy.

While her parents were busy, she said, "Loch. I'm sorry. I just found out today."

"Is it Ciar's?" her brother asked.

"Yes." Not giving him a chance to push her off, she wrapped her arms around his waist and rested her head against his broad, youthful chest. "I love you. Please don't be disappointed in me."

"Damn it, sis. Nothing could make me disappointed in you. Ciar, however, better watch his fucking back."

"Language," her mom scolded.

Gray didn't realize that her mom and dad had moved back to the island and had been watching their children.

Both Coll and Laith appeared rigid and expressionless. Her aunt Cat, though, gave Gray an encouraging smile.

"Dad," Gray implored, his usually stoic countenance appeared devastated. He did take several steps closer to his daughter, at least.

"I just found out today, Dad, I swear. I decided I'm going to try to work things out with Ciar, but if I can't, I can promise you that I'll bloody well do it on my own and do a damn good job of it."

And because she refused to bow to her father's possible judgment, she added, "I would have liked to come to you with this announcement in a better place, Dad, but as I'm a woman grown, and one who has proven her worth in Mom's family business, I won't apologize."

Her dad took the final steps that separated them and gently touched her cheek. "I will love your child as I have my own. I only wish that you would have used that big brain of yours to remember contraception, or at the very least, choose a better partner."

Gray gasped, Cat gasped, and her mom hissed, "Thomas."

Her brother even stepped forward and said, "Da. Enough," which was mild compared to her father's sister.

"Tom, you say one more fucking word like that, and I will never speak to you again. I can't speak for Coll and Laith, but if you don't apologize to Gray, I will walk out that door," she pointed to the carved wooden entrance, "and you won't see me again."

"Cat," Coll began.

"Don't you Cat me. If you think the shit my brother just said was correct, you can find a new place to sleep. I'll also remind you, Coll Barr, that you were the one without a care for contraceptives, which is why I was pregnant with Blair when we'd only just started sleeping together," her voice raised when she added, "behind our family's backs too!"

"Christ, Mom," Laith groaned, embarrassed to be hearing about his parents' sexcapades.

Coll, smartly, put his hands up in surrender. "Forgive me, my love. I wouldn't change a thing about how we started out, which you better damn well know," he growled.

Catriona sniffed and clamped her lips tight, but she did give one shaky nod of agreement. Seeing that, Coll pulled her tight to his front, holding her close.

"Christ, Loch, can we bounce yet?" Laith whined.

Her brother didn't answer because her mom suddenly had the floor. "Are you saying," her mom began stiffly, "that when you had sex with me on the plane, when my birth control was screwed up, it's because I wasn't being smart?"

Lochlann mumbled, "Jesus, my ears."

Her dad looked like he'd been shot between the eyes. "No. No, that's—" He raised a hand to touch Gray's arm, but when he reached out to touch his wife, her mom took a step back.

He looked between Gray and her mom, deflating when he saw their tears. "I'm an idiot. I spoke without thinking." He tugged Gray close, wrapping an arm around her back to bring her close for a hug, using one of his beefy hands to push her head to his chest.

Gray hadn't realized how badly she needed a hug from her dad until that moment, feeling silent tears trickling down her cheeks to soak his shirt.

"Jo. Please." He motioned to his wife. She hesitated a moment before joining Gray on her dad's other side. "Will you girls forgive me? It was one of the best days of my life when you told me you were pregnant, Jo, and Gray, I forget sometimes that you aren't a little girl anymore."

"Clearly," Laith snorted, "since she's knocked up."

"Shut the hell up," Lochlann started to say something else, but Laith wasn't finished.

"I can't believe your folks are part of the mile high cl—" Loch's fist to his best friend's stomach finally shut Laith up.

"And how do you know your parents aren't members?" Cat asked her son sweetly, who moaned something about needing to vomit.

Her dad kept talking, ignoring the company. "I'm mad at Ciar, not about the pregnancy. I think he's shit and doesn't deserve you. I took my anger at him out on you. It won't happen again. Forgiven?"

Gray sighed in relief. "Of course. Grandpa."

"Too soon, Gray," her dad grumbled. "And you, Jo? I've never regretted the plane or anything that came after. Forgiven?"

Her mom smiled at Gray across the expanse of her husband's chest. "Men can be so dumb," she announced before twisting from his arms to reach up and kiss him gently. "I love you."

Cat clapped her hands and grinned. "Now that's over, how far along are you, Gray?"

"The test said eighteen weeks."

"Christ Almighty," her dad spluttered, "she is definitely your daughter, Josephine."

Her mom giggled and elbowed his side. It was kind of funny that her mom found out she was pregnant with Gray at around the same time.

"It's because you both are so lovely and tall with so much more room for a baby to grow than simply out. I swear, Coll caught me a million times from tipping over face-first. Having that heavy belly threw my equilibrium off something terrible." Cat smiled at her husband, who grinned back. The memory was a fond one.

"What now?" Lochlann asked.

"I'm changing my flight. I'm going to London in the morning and see what's really going on with Ciar, and then once I'm back to Dublin, I'll find a doctor. The rest is TBD."

Lochlann stepped forward, looming almost as large as their dad, and said, "I'll go with you. To London. For moral support, that is."

She gave him a big hug where he awkwardly patted her back. "Thanks Loch, but I'm not letting you or Dad anywhere near this child's father until things are sorted." She knew she'd made the right call when her dad and brother exchanged looks of disappointment.

"Oh, and Cat, please don't say anything to Blair. I'll tell the girls when I get home."

"The sooner the better, because as soon as the girls know, we can call the Byrne sisters to get their recommendations for doctors," Catriona grinned, excited about the baby.

"Also," her mom added, "would you mind, Gray, if we had Aileen and Charles come over so you can tell them the big news? She would never tell Mags if we ask her not to."

"Of course we should," Gray agreed.

Twenty minutes later, the kitchen was more crowded, including Mirren on a video call. Aileen cried and congratulated Gray. "I'd better not get news like this from Mags for several years, though," she laughed.

"Do you remember calling me when you found out, Jo?"

"You listened to me bawling in my car in the doctor's parking lot for what felt like hours. You made me feel like I could conquer the world or at least your ex-husband," her mom joked.

Gray felt lightheaded at the speed with which the day had escalated. It started with a relaxing barbecue with the family, led to a positive pregnancy test, and finished with a big family reveal.

Her mom was right. It was a relief that her father knew. Waiting would have been stressful, and worse than that, it would have hurt his feelings.

Before she went to bed, Gray booked an early flight to London in the hopes of cornering Ciar before he went to work for the day.

Even before she found out about the baby, she wanted a reconciliation. No matter how she'd tried to snuff out her feelings, she still loved Ciar Murphy—add to that a baby, and she was beginning to feel twinges of desperation.

He'd better cough up every secret he'd ever hoarded.

He'd better want their child.

He'd better still care about her.

thirty

CIAR

CIAR HADN'T SLEPT for more than two hours a night since Jonathan's call three days ago. Jon had promised to let him know when Gray was back in Dublin.

The plan was to fly out immediately and then tell her everything. He refused to do that over the phone.

It had been a shock to find out that his friends knew he had a child. Jonathan had every right to be angry with him. There was nothing that Jonathan said that Ciar wasn't already castigating himself for.

His mind had been circling itself, considering the best way to make Gray understand that he cared for her deeply, but that he couldn't—wouldn't—walk away from an innocent child.

Ciar compounded the shitstorm that he'd created with his silence to the point where an explanation that sounded plausible was nearly impossible.

Would he give her the same benefit of the doubt if the situation were reversed? He wasn't sure, and that's what had put an acid ball in his stomach for weeks on end.

Gray should have been home yesterday, so surely today was the day. It was seven in the morning, and Imogen was already rocking her hungry squawk. The bottle warmer dinged, and as he positioned his daughter in the crook of his arm and grabbed the bottle, flicking off the cap with one hand, a knock sounded on the door, followed by the bell.

"What the hell?" It was a little early for a damn grocery delivery, but knowing the lovely Tina, she planned the obnoxious timing on her night off.

Tina wasn't expected for another thirty minutes. "Hag," Ciar muttered as he made his way to the front door.

He was already opening the door, explaining, "Sorry, I wasn't expecting a delivery this morning."

It wasn't a delivery.

It wasn't Tina either.

"Gray."

She stood still, as stunned as he was. He noticed she wore slouchy jeans and an oversized tee, the handle of a rolling carry-on gripped in one hand.

Her hair was loose, and her face was clean and fresh and stunning. It had been months of indescribable pain being away from her, and now here she was. On his doorstep.

She was looking at him with her mouth parted in surprise, and he was looking at her in desperation.

He wasn't sure how long they stared at each other, but finally, the sound of Imogen sucking greedily on air, having finished her breakfast in record time.

He pulled the bottle from her mouth and, with the skill of a single father, propped her up against the oversized burp rag that never quite caught all the spit-up. He gently patted her back while Gray remained frozen in place.

"Gray, please, come in," he implored.

"You have a…child."

"Yes, but please come in and let me explain." Imogen's loud belch made Gray flinch and Ciar moan in desperation.

"Jon was to tell me when you were back in town, and I planned on coming to you. To explain everything. You're here now," he fumbled to get the right words out, "so I can do it now."

"Jonathan knows about," she swept her hand up and down his body, encompassing his daughter, "this?"

"Only just. He would have told you if I didn't, which I planned to do," he added quickly. Again, he tried to urge her forward. "Come in."

"When was the baby born?"

"Imogen. Her name is Imogen." Gray shoved her fist between her teeth, and a keening wail ricocheted off the flat's walls and the hallways beyond.

"I have an explanation for that too. Just let me explain. Please, Gray."

As if it couldn't get worse, Tina's scowling face showed up at Gray's elbow. In the nanny's true obnoxious form, she bustled by Gray, sidestepped the suitcase, and took Imogen from his arms.

"I'll get this sweet girl cleaned up and dressed." Tina didn't wait for confirmation but stomped her way to Imogen's room with a soldier's cadence.

"When was she born?" Gray asked again.

He refused to lie and gave her the date. Her face went impossibly white, and she swayed. When he held out a hand for support, she held hers up in a stop gesture.

"The last night we all went out to your dad's for drinks."

It wasn't a question. "In the early morning hours," he confirmed. "Marie called, and I—"

"Please do not."

"Let me explain. I should have explained months ago. I...I

care for you so deeply. I couldn't stand the thought of hurting you."

"That night you left me in my bedroom, naked and alone, you knew you were going to the birth of your child?"

He nodded reluctantly, hearing how badly he had handled the situation was disgusting. "Yes, but—"

"No," she stopped him. Her grip on the suitcase handle was white. "Good on you, Ciar. You scored one last piece of me on your way out."

Now, it was his turn to sway.

"I'll make sure Daniel, Jonathan, and Dagr let me know when you're in Dublin. I expect you'll do me the kindness of letting them know so our paths never cross.

"Goodbye, Ciar."

thirty-one

JOSEPHINE

"I WILL FUCKING RUIN HIS LIFE," her husband said quietly as he leaned against one of their wraparound balustrades, watching the sun set.

Usually, Josephine would have scolded Thomas' aggressive threats.

Not today.

Her eyes were raw from crying. Ever since Gray had called her from the airport, she'd been paralyzed.

Parents didn't want their children to suffer, and their daughter was suffering.

Jo tried to talk her into coming back to Scotland, but she insisted she had to get back to school and decide how to tell her friends about the baby. Not about the child Ciar already had—that sonofabitch—but her own.

She didn't push on what Gray meant to do now. It was too raw and too soon.

Gray wasn't alone. She would never be alone, and together, as a family, they would figure it out.

"He named his daughter Imogen. Why, Thomas? Why call her by our daughter's middle name? I can't make sense of it."

Thomas left his silent vigil of counting the stars that had begun to fill the sky to pull her into his arms. "He'll regret his life choices, never fear, Jo, but for now, we have to help our girl.

"I spoke with Bran and Patrick." Thomas' rumbling voice at the top of her head made her feel safe, less panicked. "The O'Faolains still have a seat on Trinity's board as one of their largest donors. If Gray can get through the end of the year, they think they can get her a special dispensation for her final months to be online. I want her to move home."

Jo sniffed back tears. "I want her home, too, but she's as stubborn as her father."

"She'll come."

thirty-two

GRAY

GRAY'S biggest regret of her life to date—calling her mom while she was hysterically crying after leaving Ciar's flat.

That single misstep would cost her. Her parents were likely planning World War III, and they would only have one target. Ciar Murphy.

She'd texted her mom as soon as she'd landed in Dublin and told her that she'd overreacted.

> Gray: It was a surprise.

> Gray: He never said he loved me anyway.

> Gray: Once I tell my friends about the baby, I'll figure out the Ciar thing.

> Gray: No worries. Tell Dad I'm fine.

And her only hope.

Gray: Give me a few days, please.

Her mom's only response.

Mom: We love you.

Evasion.

"Fuck," Gray muttered as she tossed her suitcase and backpack on her bed. It was great to be home, but her parents weren't the only shitstorm she was dealing with. One was waiting for her in the living room, making the binding of dread across her ribs tighten.

It was early evening by the time she'd disembarked and ordered an Uber to take her home. During the lift, she'd texted her friends to meet her. As she came out of her bathroom, she heard their conversation filtering through the house.

Reminding herself that it would be easier to tell her friends than it had been to tell her dad and brother, she took a deep breath and walked toward the voices.

As soon as they saw Gray, Bébhinn, Mags, and Blair jumped up and ran to her side.

"Missed you." Mags hugged her tight.

Blair only gripped Gray's hands and squeezed. They didn't need words.

"It feels like you've been gone forever." Bébhinn kissed her cheek.

Dagr, Jonathan, and Daniel were at the kitchen table looking way too much like triplets, much to her amusement. The only amusing thing about the day.

"You've been crying, Gray. Best tell us what the hell this is about, before I lose my shit," Daniel said evenly.

Gray winced, thinking that it wasn't that many months ago that he and his family were told surprising news that ripped his family apart. Her news wouldn't change his family, but it would definitely shift their friend dynamic, and Gray hated that.

The girls sat in the empty chairs with Bébhinn perched on Dagr's lap. All eyes were on Gray. No turning back now.

"I'm almost five months pregnant, and Ciar broke up with me because he had a baby with another woman. I went to his flat this morning and saw for myself. I know you know, Jonathan, but I didn't know if anyone else did."

In the silence, she said, "I learned about my baby last night and about Ciar's only hours ago."

"Holy shit!" Blair signed.

"What the hell? Oh my God! I knew things are topsy turvy, Gray, but a baby. How wonderful." Bébhinn covered her mouth, clearly stunned.

"How in the hell did you just find out?" Mags, of course.

Daniel looked at Jonathan, anger painting his features. "Why didn't you tell me? Why didn't fucking Ciar tell me?"

"The girls staked out his place in London a few days ago and discovered he had a baby. Blair came to me for my opinion. They couldn't decide whether to tell her immediately or wait until she was home," Jonathan explained.

"I would have called Gray first and then flown to London to kick his ass," Daniel replied furiously.

"Exactly, Dan. You would have railroaded the whole thing. We were trying to do what was best for Gray. I promised to tell Ciar when she got back, he planned on coming to see her and explain."

"I don't give a shit about Ciar right now," Bébhinn growled, sliding off Dagr's lap to come wrap her arms around Gray. "Our best friend is pregnant. We're going to be aunties and uncles. My God, Gray, there's barely time to decorate a baby's room. I'll get Mom and my aunts on it."

Mags stood, lending her support. "You're pregnant, Gray.

Like, a few months from giving birth, pregnant. Jesus. Had you left it much longer, we would have had to have this conversation at the hospital while you were in labor."

Blair laid her hand over Gray's flat stomach before smiling and signing, "Tall bitches get all the luck."

Gray burst out laughing and crying. The release of emotion was exactly what she needed. It'd been a hell of a day. "I have so many things to figure out. Where will I live? Will I stay in Dublin? If I know my father, he's already sending a moving company to drag me back to Scotland."

"Why can't you stay here, Gray?" Mags asked. "We would all love to help with the baby. You'll have like your own team of nannies."

Blair asked, "Did you tell Ciar this morning?"

Gray could only shake her head, tears pricking her eyes again. Blair simply said, "I understand."

Gray slid into one of the dining room chairs and faced the men. Daniel was still pissed, Jonathan was looking at her in sympathy, but Dagr looked like he had something to say.

"What is it?" Gray asked him, blotting her eyes with a tissue that Bébhinn placed in her hand.

He glanced at Bébhinn first before admitting, "Bébhinn doesn't think I'm right, but...well, I know I'm new to this group, but I think it's given me maybe a perspective that you all don't have, as you're so close.

"I've watched Ciar and how he is with Gray. He was fully committed. He bought them a house for fuck's sake. That is not the action of an uncommitted man. I don't think he had any idea about the baby until after Colorado.

"I think the man is an idiot when it comes to communicating. He's more closed off to his feelings than anyone I know besides my father. I just, well, I think there is more to this story.

At the risk of pissing Bébhinn off, I think you should at least let him explain his actions.

"All we've got is speculation, Gray. If nothing else, you can finally have the truth. You are going to tell Ciar about your baby. Eventually anyway. Talking to him is the only way to open up communication. He's the father of your child. He's going to be in your life whether you like it or not. Make it on your terms."

It had been almost two weeks since the day of the big reveal, and Gray was still dodging the question of whether or not she would or could reach out to Ciar. Dagr was right. There was no 'if' she would, but "when."

The fact that he had so coldly cut her out of his life and hid a baby of all things wasn't something a woman would or could get over quickly.

Her parents had agreed to give her a few weeks to let everything sink in before her dad tried to bulldoze his way in. Her mom had found an obstetrician's name, and Gray had an appointment at the end of the week.

If the pregnancy test was accurate, she should be all of five months along. Her lower stomach had a slight swell, only noticeable to her, she was sure, but Gray was thrilled. The baby had been a shock, but after almost two weeks of knowing, she'd become ridiculously excited.

As long as she didn't think about the father.

Christmas was around the corner, which meant she'd been studying for final exams like a crazy person. They all had. She was kind of sad that it would be the last classes she had on campus.

Daniel and Jonathan had come by last week to explain what Gray's dad had asked their fathers, Bran and Patrick, to do. Gray was far from shocked. They explained that Trinity would allow her to finish out her degree online and through virtual meetings with the professors.

It was a relief. School from home would allow her to focus on getting ready to have a baby. There were a million things she would need and a room to decorate. Somewhere.

When she'd called her dad to bark at him for going behind her back with Bran and Patrick, he'd remained silent. Clearly, he wasn't going to apologize.

When he was done listening to Gray rant, he followed with, "Your mom and I want you to move home."

That shut her up. "I'm not ready to make a big decision like that, Dad."

"You don't have very many months left to make it, sweetheart. I only want you and the baby safe."

Her dad's heartfelt plea pulled at Gray's heart. Still... "I know. I promise to figure myself out sooner than later. Okay?"

"So, should I cancel the movers?"

"Dad," she growled.

That was five days ago. Gray was living in fear of what his second battle would look like. Daniel's mother, Raven, was taking her to look at a gorgeous loft flat that a friend of hers was putting up for lease in January.

Her friends really wanted her to stay at the townhouse. There was an extra bedroom for the baby as Bébhinn had moved out two months prior. Gray struggled with wanting to stay where she was comfortable and not wanting to put her friends on nanny duty.

Blair barged in from the door that led to the back garden. For such a tiny woman, she could make a clatter. She caught her friend's eye, signing that Blair was covered in her work. Blair only grinned and swiped her fingers across her cheek, covering herself in even more soil and debris.

"Are you ready for your INCC internship? I hear Dagr's father is a handful." Ulf Griffiths, Dagr's dad, was heading up a new nature and hiking preserve in Wales for the Initiative for Nature Conservation Cymru, and Blair had scored the coveted internship.

"Two months," Blair grinned. "I can't wait. They're doing their conservation process all wrong. I can't wait to bitch slap them into the twenty-first century. I have so many plans, I can hardly sleep.

"From March on, I'll be in Wales until graduation. This project will be the groundwork for my thesis over the next two years."

"The fact that you're graduating uni a year early and already have your thesis squared away for your master's disgusts me. Such an overachieving bitch," Gray teased.

Blair fanned her cheeks like she was overwhelmed with the compliment. "Never fear. I put in vacation days for the birth of baby MacGregor."

"Since I'll be finishing my last year's school projects online, I hope to have a couple of months to still pick up some jobs for O'Connor's before I need to buckle down and figure out what my new circumstances look like." Gray smiled, patting her stomach.

"A word of warning," Blair started, "the Byrne sisters are planning a three-pronged invasion into your life."

Gray felt her eyes widen. "What does that mean?"

"Bébhinn would have warned you by now, but our friend can't seem to take the time away from riding Dagr and working, so I'll do it for her.

"I believe stage one is a party to announce the pregnancy, which means you'd better have spoken to Ciar before that, because his dad will hear about it."

Gray felt her stomach clench. Every time she felt like she

was getting a handle on her new situation, Ciar's shadow swooped in to ruin it.

"The second stage is a baby shower, of course. The last stage of the Byrne BabyPalooza is finding the perfect home for you and decorating it. I don't think the last stage will pan out because your parents are fighting hard for you to move home, and your mom is threatening her own war with the Byrnes if they try."

Gray dropped her head in her hands. Blair touched her head so she would look up and Blair could speak to her.

"I was teasing about Bébhinn, well, kind of. They do have a ton of sex, but she did tell me that she planned on pushing pause on her mom and aunts' plans until you decide what you want." She emphasized "you" by bopping Gray's nose.

"Oh, thank God." Gray felt her body relax again.

"I'm not joking about Ciar, though. You know it's time. He's a complete dick, but if what you said about how he handled his baby is true, he'll probably be a good father if nothing else."

Gray had nothing to say to that, only, "Why Imogen, Blair? Why?" Ciar had hurt her in so many ways, but to name his child after Gray was brutal.

Blair shrugged, blowing out a breath of her own frustration over his behavior. "I don't know. Hopefully, that is one of many things you'll find out. Nothing that man has done after Colorado makes any sense."

"He's never missed Christmas at Murphy's Pub, and I know he'll want to make an appearance or two at Gray Eyes." At least Gray didn't wince at yet another reference to herself. His pub... his daughter.

"I will ask for a moment of his time over the holiday."

thirty-three

CIAR

IF HIS LIFE could get suctioned any deeper down the shitter, Ciar would be impressed. With Tina's hateful assistance with Imogen—to be fair, Tina was generous and loving to his daughter. He was managing work and fatherhood well.

His boss, Anders, had promoted him, not just promoted, but he made Ciar a shareholder of the business. The man was creative in every aspect of his life except for the name of his company—Anders.

Ciar managed his own team and collaborated closely with Anders on major client accounts. He was in a plane flying all over the world more often than sleeping in his bed, but he made sure to only fly out after Imogen's bedtime and never be gone more than two to three days.

He felt plenty of guilt for missing any moments of her day, but he made every moment count when he was home. Nothing fell outside his duties; bathtime, story time, bottles, and poopy diapers.

He'd just gotten in early that morning from a quick trip to

Spain, where Anders had him look over a brokerage that was wanting to sell. There was a meeting at the office in the morning, which meant he had the whole day home to spend with his wee one.

Tina had just stomped out the front door, as though his presence offended her, which it must, because she'd never warmed to him, when the doorbell chimed. He hurried to answer before it woke Imogen.

He only placed a formula order thirty minutes ago. Must be a slow morning. He tapped the video monitor next to the door and saw three frowning, white-haired faux triplets.

Oh, shit. Dagr, Daniel, and Jonathan.

The door opened, and he was greeted with a hammer fist to the face. Daniel. Jonathan growled, "Fuck, Dan. Not the plan, bro." Ciar retaliated and punched Daniel in the stomach, knocking the air out of him.

Jonathan punched Ciar in the stomach, and Ciar punched Jonathan smack in the left eye, causing Jonathan to swear. Dagr barked, "For fuck's sake," before he entered the melee.

It became a free-for-all as the four men wrestled across Ciar's foyer. At that point, he had no idea where his punches were landing and who was taking swipes at him. He was pretty sure everyone was punching indiscriminately at that point.

Until "The fuck," Daniel yelled. Ciar pried his swollen eyes open as far as they would go in time to get doused with water. Squinting, he managed to make out Tina dumping water over the lot of them, her face red and rigid.

"Of all the imbecilic, juvenile behavior," Tina muttered. "I have never witnessed anything so ridiculous in my life. Get your arses off that floor and park them at the kitchen table before I make more use of this glass vase than watering you toddlers."

None of them dared naysay Tina's orders and, with moans

and groans, gingerly separated their limbs from one another to limp to the flat's only table.

Tina stood with her hands on her hips, practically vibrating with censure. "Do you knuckleheads hear that? Do you?" she hissed.

Ciar could hear the faint stirrings of Imogen stirring in her crib and groaned.

She stomped into the kitchen proper and sat about making a bottle. "You have woken a child up with your nonsense. You boys," and she pointed at all four of them, "will behave and shake hands, or I will set about to box all of your ears."

She slammed her hand on the counter, causing all of the men to flinch. "Have I made myself clear?"

"Yes, ma'am," they chorused.

Before she could take the bottle to his daughter, Ciar said, "I thought you were gone for the day."

He blanched when she turned her furious gaze his way. "Do not sass me, boy. You'll regret it and then some."

"Christ Almighty," Daniel groaned.

"Ballbuster," Jonathan muttered while dabbing his bloody lip with the tail end of his shirt.

Dagr was touching the swelling around one of his eyes and cheek, before grumbling, "We had one plan. One."

Ciar carefully got up, barely holding back whimpers of pain, to lay out several kitchen towels and fill them with ice.

He handed the packs out like treats before finding his seat again. Nothing was said for a few minutes, and honestly, he was glad for the silence. This wasn't a social visit, clearly, and he wasn't in a hurry to hear what they wanted.

After five more minutes had passed, Dagr broke the silence. "We came here to speak with you, Ciar."

"My broken face and ribs say different."

"Gray's been crying. You deserve worse, you piece of shit," Daniel barked, groaning as his split lip started to bleed again.

Hearing that Gray had been crying destroyed him. Christ, but he hated himself worse in that moment than any other.

"You've done nothing to fix this, Ciar," Jonathan slammed his fist on the tabletop to drive his point home.

Tina came storming out, holding a drowsy Imogen in the crook of her arm. "One more outburst," she threatened. No one wanted to hear the end of her threat.

"Apologies," Jonathan shook his head in regret.

Dagr asked, "Can we see your child?"

Tina answered before he could. "I'm not letting this sweet girl anywhere near you streetcorner thugs. Finish your business," she sneered the word business, "and get out."

Ciar didn't bother getting on to the older woman. He wasn't that brave.

"It's still weird to see three of you," Ciar wondered aloud.

They ignored the reminder that Dagr and his dad were new family. "We're only here to know whether you plan on letting Gray go for good. She is under the impression that you two are long done." Dagr gave his best badass solicitor's stare—or as badass as he could give with one functioning eye.

"I'll never be done with Gray. I understand that I've blasted every good intention to hell and beyond and have not done one thing right when it comes to her. I had so many dreams and ideas. I still have them, damn it.

"What can I do? She came here and saw Imogen and thought the worst, and I never got a word in."

"She thought the worst," Daniel huffed in fake amusement. "Of course, she thought the fucking worst, you moron."

"She doesn't know everything. She actually knows next to nothing of it," Ciar slung back.

"Did having a child make you a pussy, Murphy? You can't

make one woman listen to you for five minutes?" Jonathan demanded.

Ciar didn't immediately defend himself. Truly, he didn't have a leg to stand on, but it did kill him to hear what his best friends thought of his behavior.

"The building you purchased for you and Gray is finished?" Dagr asked, the most even-keeled of the three cousins.

"It is. She doesn't know." His dad had encouraged him not to let go of his dream, and even though he didn't know all the details of what was between him and Gray, he never failed to support his only son.

"Then you have somewhere to move your family and work on getting Gray to hear you out. Christ, Ciar, if this were Bébhinn we were speaking about, I would lock us in together until she agreed to listen. It's your only chance, and only if you truly have a good reason for all the lies," Dagr shrugged, giving him some benefit of the doubt.

No one knew why he made the decisions he made, and he wasn't sure if he wanted them to. Even Gray, as much as he died inside when he thought of never holding her again.

"Your only chance," Daniel echoed.

A look passed between Daniel and Jonathan that Ciar couldn't decipher. They were keeping something from him. Could Gray have moved on? He tried to swallow the rage that threatened to erupt.

"I can only move if Tina agrees to come with us. She hates me, but she loves Imogen."

"I'll move, you idiot," Tina announced as she walked out of the hallway, where she'd obviously been eavesdropping. "This apartment is too small. I need my own space." Sniffing, she disappeared as soon as she'd appeared.

"Well," was the only thing Ciar could fumble out. "It looks like we're moving to Dublin."

thirty-four

GRAY

"CONGRATULATIONS, GRAY. YOU'RE HAVING A BOY," her doctor announced during the ultrasound. Bébhinn, Mags, and Blair stood next to the exam table as the doctor rolled the ultrasound device over her lubed up stomach.

"Oh, Gray," Mags sighed. "A boy. I'm so excited to embroider something special for him from his Auntie Mags."

Blair simply touched Gray's forehead and made the sign for love.

"Mom swore it was a boy. I can't wait for you to tell everyone. I'm so excited for you, Gray. So excited," Bébhinn repeated as she blinked back tears.

A boy.

She was going to have a son.

"You nailed your due date. You are right at five months, and baby MacGregor is just the size we want him to be. I'm putting your due date as April thirtieth, though every woman's body decides the day. He might want to come before that, or he might decide he likes it in your belly and come later.

"You still have a ways to go and plenty of time to prepare. Unless you have any issues, I will see you next month." The doctor wiped off all the gloop from her belly and clapped her hands in excitement, which made Gray smile.

It was exciting.

"You're sure he's the right size? I know she's tall, but..." Blair trailed off.

Mags translated for the doctor, who laughed at the concern. She made sure to look directly at Blair, so it was easier for her to read her lips.

"Moms come in every shape and size. Think of your baby space like a twin-size bed," she pointed toward Blair's middle. "There's really only one direction the baby can grow, and that's out.

"Now, Gray's son," she pointed to Gray's middle, "can enjoy a queen-sized bed, more room to stretch. Both are healthy and perfect for mother and child."

"What size bed are we?" Mags asked, pointing between herself and Bébhinn.

Without missing a beat, the doctor studied the girls. Pointing at Mags, she announced, "A double, smaller than a queen, but bigger than a twin." She turned to Bébhinn. "Twin."

They were all hooting with laughter as Gray thanked the doctor, who left the room so that she could get dressed. Her friends were all buzzing with excitement, asking a million questions, and teasing each other about their belly beds.

"Lord, I needed to laugh. My life has been way too serious lately," Gray admitted.

Blair asked, "How do you feel, Gray? Really?"

How did she feel? Specifically, how did she feel about being a single mother? "I feel like I've got this. I know I've told you, but I feel peace about telling Ciar. He won't be in my life, but he will be in our son's. I can be nothing but okay with that. I don't have a choice."

"We're meeting the boys for lunch," Mags reminded them.

If they didn't get a move on, they'd be late. "You'd better call your mom and dad before we meet them, because those tattlers will be calling out the sex of the wee one on street corners the minute they hear."

"Truth," Blair grinned, agreeing.

"Dagr might tell his dad, but that grumpy curmudgeon won't tell anyone." Bébhinn crossed her arms and rolled her eyes.

They all loved Ulf Griffiths, but he was an acquired taste.

Thirty minutes later, she and her friends were walking into an old-school pub that only locals knew about. The proprietors could fry a cod fillet like no one else.

Normally, Gray could take or leave lunch. A protein shake was good enough for her, but baby boy had been insisting on heartier fare. Who was she to deny a child?

The girls jostled against one another as their feet suddenly stopped moving. The guys—minus Ciar, which she tried to tell herself didn't hurt—sat there looking like men who made their living in a dark alley. They were sporting swollen eyes, bruised jaws, and split lips.

Gray assumed their bodies were equally roughed up because they winced while lifting their glasses of whiskey. Their attempt at playing it cool failed.

Bébhinn ran forward and clapped her hands on each of Dagr's cheeks, causing him to moan. "What in the hell happened? You've only been gone a day and a night!"

Blair drilled her steady gaze toward Daniel, who swallowed thickly. He hated disappointing Blair, as all the boys did. She signed, "Did you go to London?"

Gray gasped at the implication. "You didn't," she gasped. It went without saying that she would love to punch Ciar for his lying, cheating ways, but that didn't mean she wanted him to be jumped by three men.

"If you went to kick Ciar's ass, why didn't you call me?" Mags asked. "I am confused, though, how in the hell are all you beat to smithereens if it was three against one?"

Gray was wondering the same. She shouldn't care about Ciar's well-being, but clearly, the baby boy's father had to have been involved.

"Well?" Bébhinn insisted, looking at her fiancé with a frown.

Jonathan caved first. "We did go to London."

"And?" Gray prompted.

"Daniel fucked up our plan right off the bat." Dagr grinned when Daniel flipped him the middle finger.

"In our defense," Daniel began, "we hated how he handled you, Gray, and we wanted answers. He's never lied to us before."

"We wanted answers," Jonathan finished.

As they sat down, a waitress came to take their order. Once she walked away, Gray asked, "And did you get answers?"

Daniel and Jonathan shook their heads no. Dagr lifted a hand to stop them. "Not necessarily true. We know how he feels about Gray. I think we also know he is struggling greatly with whatever he isn't saying."

It took everything in Gray not to ask how he felt about her, but she refused. After his treatment of her and his lies, she wasn't sure it mattered. She did ask, "Did you tell him about the baby?"

"God, Gray," Jonathan started, "of course not."

Gray wasn't sure if she was relieved or disappointed. She really wasn't looking forward to that conversation.

"I plan on telling him in a few days over the holiday. I was only waiting to finish the end-of-year tests."

"In other news," Dagr looked like he was about to fall on a sword, "Ciar is moving himself and his daughter to Dublin."

Gray felt her heart begin to pound out of her chest. "Not with you, surely," she looked desperately toward Daniel and Jonathan. Being neighbors again would be a step too far.

"No," Daniel told her gently. "He had the building he bought for you both finished. It's move-in ready, I guess. Not decorated, but well enough to move in."

She felt her cheeks burn. Yet another thing he'd done behind her back. "I see."

"What a prick," Mags sneered. "Why can't that asshole stay in London? I'm sorry, Gray. Unexpected and not easy news for you."

Blair signed something quickly to Bébhinn that Gray missed, but Bébhinn cleared her throat and suggested, "Why don't we drop this conversation for now. Mags is right, it's unexpected and needs some digesting. Besides, we have something to celebrate."

Signing slow for Dagr, Blair said, "It's a boy!"

thirty-five

JOSEPHINE

"ACCORDING TO THE MOMS, the kids are all saying the same thing," Josephine said while cutting up vegetables for a beef stew for their dinner. Making the correct quantity was always tricky. She never knew whether her son would eat at home or at Laith's, or whether both boys would show.

In a house with large, starving Scotsmen continually waltzing in and out, food never went to waste. She glanced at her husband, who had yet to acknowledge she'd spoken. He was brooding. He'd been brooding since he realized their dream of having Gray home was slipping through their fingers.

Jo set her knife down and joined Thomas at the table. "Scootch back." He eyed her warily but pushed his chair from the table.

Jo sat in his lap and looped her arms around his neck. "Kiss me," she whispered against his lips.

She yelped in surprise as he took her mouth quickly. It was her intention to relieve some of the stress tensing his shoulders, but the assault of his tongue and hands relieved her of everything, including her mental faculties.

Somehow, her clothes littered the kitchen floor, and she was straddling her husband's lap, where he used her hips to glide their clothed sexes together. "Christ, Thomas, your mouth is sinful."

He let one of her nipples pop from between his lips to kiss her again. She sucked in deep lungfuls of oxygen when he finally let her up for air.

"Take me out, baby. I want you riding me right here, right now," he growled, nipping her bottom lip.

Thank heavens for sweatpants and well-hung men. He was already halfway out of his pants. It had been months since they had been this ravenous for one another.

He lifted her easily and lowered her down slowly until his hard length disappeared inside her. "Thomas," she moaned as her body adjusted.

"Josephine," he hissed her name between clenched teeth. "I'll never get enough of you."

This was one of those times she loved her long legs. She was able to plant her feet on the floor and ride her husband to her heart's content. Every time she bottomed out, she would give him her full weight and circle her hips.

"I won't last," he gasped, "if you keep moving like that."

"I'm not going to last either," she panted, feeling her orgasm begin to shake up her thighs.

"Touch yourself," he demanded. When Jo complied, she groaned at how good that felt.

"Come for me, baby, and then I'm going to fill you up." Thomas took control of the momentum because she could no longer keep pace.

One moment she was riding the edge, and the next she was crying out. Her orgasm had her back bowing. A hoarse cry left her mouth just as Thomas roared his release, and she would swear the dishes rattled.

She let her head drop to his shoulder while he rubbed her back in soothing circles. "I love you," she said, kissing the side of his neck.

"Christ, Josephine. Love has never been a strong enough word for what I feel for you."

All these years together, and he still surprised her with his romance. "I'd better get dressed before your son gets home, and our current state burns his eyes out."

"Fine, but I'd rather stay inside you."

"There's always tonight." He gave her behind a light slap when she bent over to pick up her clothes to dress. "Now, Mr. MacGregor, I'm going to work on dinner, and while I do that, you and I are going to discuss your daughter."

"Fine," he grumbled, rearranging himself beneath his sweats.

The front door slammed open, surprising them both. Laith and Lochlann came tumbling into the kitchen, dumping their rugby gear in an untidy heap on the floor and going straight to the refrigerator for drinks.

Josephine tried to quickly do up the rest of her buttons. "What are you boys doing home so early?" Two minutes earlier, and they all would have had an embarrassing moment.

"Coach's daughter puked all over his shoes. He called it," Laith offered.

"What's for dinner?" Lochlann sniffed, opening the pots on the stove.

Before she could answer, Laith answered. "I think your parents already had dinner if your dad's semi and your mom's crooked buttons are any clue."

Thomas lunged out of his chair and had Laith's shirt fisted in a heartbeat. "You want your ass beat, boy, keep running your mouth about my wife," he threatened. "Get your asses upstairs."

"I'm going to order pizza for us, Ma," Lochlann muttered. Both boys took their sports drinks and gave Thomas a wide berth as they exited the kitchen.

As the boys started down the hallway, she heard Laith say, "Good call, Loch. Who the fuck knows what's on the table."

"Shut your mouth, Laith. I saw your dad last month taking Aunt Cat against the side of one of her greenhouses."

"No, you didn't," Laith replied hotly.

"I did. She was screaming your da's name just like in the mov—" Lochlann was cut off from describing the event further —probably from a jab to his side from Laith. *Thank the Lord.*

"I'm dead. How mortifying."

"Loch," Thomas hollered after them, "order your mom and me a pizza. We have unfinished business this evening, and it will free up her time."

"Not a word, dickhead," Lochlann hissed before his bedroom door slammed shut.

"Thomas," she whined. "He shouldn't even know about sex."

"He's a month from sixteen, love. There isn't a whole lot he thinks about that doesn't involve sex. Coll and I spoke with the boys last year."

"Fine, but it had better have only been the highlights. I don't want to discuss any of," she hesitated, "that." Scooping the cut veg she'd been working on into a plastic zipper bag, she turned to her husband, who was smirking, clearly thrilled with tugging the boys' tails.

"Now we've the time, sit and I'll tell you what the word is from Dublin." She poured each of them a shot of whisky to complement the tall glasses of iced tea. She'd finally converted Thomas into an unsweetened iced tea connoisseur.

Ripping the band-aid off, she started with, "Ciar is moving to Dublin with his daughter this week. The building he bought for him and Gray, which she had cancelled plans for, he actually finished.

"According to River and Raven's boys, he's moving back to Dublin, with his child, to try and convince Gray to take him back. He doesn't know she's pregnant. She's supposed to tell him before she comes here for Christmas break.

"I don't know more than that, really. Gray is being tight-lipped. Probably afraid we plan to snatch her from her bed in the dead of night."

Thomas ruminated over the information dump, steepling his fingers under his chin. "I'll give Gray the time to tell him as she will. His response will determine mine."

"He'll always be Gray's son's father," Josephine said quietly. She was exuberant about becoming a grandmother and knew Gray would take to motherhood as she had, but the Ciar issue clouded the excitement with concern.

She had no doubt that Ciar would take responsibility for his son, as he had for his daughter, but where did that leave Gray? Her daughter was a strong woman, but as her mother, Jo never wanted her to feel unwanted or not good enough.

Jo waffled between begging her to come home and encouraging her to take charge of her new life. She also wanted to visit Ciar and bash him upside the head with a rolled-up newspaper.

Plan C, and it was beginning to look like the promising choice, was to send her own mother to Dublin to sort things out.

Grandma Mary O'Connor would descend on Gray's life like an avenging angel, having her in a fashionable home and hiring a nanny, chef, and house cleaner within hours. Her father, Dean, would have security posted along the perimeter to ensure there were no unsupervised visits to his granddaughter and great-grandson.

She was leaning closer to Plan C every day, but that level of interference had to be reserved for drastic times, and Thomas was right, it all came down to Ciar's response to Gray's announcement.

Jo picked up one of Thomas' heavy hands from the table, bringing it to her mouth to kiss his knuckles before resting her cheek against his palm.

"No matter what, we're going to be grandparents. I can't wait."

"Our grandson," Thomas said quietly, switching their position and bringing her hands to his lips. "I can't wait either."

thirty-six

CIAR

CIAR, Imogen, and Tina were installed in the Dublin two-story. That might be overstating things. They had beds to sleep on and were surrounded by what could only be thousands of moving boxes.

Tina was doing her best, in her special, hateful way, but it was clear she needed help. Since being back in Dublin, Ciar had spent hours at Gray Eyes catching up on how things were running.

The numbers were promising. Extremely so. It had fast become "the hangout" for old money and new. He was amazed to see Gray's vision in real time every time he walked through the pub's door.

He still worked hours a day for Anders, taking most meetings over video, but traveling was inevitable and often.

None of the details mattered. None of them.

Gray had reached out to meet him. She was due to arrive in minutes.

He'd been a blithering idiot since the moment he'd received

her text yesterday. It only said that she would like to discuss something with him.

He didn't know what she wanted to discuss, but he had at least twenty different things he wanted to explain. He wanted her back so bad. His stomach was cramping, and his sweat glands were working overtime.

Ciar told Tina that, unless there was an emergency, she needed to have everything Imogen could ever imagine wanting in the smaller kitchen upstairs, where Imogen's room was located, as well as Tina's small nanny apartment.

He hoped Gray would let him show her around the space. He especially wanted her to see how he'd finished out their downstairs bedroom suite. From their past talks, he believed she would be pleased that her vision had been realized.

After she canceled the contractors, he'd rehired them and given them her house plans. There was no décor or, well, there was nothing really, but he dreamed of Gray making the final touches to their home.

Tina walked out in a gaudy bathrobe wrapped around her stout frame, gunmetal gray hair sticking up in multiple directions, and an empty coffee mug in her hand like she owned the space and everything in it.

"Tina, for fuck's sake, I've company soon. Please stay with Imogen."

"First, language, young man. My outlets in the upstairs kitchen are on the fritz. Never fear, I put in a work order. Secondly, the wee mite is sleeping, and I want a bloody mug of tea."

And of course, the bell would ring at that moment. Of course. "Christ, Tina. I'm begging you. Disappear."

She simply sniffed her snub nose and proceeded to the kitchen. There was nothing for it. He had to answer the door.

Ciar pulled the heavy door open so quickly that he almost

took the tips of his booted toes off. And there she was. "Gray," he spoke her name reverently.

She was dressed in loose jeans, a heavy sweater, and a wool coat. Dublin winters were not a light layering season.

She was stunning. Glorious. Her golden waves were clipped back on the sides, with the rest draped over and about her overcoat.

"Come in. Please," he stupidly waved her in like a hotel concierge. He asked to take her coat, and in his worst nightmare made reality, he tripped over his own feet and fell into her side, pushing her against the door's frame.

"Fuck," he cursed as she let out an "Oof."

"I'm sorry." Grasping her upper arms, he gently separated her from the wall and carefully helped slip her coat off her shoulders.

She'd yet to speak a word. Her pinkened cheeks spoke of more than the wintry chill, however, and he wanted to wrap his arms around her so badly he shook with it.

"Would you like to go to the master suite's sitting room?" He cursed the suggestion as soon as her shoulders stiffened. Presumptuous bastard.

"Or here," he waved toward the kitchen where his obnoxious nanny stood in all her bed-haired glory, making tea. "I could make tea once the pot is free," he growled, his wrathful gaze locked on Tina. Never mind that there was a kitchen upstairs.

"Don't mind me, lad," the bit—woman, he corrected mentally, snidely commented.

Tina finally vacated the kitchen but stopped before a wide-eyed Gray. "I'm Mrs. March, Miss Imogen's nanny." She stuck her hand out for Gray to take, and though she looked horrified, she politely took the outstretched hand and shook it firmly.

"Nice to meet you, Mrs. March. I'm Gray MacGregor."

"And who are you to Mr. Murphy, lassie?" Tina rudely asked.

"No one special, ma'am, I assure you." Ciar was furious with Tina and gutted by Gray's answer. She was so far from "no one special," he wanted to roar his denial.

"That's enough, Mrs. March. You will retire now or find other accommodations for the night." His threat widened her eyes, but she managed to sniff arrogantly, twice, before spinning on her heel and finally leaving them.

"I apologize, Gray. She's—" he hesitated "—horrible."

"No problem." Gray sat on one of the barstools lining the center island.

"Tea?"

"No. Thank you."

She was wringing her hands and biting her lip, so uncomfortable that he wanted to beg to start the meeting over.

"I'm sorry. Tina is an acquired taste."

"I'm sure she must be good with your daughter, or you wouldn't keep her. Now," Gray said with conviction, laying her hands flat against the counter in front of her, "I hoped we might come to an understanding."

"An understanding?" Ciar sat, too, as he felt his legs start to give way.

"We have mutual friends. I have no wish to make every gathering we have together miserable for everyone. I would like us to wipe the slate clean between us, is what I'm trying to say, I guess."

"Wipe the slate," he repeated dumbly.

"Exactly," she nodded her head as though he'd solved the riddle to algebra. "I have something important to tell you, and I know it will be...a surprise, but—"

"Mr. Murphy," Tina's aggravating voice rang out, "Miss Imogen, your sweet daughter," she emphasized unnecessarily, "is inconsolable. She needs her father's soothing touch before she can go back to sleep."

Gray's face drained of all color, and she stiffly stood, tugging on the hem of her sweater. "I've...I've taken up too much of your time," she stuttered, backing away from Tina, who was holding a perfectly content-looking Imogen in her arms.

"No, Gray, please. Please don't leave." He could tell that no amount of pleading would make her stay. He took Imogen into his arms. "You wanted to tell me something. Please."

It was too late.

The opportunity was ruined, and he was too much of a piece of shit to salvage it.

"It's not," she took a deep breath before continuing, "important, after all. Have a merry Christmas. I'm flying to Scotland tonight for the holiday."

She grabbed her coat and ran out the door before another word could be uttered. He sat down heavily, his breath catching on a swallowed sob.

What now? "What now?" he whispered in Imogen's tiny ear.

thirty-seven

CIAR

TWO MONTHS after the night Gray ran out of what was meant to be their house, Ciar and Imogen were enjoying a quiet Sunday afternoon watching television and playing on the couch.

It was Tina's afternoon off. He'd barely spoken to the woman after the stunt she pulled with Gray. She finally unbent a couple of weeks ago and apologized. Not a great apology, but it was something at least.

He was still furious, more so with himself. Had he taken control that night and told her everything he'd done, everything he hoped for, and all the things he was sorry for, it might have ended differently.

Instead, he froze, became tongue-tied, and gave Gray nothing. She had been the one to reach out first, and he crashed and burned.

As Imogen gnawed her soft bunny into a slobbery mess, he leaned his head back on the couch. Why couldn't he just tell her how he was feeling?

For weeks, he'd gone over every word she'd said that night. It was possible that she had come hoping he'd fight for her, and when he didn't, she asked for a clean slate between them.

For the most part, his friends avoided him. He didn't blame them. When Daniel, Jonathan, and even Dagr spoke to him after that night and found out he hadn't explained anything to her, Ciar was very aware of their disappointment.

His dad had come by last week to visit his granddaughter and stayed after Imogen went down for her nap.

His dad asked, "Why are you doing this, son? Your silence is hurting both you and Gray. Hell, it's hurting all your friends.

"They rarely come into Murphy's, and I haven't seen Gray since our last meeting about Gray Eyes. It's like everyone's holding their breath, afraid to hope, but afraid to let the idea of you two go.

"Don't you still love her?"

Ciar startled at the question. "Love her? I never, that is, she might have—"

"Christ Almighty, boy. Did you never tell the girl that you loved her?"

"I didn't," he replied hotly. "I don't. I care for her."

Love was pain. His mother taught him that.

"Cut the shit," his dad demanded, slapping his palm against the kitchen counter where they were seated. "You've mooned over that girl for years."

Ciar gritted his teeth, swallowing the denial. "How did you know that?" he asked instead.

"I'm your father, and I watched you watch Gray. I knew why you didn't pursue her initially. You were older, but once she was of age, I never understood why you didn't."

"She didn't think of me that way, and I didn't want to ruin our friendship over trying," he admitted, leaning back in his chair and crossing his arms over his chest defensively.

"Children," his dad muttered under his breath. "Gray watched you every second you weren't watching her. She always loved you. I imagine she still does, you idiot. What are you so afraid of? Why can't you admit your feelings? If not to her, then at least to yourself."

"I don't know." What a childish, lame excuse.

"Is this to do with," he hesitated, and Ciar instantly felt his body flush with red-hot fury, "before you came to live with me?"

Ciar stood so quickly that the tall, heavy barstool flew back, crashing to the floor and probably waking Imogen. He rubbed his shaking hands over his buzzcut, feeling the prickly ends sting his fingertips.

"Go home."

"Ciar," his dad said sadly, "I didn't mean—"

"Go home," he repeated, not looking at his father.

Sighing, his dad stood and walked to the entrance. He paused in the open doorway but didn't turn around. "Don't let your past destroy your future, son. More than you've already let it, because you do love Gray MacGregor. Time to face your demons, boy."

And then he was gone, and Ciar was wrecked. He would have grabbed the bottle of vodka from his liquor cabinet had his daughter not chosen to wake up screaming for his attention.

One week had gone by, and he was still shaken from his dad's words. They had bored into his chest and sat there aching.

Looking at Imogen lying on the couch cushion by his side, her delighted smile as her chubby feet held her bunny over her head couldn't even relieve the pressure. He absently rubbed his chest, but nothing soothed the pain.

It was dinnertime, and Ciar was contemplating a plate of cold lasagna in the refrigerator when his phone buzzed. He would have blushed had anyone been there to see him dive for his pocket. Loneliness wasn't a good look on him.

His brows lifted in surprise. It was a text from Mags.

Mags: What are you doing?

Ciar: Nothing. At home.

Mags: Buy me dinner at Gray Eyes. I have something I want to discuss with you.

Mags: I'll be there in twenty.

Ciar: Okay.

"Holy shit," he swore as he lifted Imogen up to his face. "Daddy's got plans, little one." Imogen patted his cheeks with slobbery hands as he ripped across the room and ran up the stairs to bang on Tina's door and asked her to give Imogen her dinner and bath.

Mags surely wanted to speak to him about Gray. Surely.

In the downstairs primary, he tore his clothes off, leaving a trail to the bathroom and was showered, shaved, and redressed in slacks and a dress shirt in twelve minutes.

He texted Tina as he slipped into his leather shoes, saying he was going out for a couple of hours and to call him if she needed anything.

He ran out the front door just as his Uber was pulling up. He could have easily walked the few blocks, but he was down to seven minutes, and he refused to show up sweaty and winded.

Mags' Uber pulled up right after he exited his, so he walked to her door and helped her out. Her usual mischievous grin or trademark glare were missing. Her features were purposefully smooth, devoid of emotion, but he noticed she was gripping her purse with excessive force.

She was nervous. This might not be a conversation he wanted to hear, because it was clear she didn't want to have it either.

As they walked toward the entrance, he asked, "Why did you want to meet here and not somewhere closer to your house?"

"I've heard the food here is to die for, and I wanted to try it and let you pay for it. Starving artist here." She raised her hand like she was in school.

Ciar only grunted. He forgot sometimes that not all of his friends were wealthy. He wondered if Mags ever minded the disparity. Knowing her, probably not at all.

The host recognized Ciar and took him to a small table near the back bar. Mags ordered a rum and Coke, and he asked for his regular Absolute over ice with a squeeze of lime.

When drinks arrived, and they placed food orders, she still hadn't said anything besides to tell him his place could use some embroidery.

He agreed. They lapsed into more silence, causing Ciar to fidget in his seat. Finally, he asked, "How is everyone?" How was Gray?

Mags held up a hand and started ticking off her news one finger at a time. "Blair left today for her internship in Wales with Dagr's dad. She won't be coming home that often. We plan on visiting her, though. Bébhinn has taken on several new jobs for Triskelion that she loves. Daniel and Jonathan have been in Oklahoma this past week, checking on some of the O'Faolain properties and businesses. They're due back.

"Dagr's still traveling quite a bit between London and here, but his firm here in Dublin is doing very well. And last but certainly interesting, Ulf Griffiths is spending time with Bran and Patrick."

"I still can't believe they just found one another after all these years. Besides the white hair, their mother must have had a thing for big men."

For the first time that night, Mags cracked a smile. "I think Ulf helps to fill a little piece of what they've been missing since Hugh's passing. The other night, Bébhinn told me that Bran and Patrick let Dagr know that they hadn't been happy about him not asking their permission to marry Bébhinn.

"Dagr told them that their oldest brother gave him permission, which made the table burst into laughter. I'm happy that Bébhinn and her family are finding things to laugh at again."

"I got the wedding invitation in the mail for Bébhinn and Dagr. They decided on the end of May. I'm surprised it's not before then, honestly." Mags only shrugged.

The food arrived, and his dinner companion tucked in. Ciar mentally groaned. She clearly meant to finish her dinner before resuming any small talk.

Eventually, the server cleared their plates. He refused any more small talk and folded his hands in his lap, willing to wait patiently.

"Gray said that when you two met at your place, you didn't try to explain anything about the reason why you cut her out of your life or why you lied about having a child."

The waitress had just set down fresh drinks on the table. He was tempted to down his in one go. "I tried. I..." he paused, taking a deep breath, puffing out his cheeks, and exhaling slowly.

"My nanny interrupted us. Twice. Gray said she wanted to be friends, or something akin to that, and then she was running for the door before I could get anything out."

Mags flicked the top edge of her rum and Coke's crystal

glass, annoyance and perhaps anger darkening her features. "Bullshit. Lie to yourself, Ciar Murphy, but don't fucking bother me with that load of shit," she hissed across the small table.

"You're trying to tell me that if you had wanted to, truly wanted Gray to hear the truth, that you wouldn't have made sure it happened. I don't buy it, none of our friends buy it, and though Gray never speaks about you anymore, I know she didn't buy it either.

"Truly, I think she believes that you never cared enough about her to begin with and that you think she doesn't deserve answers."

Ciar felt sick. She was right, of course. He hadn't wanted to tell her the truth, so he hadn't. He still didn't want to.

Mags put her hand palm up on the table, and when he didn't do anything, she demanded, "Take my hand, dumbass."

He hesitantly clasped their hands together and felt his cheeks redden in discomfort. "Ciar, listen to me. As your friend, hear me. I may fly off the handle at times, but I know you as well as you know me. You are hiding something, and it's hurting two of my best friends."

She clapped her second hand over his, tightly sandwiching them together. He was all too aware that this conversation all but mirrored the one with his father the week before.

Ciar felt months of suppressed emotion prick his eyes. He turned his head to the side and willed the moisture to reverse.

"Ciar," Mags said gently. More gentle than he'd ever heard from her. "You love Gray, and she loves you. Not that I can understand why, as you are the biggest douche I've ever met, but still, she does. She told you in Colorado, and you didn't tell her back.

"I won't ask you why because I know that you don't know. I've not wanted to interfere between you two, but...your chances to make this right are coming to an end."

He did look at her, then, trying to decipher what she meant by that. "Why do you say that?"

She patted his hand one last time before pulling her hands back. "Gray will be back in town tomorrow to meet someone for lunch."

Oh Christ, no. "Who?" He all but shouted the question, drawing attention from nearby tables and servers.

"Cannon Micheals."

The name hit him like a bomb detonating in his chest. He knew that name. Her one and only boyfriend before Ciar.

The one man she'd loved before him and had only broken up with because he moved to America.

"Gray doesn't love him anymore. She said she loved me. She told me to my face that she did. Fuck that cunt, Cannon."

"Ciar. Settle down," Mags warned, glancing at their audience. "I'm usually the last person to give a shit about public appearances, but you happen to own this swanky place. People will talk."

"Why?" he finally ground out, lowering his voice, though the business was the least of his concerns.

She gave him a pitying look before folding her napkin and placing it on the table next to her empty drink. "You threw her away months ago. How long did you expect a gorgeous woman like Gray to stay single?"

She stood and smoothed her dress. Before she could turn and leave, he asked, more like begged, "Where?"

"Fitzwilliam Hotel."

thirty-eight

GRAY

GRAY HAD BEEN LIVING with her parents in her childhood home since Christmas. After the disastrous meeting with Ciar, she couldn't bear to live in the same city with the father of her child, who was living his best life with his daughter in the home that had supposedly been meant for her.

There were too many insults to her already severely injured heart for that level of bullshit. She'd run like a little girl and not the successful woman that she was. Had it not been for her loving parents, she would have leased one of the Zurich spa homes to spend the rest of her pregnancy in.

Giving birth in healing waters surrounded by Zen gurus sounded pretty darn good. Alas, her mom and dad were so supportive of her "single and pregnant" life that she couldn't bring herself to leave.

Hiding from Ciar was an added bonus. She swallowed her regret at their situation and patted the firm basketball she was sporting, whispering a quick, "I love you, sweet boy."

Her son seemed to love Scotland and excitedly kicked

whenever he heard the deep voices of her father and brother, which thrilled them to no end.

Her dad struggled with her need for independence. It was like, once she moved back in, he wanted to treat her like she was back in high school. Her mom advised humoring him. That worked well most days.

Was she hiding from Ciar? Yes. She had underestimated his lack of feeling for her and paid the price. The night she'd gone to his home, she had romanced the idea of him explaining himself, her forgiving him, and then getting back together to become a happy family.

The worst part, or the best part for his daughter's sake, was that he was clearly a fantastic father. The visual had wounded her doubly to see him so easily cradle his child to his chest while his son had been sleeping beneath her sweater, wanting for his love too.

As she'd run from him, and she had run as embarrassing as it was to admit, she made up her mind, right or wrong, that she would let him know once their son was born and not before.

Ciar had no say in her life. He'd made that painfully clear over and over and over again. She did not need his input or forced support these last few months of her pregnancy.

She was back in Dublin for a doctor's appointment and, as ridiculous as it sounded, she had agreed to meet her ex, Cannon, for lunch.

He was in town for his sister's wedding and asked to meet up. He was moving home that summer. Gray wasn't a fool. She could tell he was interested in rekindling their relationship.

She wanted to meet him in person so he would understand that they would never be an option and show him irrefutable proof—her baby bump. Even though Ciar broke her heart, she was not interested in moving backwards.

Her mom had suggested the Fitzwilliam because there was

a slim chance of meeting Ciar, who had his own posh pub and his father's pub to eat at.

Gray sat fidgeting at a lovely table overlooking the windswept courtyard. Had she not been so nervous, she would have soaked up the warmth of the dining room and the sweet fragrance of roses that drifted through the air.

She knew the moment Cannon arrived because she was staring at the only inside entrance to the restaurant.

He noticed her immediately. His easy smile made her smile in return. He was more handsome than she remembered, but he wasn't the man she craved, unfortunately.

The moment she stood, he would see her bump. She hoped they could remain friends, but if he was hoping for a reconciliation, baby boy should nix that right off.

This was it. Arms wide, he stood next to her. "Gray, Christ, you're more beautiful than my memories made you."

She stood and allowed Cannon's arms to wrap around her back. The moment her tummy pressed into his middle, she felt his body stiffen and still.

Leaning back, his hands slid from her back to her sides. "I think this lunch is going to go way differently than I imagined." His smile faltered in disappointment.

"Sit, Cannon. I think we have a lot to catch up on."

He studied her in confusion as the waiter took their drink orders. She couldn't blame him. Hell, she struggled with the knowledge that she was growing a child in her body too.

"How has America treated you, Cannon?" She hoped her query would jog her lunch date from his shock at finding his ex-girlfriend pregnant.

"Well," he nodded jerkily. "Gray, you're...you are...a baby," he finally managed to get out.

"Yes. I'm pregnant."

"Who is the father?" he asked carefully, clearly not comfortable asking after the man who had replaced him.

"An old friend," was the best she could come up with.

"Are you not with him?" Cannon asked, frowning.

"No." Gray hoped her blunt answer would end that line of questioning.

"I can't believe Jennifer is getting married," she announced, attempting to change the subject to his sister's upcoming nuptials.

"Yeah," he drew out the word, his frown never dissipating. "Is the baby's father not in your life, Gray?"

Attempting a lightheartedness she didn't feel, she answered, "Ha-ha, no, I seem to pick men who like to leave."

They both cringed at her honesty. *Shit.*

He grasped her hand across the table. "Biggest mistake of my life," Cannon said.

"No, asshole. Your biggest mistake is touching what is mine."

Gray almost swallowed her tongue. Her mother had been wrong. Ciar did visit the Fitzwilliam after all.

thirty-nine

CIAR

CIAR HAD BEEN WATCHING Gray from outside the restaurant's glass walls like the worst type of stalker. She was so damn beautiful. The sun haloed her from her head to her shoulders.

She used to be his. He used to be able to touch and hold her whenever he wanted. She used to smile at him.

She used to love him.

"Fuck," he muttered to himself. How had they ended up here? A rhetorical question, of course. He knew where to lay the blame.

After he'd seen Mags off the night before, he walked home, needing the time to cool his head. He needed to think rationally. He couldn't barge in on her date and demand she stay single until he decided to speak to her, give her what she needed and deserved.

Each time he argued against interfering, he immediately had a stronger argument for why he should.

He'd stared at his bedroom ceiling for hours. Looking at the stark walls hadn't helped. He hadn't allowed any décor to be bought or any pictures to be hung. Depressing.

The entire two floors were finished with white walls and warm wood floors. He only purchased beds for his room, Imogen's, and Tina's. A rocking chair for the baby's room and a couch for the living room, a small kitchen table, and a few chairs. Other than that, nothing.

He still dreamed of Gray coming in and making it a home. She'd spearheaded the opening of Gray Eyes, which had quickly become one of Dublin's hot spots. He knew that she would use that same level of detail here.

He ignored several texts from Daniel and Jonathan, a call from Dagr, and another from his dad. He still wasn't speaking to him after how badly things had ended between them last week.

Ciar had been hurt and embarrassed. He'd also been pissed because he knew his dad was right. Mags was right. His friends were right.

Agreeing with them was easy. Taking action, not so much. He was letting everyone vital to him down, and now here he was being a creep, watching Gray through a window, and she was about to have a lunch date with her ex-boyfriend.

Cannon Michaels. "Prick," he muttered under his breath.

Speaking of, he caught movement out of the corner of his eye. A man was walking to the host stand. He looked like he was around six feet or right under. Shorter than Ciar. He supposed women might think he was good-looking. Ciar didn't.

He sported neatly trimmed light brown hair. Gray loved scratching her fingers over his extremely buzzed scalp.

The guy looked fit, Ciar would give him that, but his clothes screamed university professor. No visible tattoos. Clearly not adventurous.

Cannon was nothing special to Gray's extraordinary.

There was no way she would consider going back out with that guy. What the hell was he doing back in Dublin anyway?

The interloper was almost to her table. She smiled and waved when she noticed him. She began to stand, but that asshole blocked his view of her. They were hugging. It looked like he was resting his hands on her hips.

Her hands clasped his shoulders, and that was that.

Ciar saw nothing but red. A haze of fury at seeing Gray in the arms of another man was too much. He tore his gaze from Gray and made his way to the host stand.

"Good afternoon, Sir. Do you have a reservation?"

"Gray MacGregor."

"Right this way."

He entered with the host, told her he saw his friends—calling that idiot a friend irritated him—and said she didn't need to escort him further. He preferred privacy in case things went sideways.

Gray didn't see him approach, too enraptured by Cannon holding her hand across the table and telling her what a big mistake he'd made, presumably talking about breaking up with her. *No shit.*

"No, asshole. Your biggest mistake is touching what is mine."

Cannon and Gray both looked at Ciar looming over their table with similar looks of surprise, all wide eyes and parted lips. "Let go of her hand, or I'll break it."

He made no move to let her go, and Gray appeared too shocked to realize. "Gray." He put enough demand in his tone to snap her out of her stasis.

She quickly pulled her hand from under Cannon's and focused on Ciar. "How did you know I would be here?"

"It doesn't matter. What matters is that you shouldn't be here. At least, not with him."

Her eyes narrowed. "And why is that?"

"In Colorado, the first night we slept together, you promised you'd stick by me even if I fucked up. You promised."

"You promised me a lot of things too," she whispered, tears sparkling on her lashes, gutting him.

"Is this the prick that left you when he found out about the baby?"

If they hadn't been in the middle of the fucking Fitzwilliam, he would have made sure Cannon regretted ever speaking of his daughter.

"Cannon. Please," Gray started, "that isn't what happened."

"Oh really," Cannon scoffed. "Then tell me why you're sitting here with a round belly and this," he looked Ciar up and down with a sneer, "thug left you alone to deal with his mistake alone."

Ciar was too dumbfounded by what Cannon just said to deal properly with the insulting way he spoke. When Gray turned a murderous glare Cannon's way, Ciar felt more turned around.

"Enough Cannon. I appreciate that you're trying to help, but you aren't. I also want to be very clear that a baby is never someone's 'mistake.' Please leave. I'll call you later."

"No, she won't. You heard Gray. Get out."

Cannon stood stiffly, noticing for the first time all the wait-staff hovering near their table, causing his cheeks to flush in embarrassment. *Pansy.* Ciar didn't care who heard him claiming Gray.

Ciar didn't take the vacated seat but chose the one closest to Gray, smirking at Cannon while he made himself comfortable, putting his arm around the back of her chair.

"I don't know what game you're playing here," Cannon spoke to Ciar, "but you seem awfully proud of yourself for someone who left a woman to go through pregnancy alone."

He turned his gaze to Gray. "Don't take him back, Gray. I will be there for you. I'll move home, baby. I swear I will. He doesn't want you. He's just selfish enough not to want anyone else to have you. Please call me tonight so I won't worry."

She nodded in agreement, causing a growl to rumble up his throat. Cannon turned abruptly on his heel and left. Finally.

Now that the threat to his relationship with Gray was gone, his brain was starting to come back online. He was missing something.

He removed his arm from around her stiff shoulders and turned her chair slightly toward his so that it was easier to speak. "What was all that about? What did he mean by me leaving a woman alone and pregnant? I," he hesitated and had to clear his throat twice before he could get out, "didn't know Imogen's mom was pregnant. You know that."

Gray shook her head and huffed in disbelief or disgust. "Back up. You're too close."

She was pissed, so he obeyed and moved back enough where their legs no longer touched. He felt the loss of her warmth down to his bones.

"I didn't leave you when I found out about the baby. I know things have been difficult, but I didn't leave you. I want you to be mine again. Badly."

Gray's jaw clenched, and she shook her head. He had never felt so confused in his life.

"Not everything is about you. Nor about your daughter or your daughter's mother. I don't know anything about your life now because you've made sure I don't."

Ciar winced. He was such a selfish piece. "I'm sorry, I just... what did he mean then?"

Gray placed her hands on the table, her face going from red to white. He was afraid she was going to faint. He caught one of the server's eyes, and they rushed over.

"Could we have some ice water, and," he touched Gray's arm, "what would you like to eat, Gray?"

"I'm not—"

"No," he stopped her, "you're very pale. Salad with grilled fish?"

"Sure."

"We'll both have whatever salad is your favorite," he told the server.

"Of course, and here's Kit with your water. Let us know if you need anything else." She sent a worried glance Gray's way, but she left without comment. Who knows what the staff thought about the altercation between him and Cannon.

He placed a glass of water in Gray's hand and was relieved when she took several sips. "Do you feel like talking, or do you want to wait until after we eat? I don't want to push, I'm just confused as all hell right now and feeling like you're keeping something from me."

That statement brought color back to her cheeks. "That's rich coming from you. You've lied to me since Colorado. Don't you dare act as though you deserve any of my secrets. You don't deserve a damn thing from me."

If words could make a person bleed, he should be close to death. "I want to tell you everything. I've wanted to before now."

"Forgive me if I don't hold my breath."

"It's not a conversation for here."

"When then?"

He felt the floor open up under his feet, and his guts rushed to his throat. "Gray," he pleaded. For what? He hadn't a clue.

"Exactly. I will tell you what Cannon and I were discussing, because I've been wanting to tell you for quite some time. After you broke up with me, it's become difficult. I tried to tell you that night at your house."

"Our house," he corrected.

"You're deluded, Ciar, if you think any woman would be treated the way you've treated me and agree to anything."

The salad's arrival paused their conversation. The server explained the dish. "This is our house smoked salmon over a bed of fennel salad, caper salsa, and fresh brown bread on the side."

"Thank you. It looks amazing." Gray smiled kindly.

"I'll leave you to it then."

Alone again, Gray didn't resume their discussion, contentious as it was. Instead, she slathered butter on a piece of steaming bread.

"Mmm," she closed her eyes and savored her first bite. "I needed that. I'm starving."

He barely touched his food, his gaze seldom leaving the woman seated beside him. After twenty minutes had passed, she had eaten just over half her meal but seemed content, setting down her fork and gently blotting her mouth with her napkin. This was the second time in two days that a woman had tortured him with a meal.

He placed his cutlery down so the servers would know they could clear the table, which they did moments later.

"Well, I guess there's no putting it off anymore." She watched him with an intensity that made him uneasy. "I'm pregnant."

Had he been standing, he might have fainted. He heard her, but the words were like a language he couldn't understand.

"I don't...what...but we haven't... Please explain."

"You didn't just walk away from me, Ciar. You left your son too. While you set up house with your other family, I've been alone."

forty

GRAY

NO MATTER how many times Gray told herself, her family, or her friends that she was ready to move on from Ciar, until she said the words to him, "I'm pregnant," she hadn't realized just how furious she was at him. She hadn't moved on at all.

It was irrational to blame him. He hadn't known, but rational thought had no place where the man who threw her away stood.

His confusion only pissed her off more. He'd been so busy keeping his secrets and taking care of his daughter that he'd never considered what her life looked like now. Gray knew he wouldn't have abandoned her had he known about their baby, but she didn't want a man who was only doing the right thing.

Ciar claimed he'd been hoping for reconciliation, but as the months passed, her hope dimmed, and she became ashamedly bitter. His daughter had his love and attention, which she should, of course, but what of the baby's mother? Did she have his attention as well?

Was there any room left in his life for another baby? And the more selfish question, was there any room for her?

Loving a man who gave nothing in return was a lonely and painful road. He wanted her to explain what exactly? How she got pregnant? Surely he remembered. They were both involved.

"What do you want me to explain, Ciar?"

He opened and closed his mouth several times, and finally settled for, "Whose baby is it?"

Dumfounded. Flabbergasted. Stupefied. Thunderstruck. Dazed. Stunned. Pick any or all of them. She felt them all.

He thought she'd had a child with another man. What? Simply because he did, she chose to as well? Disgusting.

Clamping her teeth together until they hurt, Gray forced herself to swallow her hurt and tears, scooted back her chair, retrieved her purse from the floor at her feet, and stood. Her coat was in the cloak room. She'd need to grab that on her way out.

She chanced a last look at Ciar, who was staring wide-eyed at her belly. Maybe that answered who the father was. *Asshole.*

"Please pay for lunch, Ciar. I've an appointment to get to." She was wearing a flowy, light wool dress, and, feeling petty, cupped her hand under her belly to emphasize the size.

One of the hosts saw her coming and fetched her coat. "Thank you," she murmured, slinging it around her shoulders as quickly as she could. The Fitzwilliam Hotel always had cars for hire. She would flag one down the moment she stepped outside.

Ciar wouldn't stay stunned and silent for long. Not nearly long enough, as she heard him yell her name the moment he rounded the corner. She walked through the automatic glass doors right as Ciar pulled her back into the warmth of the hotel's lobby.

"Gray, please. Please, for fuck's sake, talk to me." He spun her around until they faced one another. "I was shocked, but I never should have questioned who the father is."

He took her hand and led her to a semi-secluded seating area near the front. Numbly, she sat next to him on a small sofa, the realization that the time for hiding was over, sinking in.

"No. You shouldn't have. I haven't been with anyone since you left." He hated her bringing up when he left her, which is why she kept doing it.

"How, though? I mean, I know how, I just thought we were protected."

"I don't know if you remember, but right before the Colorado trip, I got so sick and stayed in Scotland to recover. Mom said I probably threw up some of my birth control pills. I never thought…" her voice tapered off.

"We never thought, Gray. We," Ciar corrected.

They were turned into each other, knees touching, both of them probably wishing they could have this conversation somewhere more private.

He held his hands palms up between them. "Can I?"

When she nodded her consent, he placed his hands almost reverently on either side of her belly. The look of wonder on his face was beautiful.

"When are you due?"

"End of April. Mom was usually right around thirty-six weeks. You probably know this," Gray tried to keep the sadness from her voice, "but if you push my belly a bit, he'll likely give you a kick."

Ciar glanced up sharply. "I've never touched a woman's pregnant belly before."

How was she to know? He went back to studying her tummy and did as she suggested. He pressed too lightly, so she covered his hands with hers and pressed and manipulated her stomach from side to side.

Bingo. His shocked gasp made her smile. "That's our son. Gray, can you believe that? We did that. My God. I'm still so... I'm blown away."

"I'm excited to meet him," she said, dropping her hands from his. He didn't let go immediately but hesitantly massaged his big hands over the mound. The gentle circles felt wonderful against her tight skin.

"I have so many questions. Like, have you thought of a name? Do you have his room decorated? Do you have all the baby stuff bought? Or did you have a baby shower?" The last made him pause, and his hands stilled.

"Everyone's known. This whole time, and they've not told me. Daniel and Jonathan?"

She didn't like how hurt he sounded and tried to explain. "I only found out six weeks ago—this bump grew overnight. I wasn't showing before that.

"I wanted to be the one to tell you, so I asked everyone to keep quiet. I did try that night at your house, but you didn't have the time to listen. I decided that it would be easier if I just let you know after the birth.

"I think that when the boys paid you a visit, and you somehow all managed to beat each other up, it was their way of getting you to come home, or admit to, you know, feelings for me or whatever.

"You did move home, I guess. They managed that much," Gray shrugged.

"I admitted I had feelings for you too," he let his hands fall from her bump to place them on her knees.

It was odd to have him touching her body. Wonderful, but weird after so long.

"In answer to your other questions, I haven't picked out any names. I refused a shower until I decide where he and I would be living, Dublin or Inverness, which means I don't have a room decorated, as much as it's upsetting my mother, and I don't have a single thing purchased.

"I moved out of the townhouse and live with my parents since I'm doing these last months of uni online. I only have one major project left and a few papers to finish. I figured I could get everything figured out before he comes."

He clasped her hands in his. "I'm gutted, Gray. Fucking gutted that you've been doing this alone. Please tell me that you want me to be a part of his life. I want to be."

And there it was. Ciar wanted to be a part of their child's life. No mention of being a part of hers. She expected it. Truly, she did, it was different thinking it versus hearing it, though.

"Of course. I will have my family's solicitor contact yours. I want to be fair with you, as I hope you do with me."

He looked so taken aback, Gray was instantly confused. She handed him precisely what he wanted. Shared custody unencumbered by the child's mother.

"That isn't what I want at all, Gray, and you know that damn well. There's been no one for me since our first kiss, and there won't be either. Can't we be a family?"

Can't we be a family? It's what she wanted more than anything, except... "I want that, Ciar, but not with a man who doesn't trust me. One who lies to me and leaves me with no explanation. No. I don't want that."

Even though he looked devastated, she couldn't cave in. Their future, if they were to have one other than that of coparents, meant starting the way you wanted to continue.

And she wanted the truth. He was hiding, from what, she hadn't a clue.

To soften the blow, she touched his knee. "I'm relieved you

know." She checked her phone and realized she had only fifteen minutes before her doctor's appointment.

She stood quickly. "I've got to go. I have an appointment with the baby's doctor. We'll talk soon."

Ciar caught her arm. "Can I come with you?"

He looked so hopeful, despite everything between them, she couldn't tell him no. "Fine. Get us a car."

forty-one

CIAR

THE CAR RIDE was silent as they traveled through Dublin's busy streets to the doctor's. Ciar was reeling. He thought he'd been going to break up a romantic lunch, but in truth, she'd not only been faithful to him during their time apart but also had been growing their child. Alone.

He was weeks away from being the father of two children. It was overwhelming but exhilarating. He loved being a father. He would love it more if Gray were by his side.

Imogen would be eight months old when his son was born.

His phone dinged before they reached their destination. Looking, he saw it was Mags.

> Mags: Gray just texted that she didn't need me at her appointment. Way to finally pull your head out of your ass.

He shook his head and choked on a laugh. Gray looked at him in question, so he angled his phone so she could read her friend's message.

"I wondered how you knew where I'd be. I'm going to kill her," Gray frowned.

"I plan on hugging her. Because of her, I'm sitting next to you. And him," he spread his fingers wide over her small bump. "I'm grateful that I get to meet the doctor. Hell, Gray, I'm grateful for anything you let me be a part of."

"Still," Gray said, her lips pressed tight. Mags would be hearing from her.

He took her hand and placed it flat against his thigh. She glanced sideways at him but left it. "Don't be mad at Mags. She loves you."

"I know. I have the best friends," she sighed.

Ciar felt her words like a punch to the gut. He had great friends, too, or he had. They avoided him because of Gray, and he couldn't blame them.

The cabbie announced they'd arrived. He paid and helped Gray out, marveling anew at how stunning she looked pregnant. He wrapped his arm around her waist as they entered the fancy lobby of the obstetrics office.

"Ciar," she warned, trying to shake his arm off. "We aren't a couple."

"We are in my mind. Let me at least have this moment." She had another think coming if she believed he was ever letting her go again.

With a huff, she entered the elevator and selected the third floor. "So, you plan on having him here instead of Scotland?"

She sighed, and her shoulders bowed slightly as if a great weight had been placed on them. "I've been indecisive, which is ridiculous considering I've never struggled with knowing my own mind in the past."

He wanted to beg her to have their son in Ireland, but it was too soon. He had to be careful not to chase her off. The door pinged and slid open, revealing a handsomely appointed waiting room and reception area.

Gray checked in and reminded the smiling woman behind the counter that she was scheduled for an ultrasound.

"Oh yes. I see that. Dr. Beckett likes to make sure the little ones are on schedule, especially for mothers who find out they're expecting later in the term, in case the date changes. Have a seat. It should only be a few minutes."

Sure enough, a side door opened, and a nurse stuck her head out and asked for "Gray MacGregor."

Ciar felt sweat prick his brow, nervous to see his son for the first time. He'd gone to a few of Marie's appointments, but that was him staying in the background. An observer, not a participant.

The nurse ushered them into a room and took Gray's vitals and asked a million questions. Satisfied, she told Gray to take her dress off and lie on the table where the ultrasound machine was waiting. There was also a warming cabinet full of blankets.

Gray thanked her while nervously glancing his way. Her dress had a side zipper, loosening the material enough to slip over her shoulders.

She caught the bodice before her lace-covered breasts were exposed. He really shouldn't be getting turned on in the middle of a doctor's appointment, but here he was. His throat was scratchy when he tried to swallow, his eyes riveted to every peek of the milky smooth softness of her collarbones.

"Ciar," Gray pleaded. "Get a blanket, please."

The "and stop staring" was unspoken but implied. He snatched a blanket from the box and was back in front of her in seconds. He witnessed when she gave up trying to get him not to look and finally stepped out of her dress.

He lost his breath, his mind, everything. Gray was the most

gorgeous woman he'd ever laid eyes on before. Now, she was a goddess.

"Fucking hell, baby. You take my breath." He dropped the blanket on the exam table behind her and, hoping she didn't swat him away, he wrapped his arms around her body, pulling her tight to his chest and pressing his hands into her bare back.

Every part of her body was lush. Mouthwatering. He palmed the back of her head and tilted her face up toward his.

"Let me kiss you, Gray. Please. Just one." The last plea was said against her mouth, her whimper setting his body on fire. When he swiped his tongue across her lips, she opened on a gasp and let him inside.

He couldn't remember where he was, why they weren't in a bed, or even his name. Gray MacGregor was a toxin and intoxicating. As their tongues twisted, he walked her step by step to the bed behind them. One moment from stripping her panties, he registered someone clearing their throat behind his back.

They jumped apart like someone dropped a snake at their feet. Gray's face blazed a brilliant pink. While she stuttered out an apology, Ciar adjusted himself, his dick a single-minded beast.

The doctor was a smiling, middle-aged woman who didn't miss a step at finding one of her mothers-to-be wrapped around a large, tattooed man in an exam room.

"Gray, you know the drill. Lie back and get comfortable. I'm happy to see that you've brought Baby Boy MacGregor's father."

Gray paused while draping the blanket over her legs, glancing at him uncertainly. He didn't hesitate. "Baby Boy Murphy, Doctor," he politely corrected.

"Oh, of course," the doctor grinned at Gray and then Ciar.

She bustled around, uncovering Gray's rounded belly,

making his chest swell, as if he were the only man who had ever put a child in a woman's belly.

While the doctor spread warmed gel over Gray's belly, Ciar took her hand in his own, holding it close to his chest while the doctor rolled the machine over her skin. Gray gave him a small, nervous smile, and he was once again weak with relief that he was there.

A loud heartbeat filled the small room, making his own heart thump. "Our son." He took her hand to his lips and kissed her knuckles.

"Would you come home with me so we can talk more about this?" Ciar laid his hand on the top of Gray's rounded belly. He couldn't get enough of touching her. Today had given him a resurgence of hope.

They were standing just inside the lower-level exit at the doctor's clinic. He was afraid that if he let her walk outside without a plan, she'd jump in a taxi and leave him behind.

"I have to fly to Japan early in the morning. I'll be gone a week," he sighed with regret at the timing. "This trip is an absolute necessity, or I would cancel it or send someone else in my place. It's a £150 million deal, and Anders wouldn't take kindly to me blowing it off."

Gray looked uneasy about his offer. He understood since he'd given her nothing that she'd asked for yet. He would, though. He would swear to Gray that he planned on telling her everything, but at this point, she wouldn't believe him.

"Umm, why don't we talk when you get back from your trip. I'm flying out in four hours and promised to visit my friends first. We can discuss how this will work over the phone anyway."

"Gray, please," he begged. "I just found out that you and I are having a baby. I don't want to separate. Not yet." He placed his hands on her hips and brought their bodies close enough that he felt their child press into him.

She looked like she might be considering going with him when his phone rang loudly in his pocket. It had to be Tina. He'd turned his phone on do not disturb and had made Tina's number the only one allowed while they were in with the doctor, and he hadn't taken it off yet.

"Sorry, I have to take this." He explained as he pulled his phone free.

Gray didn't say anything, so he answered. "Tina," he started tersely, "what is it?" He watched Gray take two steps back from him. He took two forward.

As he listened to Tina, he swore, and took Gray's hand, and walked them outside and hailed a cab. Thankfully, she knew something was wrong and didn't fight him putting her in the cab before sliding in next to her.

He gave the driver the address to his house. "Okay, Tina, calm down. I'll be there in eight minutes. Go ahead and call an ambulance. They'll have questions for you that I can't answer. Stop arguing and do as I tell you." Hanging up, he pinched the bridge of his nose.

"What's going on?" Gray asked.

He took her hand and placed it on his thigh, feeling ten times better for her touch. "Tina was on a ladder for some damn reason and fell. She thinks something is broken. She was panicked about not being able to reach Imogen if she woke from her nap.

"She hadn't even called the damn ambulance yet." He felt awful for his nanny, but the timing was terrible. He briefly wondered if she'd sabotaged his time with Gray, though he knew that was absurd since she hadn't known his plans.

"That's terrible," Gray gasped. "She must be in so much pain. As soon as we get to your place, I'll have the taxi take me to Triskelion, so I'm not in the way. Bébhinn's working today and can take me to the airport."

Ciar's mind was whirling, coming up with plan after plan, only to discard them. He might be shooting himself in the foot, but "I'll have to follow the ambulance to the hospital and help Tina get situated. She told me once, after I first hired her, that she doesn't have any family.

"If something is broken, she'll be in the hospital for a few days at least, and then will struggle to take care of Imogen. Gray," he started, praying for everything he was worth, "I don't have anyone else who can watch the baby, and I'm leaving for Tokyo at four in the morning.

"Would you please stay with Imogen until I get home?"

Gray reared back like he'd slapped her. "You can't be serious," she questioned, appalled.

"Listen, Gray, I know we have a million things to work out between us, but my ultimate goal is for you to move in permanently. I want us to be a family, and it's best you know now, I don't plan on giving up on that dream.

"You don't have to do this, Gray. I will beg one of the Byrne sisters to take her in until I can get back. It's just, if you moved in, I hoped you might start work on decorating the place. Our son's room, perhaps even Imogen's, and," he hesitated once more, "our bedroom.

"You were meant to decorate the whole place. You didn't keep your word, and you always do. So, I'm asking you to do it now."

"You made me a lot of promises, too, Ciar, and haven't kept any of them. Holding me to a separate standard is small-minded and hurtful."

Ouch. "I promise here and now, Gray MacGregor, to fulfill

every promise I've ever made to you. I promise to make new promises and keep those too. Do this for me. Move in and see what I see. Make that cold two-story building into a home for our family.

"I'll only be gone a week, but you could start. Anything you want is yours, Gray. I only need you. I'm begging you to give us a chance."

forty-two

GRAY

GRAY'S HEAD WAS SPINNING. This day just kept escalating. And now, with nothing but her purse and the clothes on her back, Ciar wanted her to move in and nanny his child, something she'd never done for any child, while he flitted off to Japan.

Oh, and he wanted her to decorate "their" home. Before she could even drum up a response, they were outside the two-story flat, thanking the driver, and hustling through the front door.

They found Tina on the kitchen floor, propped against the lower cabinets, her left leg painfully twisted at an awkward angle.

Ciar rushed to the older woman, kneeling by her side. She answered his questions through gritted teeth. Gray heard the ambulance sirens and ran back outside to direct the paramedics.

Ciar backed off as the paramedics assessed Tina and readied her for transportation. He gestured for Gray to join him off to the side, where he was quickly scratching out a list on a notepad at the kitchen bar.

"I'm not sure how long I'm going to be, but here is a list of how to make the formula and use the bottle warmer," Ciar said before handing her the pad.

"Imogen should wake up any time, she'll need her nappy changed, and then she'll want her bottle. She has a million toys in her room. She also enjoys lying on the couch next to me down here. So, you might do that."

His desperation at her accepting the nanny position might have been endearing if she wasn't about to be left with a child she'd never so much as touched.

Despite their current unresolved relationship, Ciar was one of her oldest friends, and even though it went against what she emotionally needed right now from him, she wouldn't let him down. Moving in permanently, though—that wasn't happening until he made good on his promise to tell her the truth about whatever happened after Colorado.

The paramedics had Tina on a rolling gurney and were wheeling her out. Ciar touched Tina's arm when they passed. "I'll be right behind you."

Tina humphed in irritation. "That is certainly not necessary."

"It is to me," Ciar answered the older woman.

Gray could tell his answer surprised her. She clamped her lips together and nodded. The moment they were out the front door, Ciar turned to Gray and shocked the hell out of her when he gathered her into his arms and kissed her passionately.

Pulling back reluctantly, he said, "I'll let you know what's what as soon as I speak to the doctor. Call me for anything." He hesitated, clearly wanting to say something else.

"What is it?"

"I hope...I...Imogen will love you, and I hope you will learn to love her too," he said quickly.

There was nothing to say to that.

He placed his hands on their son, resting between them. "You are the most amazing woman I've ever met."

And then he was gone, trusting her to care for his infant daughter. He had more faith in her than she did.

Gray leaned against the kitchen counter. Her legs suddenly felt leaden and unsteady. She had agreed to watch his daughter and live in their home for a week. Technically, she hadn't agreed so much as not said no.

It was in that moment of silent contemplation that Gray heard the faint chuffs of a waking baby. Her spine straightened like an electrocution rod had touched her skin.

She rushed to the bottle station upstairs, neatly set up near the sink, and scanned the directions. Not sure how many ounces she was supposed to make, she decided on a full bottle. Better safe than sorry.

While mixing the formula, she texted her mother, asking her to please cancel her flight, promising to call within the hour to explain.

No sooner had she slammed the bottle into the warmer and hit start when Imogen's surprisingly lusty wail sounded over yet another monitor. Gray tore off her coat and quickly dug a hairband from her purse, twisting her long hair into a fluffy bun on top of her head.

"You can do this, Gray," she assured herself. Sure, she could, as soon as she called in reinforcements. She sent a text to Bébhinn and Mags, Blair was gone to Wales, and told them to bring her any clothes or toiletries she'd left behind and come to Ciar's.

She entered Imogen's room and found the little doll with a bumper lip and big tears dripping down her red cheeks.

"Well now, Imogen, that's not a happy face. We'll have to do something about that, won't we?" Gray crooned, which thankfully had the effect of stopping further tears from falling.

Nothing like being thrown into the deep end. Taking a deep breath, Gray put on a confident smile and proceeded to introduce herself to Ciar's daughter.

"Who has time to be a fussy pants on such a pretty day? Huh?" Gray booped her nose, earning a gummy gurgle and smile.

Not too shabby, Miss MacGregor.

"When I sold you out to Ciar, I admit that I didn't foresee this outcome," Mags smirked. "You have to tell me how Ciar and Cannon got on."

"You are a," Gray stopped before cursing over the head of the baby in her arms, "b-i-t-c-h." She would have said more, but her phone began to ring. Ciar. It had been over four hours since he'd left for the hospital.

She answered, "Hey."

"Hey, baby," he said softly. "Christ, I miss you."

Her poor, stupid heart flipped over at the sentiment. Because Mags and Bébhinn were grinning at her like maniacs, it was clear they'd overheard Ciar. She glared at them and made shooing motions with the arm not holding Imogen. They squeezed into a single chair across from the couch instead.

"Assholes," she mouthed. For Ciar, she asked, "How's Tina?"

"She tore a ligament in her knee, but not severely enough to require surgery. As it is, she'll need plenty of bed rest, elevation, and icing. After that, she'll graduate to crutches."

"Are you able to bring her home?" Look at her, a handful of hours, and she was referring to his home as hers.

"She has to stay overnight because she hit her head pretty hard. They want to monitor her for at least one night. I've arranged for Dad to pick her up tomorrow and bring her home. I wondered if Bébhinn might ask her mother if she knew of a place to hire a nurse to stay with Tina for a couple of weeks until she can get around on crutches, though the nurse mentioned she might prefer a walker for stability."

"Bébhinn's here. I'll ask her to call Rowan." She looked down at Imogen, who was lying in her lap, her head on Gray's knees, playing with a toy and kicking her legs.

It had taken all of a minute to fall in love with the baby girl. She was delicate and lovely with blonde wisps covering her head. Her mom had once told her that she thought Gray's hair would never grow past wisps like Imogen's, and then it happened overnight, and she had hair for days.

Diaper changing was an experience, especially when she pooped in the fresh diaper right away. Changing a poopy diaper was an adventure she hadn't been ready for. At least she was getting a crash course before her baby was born.

The bottle was easy-peasy because Imogen was an old pro at the eating thing. She would fuss until she was in a position she deemed worthy, and that was that. She googled how to burp while Imogen finished her bottle. The search also revealed that Gray had made two ounces too many. Imogen hadn't complained.

She sent her mother a picture of Imogen smiling in her lap and explained about Tina, Ciar's trip, and that she'd agreed to stay here and help out.

Her response was immediate.

Mom: I'll start packing your things. Mom and Dad just flew in, so I can use their jet. Mom said she is coming too. Don't roll your eyes. Your grandmother heard the words baby and decorating. Between me, Mom, Raven, River, and Rowan, you can relax and take care of Imogen and finish school. See you soon.

Mom: Call your dad when you can. He's upset and pre-mantrum.

Apparently, in less time than it took to sneeze, the word was out that she was ensconced in Ciar's flat. Mags had been studying the two-story for inspiration for her embroidery, while Bébhinn had been nonstop texting and talking on the phone with her mom and aunts.

Gray felt like she was on a never-ending roller-coaster. She didn't even know what would happen after a week. No matter what, the babies would need perfect rooms at Ciar's, whether she was here or not. He was still their father, and Gray wanted them to have the best.

Ciar cleared his throat over the phone. "That would be a big help," he admitted about Bébhinn calling her mom. "I'm leaving here in about thirty minutes. Can I pick food up for everyone?"

Gray could tell he was nervous that she would suddenly change her mind. She wouldn't, but she was definitely more comfortable discussing dinner plans than the future.

Mags, who must have the ears of a greater wax moth—one of many facts Gray learned over the years from Blair—said, "Get us a feast from Gray Eyes. You know how I like my steak." She added the last with a grin and wink for Gray.

Bébhinn asked her to put Ciar on speaker. "Hey, Ciar, you'd better get plenty, the guys are coming over too."

"Of course, free food would bring them round. I'll call the chef and have it delivered. Take me off speaker, Gray."

Mags stood and scooped Imogen off her lap and went to the kitchen, Bébhinn following. "Okay, you're off."

"I want to kiss you when I get home. Will you let me?"

"Ciar," she sighed, a huskiness to her voice that hadn't been there seconds ago. "Your house is about to be full of people."

"I don't care."

"We're going too fast. I need things to slow down. I'm here, in your house, taking care of your daughter. My life feels like it's been ripped out from under me and someone else's replaced it."

He was silent for eight heart-pounding thuds of her heart. "I don't want you to feel pressured. Christ," he stopped, and she pictured him roughing a palm over his prickly scalp. "Today was unexpected but so welcome. Well, not Tina falling, but our son, the kiss we shared at the doctor's, and you agreeing to move in."

She ignored the mention of their kiss. "See, Ciar, that's just it. I didn't agree to move in. I agreed to stay for a week. Stop twisting my words." She walked over to the gas fireplace to warm her chilled hands, frustrated that he was withholding the one thing she needed to be able to accept wholeheartedly everything they both wanted for the future.

"I've said I'll give you what you need, and I will. After Japan. The minute I get home. I promise. As to moving in, I won't lie, I'm going to do everything in my power to convince you to never leave."

Some of the tension across Gray's shoulders relaxed. "Day by day, then."

"Day by day," Ciar echoed. "I still want to kiss you when I get home."

forty-three

CIAR

WHEN CIAR OPENED his front door, the first thing to hit him was the noise. The quiet he'd gotten used to and hated had vanished with the loud conversations and laughter of his closest friends.

He stood still for a moment, enjoying the change. Christ, but he'd missed everyone. He had Imogen, and being a father was better than anything he could have ever hoped for himself, but going from a close-knit group that texted, called, or hung out daily to limited contact had been hard.

His fault, but still tough.

When he rounded the corner to his kitchen, his eyes were immediately drawn to Gray, who was dancing around with a laughing Imogen clinging to her side. With that image alone in his mind, he could have died a happy man.

Bébhinn saw him first and clapped her hands. "Ciar, come say hello to Blair." Dagr was holding up a tablet with the screen showing the image of his tiny, fiery-headed friend.

He signed, "I miss you. How is Wales treating you?"

Blair grinned and waved. "Hey, Ciar. I've made two people cry over their ineptness and discovered a new species of Snowdon Hawkweed. I'm killing it. No surprise. Take care of Gray and Baby Boy Murphy for me."

He could only nod, afraid he'd give away how badly he wanted to do just that. While the rest of the group talked with Blair, he made his way to Gray's side, her cheeks already blushing with his attention.

He took Imogen from her arms and kissed his daughter's cheeks before handing her to a wide-eyed Daniel, leaving Gray with nothing to do with his hands but touch him.

"I missed you," he said while backing her into one of the high kitchen counters until he felt her small bump press against him. He nuzzled her neck and lifted her hands, wrapping them around his neck.

"I'm going to kiss you now." He punctuated his words with a kiss to the corner of her mouth. "Will you let me?"

The moment "Yes" slipped from between her lips, he was on her, sliding his tongue past her teeth to stroke her own tongue.

She gasped once before deliberately driving him crazy with her tongue. She grasped his neck to hold him close while his hands slipped from her waist to her ass.

He heard Mags tell someone, "Make sure the angle is right for Blair." Gray stiffened where she was fused to his front. That wasn't the only thing stiff. His dick clearly remembered the heaven that was Gray's body and wanted a reunion. Badly.

"Ciar," Gray whispered, pushing her hands against his chest. "We're putting on a show."

"I don't care," was his answer as he tried to retake her mouth.

"I do," she whispered, pinching his side for good measure.

Forcing himself to let her ass go and step back, he glanced at their audience. Mags tilted the tablet screen downward that

Bébhinn still held, and then, to his horror, Mags ducked into the camera's line of sight and signed, "Oh my God. He's totally hard. What an animal."

It was safe to say that Gray was no longer the only one blushing. Maybe he'd overvalued having friends. Daniel, Jonathan, and Dagr were laughing and giving him either a thumbs up or mimicking jacking off.

"Pricks," he mouthed. Leaning down, he gave Gray one last smacking kiss before backing up and reaching for Imogen, who instantly held her hands out for her daddy.

Once tickles and nuzzles were given, his daughter was struggling to get out of his arms and was windmilling toward Gray, whose cheeks were pink with delight as she took his daughter into her arms for her own snuggles. To say he was shocked was an understatement.

Gray bopped Imogen's nose and asked, "Does my sweet Immy want her dinner and bed?" Imogen's answer was to gurgle happily and latch on to Gray's long waves and bring them to her mouth.

She glanced his way and shrugged. "I spoke to Tina before you got home and asked after Imogen's nighttime routine."

For the first time, Ciar felt peace in explaining himself to Gray after returning from Japan. There was no better partner than Gray. Even after months apart, Gray had never not been his cornerstone. She was the one who would make them a family, and if telling her what she wanted to know ensured she would stay, then he would.

There was also a chance that his revelations would have the opposite effect, and she would leave him anyway.

The food arrived fifteen minutes after he and Gray put Imogen to bed. Bébhinn and Dagr stood in the doorway of his daughter's room to "ensure Ciar didn't do anything to make them late for dinner."

Their bullshit aside, it was the best night he'd spent with everyone since the Colorado trip last summer. He sat next to Gray at the dining table as everyone passed food around and talked about what was going on in their lives.

Blair stayed with them for a while, but she needed to check on one of her "babies" before she could get ready for a date. The girls all quizzed her about the guy, discussing his physique in way more detail than surely was necessary. They missed the look that Daniel and Jonathan exchanged. Neither of the cousins looked happy about the news, which didn't make any sense.

He caught Dagr's eye, who had also noticed the look, and raised his brows and shrugged. The call ended, and the talk turned to Dagr and Bébhinn's wedding. Now he understood why the date had been pushed back. They were waiting until baby Murphy was born.

The wedding would be at St. Mary's. Family and close friends only, with no groomsmen or bridesmaids. Just the two of them standing before a priest vowing forever. Bébhinn believed that without her father to give her away, she wasn't sure she could handle too much pomp surrounding the walk down the aisle without him.

He looked at Gray more than once as they described the simplicity of their nuptials. He wanted that. Well, he would marry Gray anyway she wished. Big, small, fancy, or simple, Dublin, Scotland, or even America, it didn't matter.

An hour later, Daniel, Jonathan, and Mags took an Uber to their townhouses, and Dagr and Bébhinn to their home.

"I'd better pack. Help me?" he asked Gray, who was leaning against the counter, stretching her lower back, causing her baby bump to push against her sweatshirt.

"Okay." She smiled shyly.

They walked through the living room to the back hallway

leading to their suite. "Today's been something, huh?" she asked.

"Understatement. Finding out about our son, I feel…overwhelmed but in the best way. I also got to have my hands and mouth on you three times. Definitely a good day," he teased.

"You're a shit, Ciar."

She admonished him as she walked down the hallway to their bedroom. He looked around their home, pleased with how well the contractors followed his plans, many of which were from memory of the conversations he and Gray had had during many late-night conversations. He'd tried to remember every detail she'd wanted.

The ground floor had a large living area, with one spacious end devoted to offices that shared a bank of windows. The living room and kitchen were large and open, perfect for entertaining and ideal for cozy family time by the fire.

The gym and small spa were upstairs, as well as Imogen and Tina's spaces. He'd had the contractors build another bedroom with an ensuite bathroom meant for company, but it was clearly going to be their son's room.

Their suite had a spacious sitting room, two huge walk-in closets divided by a large bathroom with each side mirroring the other, a his and hers situation.

It was clear that Gray hadn't explored the building while he'd been gone because her eyes were wide as she took everything in.

"I didn't have anyone in to decorate any part of the place." He cleared his throat nervously because everything was glaringly plain.

"I tried to get the colors right on the walls, wood floors, and bathroom tiles. I've been hoping for a miracle and that you'd be here to decorate it the way you always spoke about.

"And here you are." Before she could correct him, he held up his hands in peace, "I know it's not all worked out yet, but I know you won't be able to stand the unfinished rooms for long."

She tried to hide her smile but finally relented. "It does need a few things, and...Imogen's room is not at all how I would want it," she admitted softly.

He swallowed three times until his grin went down his throat. Gray was feeling a definite need to take charge of the place, and he was more than willing and ready to hand over the reins.

He always kept a bag partially packed with toiletries, so it didn't take long to add the necessary clothes. Meetings in Japan were typically far dressier than even London, and he wouldn't disrespect his client by not looking the part.

"I have a car picking me up at one to drive me to the airport. I hate leaving you here alone on your first night."

She shrugged and sat on the edge of his bed. "I'll be fine."

Ciar took off his shoes and socks. When he started unbuttoning his jeans, her eyes widened.

"What are you doing?"

She started to stand, so he touched her shoulder to keep her still. "I have three hours before I need to leave. I'm getting comfortable. Slip your clothes off. Let me give you a massage. It's been a long day."

"I remember what your massages are like, Ciar. They always ended up with you—" she cut herself off.

"With me what?" He finished pulling his jeans off while he asked. Her gaze dipped to his tight, black briefs that did little to hide how badly he wanted her.

Dragging her eyes up his body, she smirked. "With you inside me. The proof is looking me in the eye."

He dragged his t-shirt over his head and looked down. "Let me take these off then," he said, hooking his thumbs in the band of his briefs and tugging. "It's really looking at you now." He was fully erect and leaking precum, so desperate for her, his stomach clenched, and his muscles contracted.

She licked her lips, and little pants of air tripped over the lips of her slightly open mouth. "Let me massage you with my hands, and my mouth, and with this," Ciar fisted his erection and pumped slowly.

"Maybe we should talk about things first." She bit her lip, though it was clear her body didn't want to talk at all.

He didn't want to talk either. Not about what she wanted to hear, at least. "When I get home. I promised you I would. Give us tonight."

"You know," she started, pulling her sweatshirt over her head and dropping it to the floor, giving him a stunning view of her silk-covered breasts and small, rounded belly, "if you don't keep your word, I'll leave."

She cupped her breasts and pinched her nipples through the thin fabric, making him groan at the sight of them puckered and hard.

Reaching behind her back, she unclasped her bra and let it fall. Her heavy breasts and pink areolas had him salivating. When he started to step forward, she stopped him.

"Not yet. You made me watch you strip, and now I'll return the favor."

On her feet now, she pulled down her yoga pants, lacy thong and all, and kicked them to the side. When she sat back on the bed, she opened her knees wide, almost making his knees buckle.

He didn't wait. He stepped between her legs and was about to lift her to move her further on the mattress when she stopped him again.

"Gray," he growled. "It's been so long."

"Just as long for me." She placed her hands on his rigid thighs, caressing him until her hands were clasping his ass.

"Oh Christ, baby, no," he begged, as she leaned forward and licked the head and slit of his rigid sex. "I won't last." His hips were already short-circuiting, small uncontrollable jerks at the feel of her hot breath and tongue.

"You don't need to," she grinned. "I'm sure you'll recover while returning the favor."

forty-four

GRAY

CIAR'S ROAR as he came was as satisfying as if she'd come herself. She let his still semi-erect length slip from her mouth.

"Fuck, Gray. Fuck."

He bent at the waist and kissed her savagely while lifting her, moving her to the head of the bed, knocking extra pillows out of his way as he went.

"Gray, baby," his roughened voice cracking, "tasting me in your mouth makes me crazy."

To prove his point, he devoured her mouth like it was his favorite treat. "Your turn," he warned, licking and kissing down her neck, across her chest, until he palmed her aching breasts.

"Yes," she hissed, the sensitive flesh more than ready for him. He spent so long on her nipples, sucking and pinching, that she felt the beginnings of an orgasm from that alone.

As if sensing she was close, he let one of her breasts pop from his mouth and kept journeying lower. His big hands cupped her belly as he placed sweet kisses over the mound. "My son," he said, lips brushing her skin.

"I'm nothing without you, Gray MacGregor."

Gray felt tears prick her eyes at his sincerity. She felt the same. She swallowed the heavy emotion, praying for the thousandth time that he didn't make her regret it.

At the first breath over her core, she gasped, instantly lifting her hips, greedy for more. The first full swipe of his tongue up her seam practically made her levitate. "Ciar, yes."

"Like that, do you?" he asked before working her body like only he could.

"You know I do," she moaned as two fingers joined his tongue. Less than five minutes later, she was screaming his name and holding his head so tightly between her thighs, she chanced suffocating him.

He lapped at her sensitive flesh until her body calmed and then stretched over her body, careful of the bump, to kiss her tenderly. He sat up, kneeling between her legs.

She grinned, glancing between his legs where he was fully erect and bobbing up and down. "Looks like you recovered just fine."

"I'll show you recovered, woman," he grinned back, positioning himself at her slick entrance.

He frowned and hesitated, which caused some alarm. Gray started to reach a hand between her legs, because in this position, she couldn't see. "What?" she squeaked, as he caught her hand and placed it back on the bed.

"Is it safe? I mean, I'm not small, and you are, and the baby is," he tapped the swell of her low baby bump, "right there."

Gray chuckled. "I'm hardly small, Ciar. I'm bigger than all my friends."

He gave her a hard look before rubbing his sex against her entrance. Her heart lurched when he said, "You're perfect."

"It's safe to have sex. Mags asked the doctor. In fact, she

asked enough explicit questions that the doctor was even blushing."

"You're sure?"

"Very," she urged, moving her hips enough that he barely pushed in, causing them both to groan.

He trailed his fingers down her chest and over her bump once more, only stopping when she gasped and caught his hand from moving lower.

"What is this?" she demanded, leaning forward to touch the side of his neck. He had a new tattoo that she'd only now noticed.

Gray almost died when the big, tough Irish-Russian brute blushed. He touched the side of his throat where two words were tattooed in swirly script, surrounded by miniature grayscale flowers.

Gray Imogen.

"Your name, but it's really for both my girls," he shrugged, like it wasn't a big deal.

He'd named his daughter after Gray. How could she ever keep that man at arm's length?

"Christ, Ciar. What if...what if we don't work out, and you're stuck with me on your neck?" she choked on the question.

"You'll always be mine." It was as simple as that.

Romantic. She traced his firm, soft lips. "It's beautiful. Thank you." In appreciation, she put him out of his celibate misery and lifted her hips enough to take half his length.

"Fuck, baby." His control snapped. "You'll tell me to stop, if you need to?"

"Yes, damn it! Now, babe," she demanded and thank the Lord, he complied.

He went slowly, giving her body time to adjust. "Tight," he groaned, "strangling me."

She felt faint tremors dancing across her skin from his

touch. He was fully within her now, holding still, their bodies already warm, flushed, and slick with sweat.

"Good?"

"So good," she moaned. And then he was moving, the push and pull of their flesh coming together, full then empty, a blessing and a loss with every thrust.

Her body remembered Ciar. Her heart did too. She'd ached for the closeness they were sharing again. "I care for you, Ciar. So much," she confessed, arching her body off the bed to meet each of his thrusts.

He moved faster and faster until they were both wrecked and quivering, shouts and moans of completion echoed off the bedroom walls.

In the silence that followed her words, Gray pretended like the ache in her heart wouldn't kill her.

Ciar lay his head next to hers on the pillow and let his body tip to one side, where he pulled her close. He didn't utter a word. He didn't placate her with words of "like." For that, she was immeasurably thankful.

Tonight wasn't the first time she'd put her heart out there and had it handed right back. She said "cared for," not "love," but he knew. He knew very well how much she loved him.

He cared for her. She knew he did. They just needed time, and hopefully when he returned from Tokyo, they'd have it.

After thirty minutes of boneless chill, they showered, which led to more intimate activities. By the time Gray had dried her hair enough not to soak the bed, her eyes were drooping.

"Lay down, baby, and let me hold you until I have to leave."

Gray couldn't think of anything she wanted more. She was wearing a short, pine green silk nightdress, the material sliding decadently over the swell of her belly and breasts. Mags had borrowed it once, so she brought it over earlier when she and Bébhinn visited, which was why she had any nightclothes at all.

"Jesus, Gray. I have to leave soon, and you're wearing that," he complained.

She rolled in his arms until they were facing. From his shaved head to his muscled body covered in tattoos, no one would believe what a sweet, thoughtful man he was. Seeing him with his daughter had proven he had plenty of love to give, and she knew he would dote on their son the same.

Was she selfish to want that love for herself?

She ran her hands over his head, massaging and dragging her nails over his scalp, before using the pads of her fingers to trace his face. Ciar closed his eyes and practically purred beneath her touch.

She traced his shoulders and chest, down the arm lying atop his side, tracing his hand before beginning on his stomach muscles and V-line. Her fingers traced the band of his boxers where his erection strained.

He didn't ask her to take him out, but his hips undulated when her touch was close to where he wanted it.

"Gray," He pleaded. "Fifteen minutes."

She knew when he had to leave. Before he could anticipate her move, she swung her left leg over his waist and sat straddling his hips.

Tugging her nightie over her head, she said, "How fast can you get us off then, baby?" she teased.

Ciar pulled his boxers low enough until his sex sprang free, and while he lined himself up with her entrance, she lowered slowly.

"Fuck, Gray, fuck," he moaned as he watched her take his length. "Never have enough of you."

"Never," she mirrored, arching her back and pushing her belly high.

"So perfect, baby, carrying our son."

He started pistoning faster from his back. She rocked,

moaning his name, concentrating on the sensation, her orgasm building faster than ever. When his thumb pressed the sensitive nub above where they were joined, her body went off like fireworks.

As her inner muscles pulsed and squeezed Ciar, his body stiffened, a satisfied "Ahh," his guttural cry as he followed her over the edge.

Once the aftershocks had subsided, he looked at her, curved over his body. Gray MacGregor was precious to him. After months apart, feeling her heartbeat against his was nothing short of miraculous.

He clasped her ribs just above her bump. "I don't want to leave you."

"I'll be here when you get home."

"Promise?"

"Yes. I don't ever want to be where you aren't, Ciar," she admitted, "but you've promised a come-to-Jesus with me the moment you're back in Dublin, and I'll hold you to it."

Gray hadn't been happy about waiting even the one week until he got home, but she did understand that they'd had a heck of a day.

Ciar found out she was pregnant. Tina tore her knee in a fall. Gray agreed to move temporarily into his home and care for his daughter *and* decorate, which admittedly, wasn't a hardship, since it was her second favorite thing to do after hospitality.

He also interrupted her lunch with Cannon, for which she still wanted to strangle him. As though he'd read her mind, Ciar sat up, keeping their bodies connected, and asked, "You won't talk to your ex again, right?"

"Of course, I will. What the hell, Ciar? Cannon and I are friends."

"He doesn't want to be your friend. He was touching you,

and as a man who understands men, I can assure you, pregnant or no, he wanted you."

"Don't be gross." Her cheeks felt fiery.

"No talking to anyone we've ever slept with. For either of us."

"Well, that's a short list for me. You, not so much."

"I mean it, Gray," his voice rumbled as he bent to suck on her neck.

She shrieked, shoving him back. "Don't you dare give me a love bite where my mom and grandma can see."

"I'll do what I have to unless you tell me you won't speak to that dipshit you were going to eat lunch with."

"You're being impossible. I would never get back with him. Obviously." She cupped her belly to make her point.

He didn't say anything else, but his features were frozen in, not so much disapproval, but hurt. The fact that he had a child with another woman, a child that she was going to be caring for, and he was worried about her letting Cannon know that "All is well. No need to worry. Have a great life." Unbelievable.

"Ciar," she began softly, shifting off his lap so that he could get dressed, "you're being unreasonable."

He stood from the bed, still gloriously naked, and pulled her to her feet to face him. "I don't think you understand just how long I've wanted you to be mine, Gray, but now that you are, I refuse to share. Even if you weren't pregnant, I wouldn't want you to spend time with him."

She expelled an exasperated breath against his chest. "I've wanted you just as long, you idiot."

"So?" he pressed.

"Fine, but we'll revisit this when you get home." Then, because she couldn't help herself, "Hurry home."

forty-five

CIAR

HE TRIED to sleep on the way to Tokyo. It was an excruciatingly long flight. He managed to sleep a few hours and also work on several of his current deals, especially the upcoming meetings with his picky, Japanese client.

They landed in Tokyo at one in the morning the day after he'd left Dublin because of the distance and time change. Gray and Imogen would be getting ready for supper.

The further he traveled away from Gray, sparks of anxiety began to zap him. Yesterday had given him everything he'd been hoping for. Gray was back, and in his arms and bed, and Gray and Imogen were bonding.

Nothing mattered but those two things, and yet he couldn't help but think that the kind of euphoria he'd experienced with Gray and having his friends back wouldn't last. How could it last?

He didn't want to talk about the past when he got home. Why go backwards? Why couldn't Gray be happy with now?

They both cared about one another. She admitted last night that she cared for him. He tried not to feel cheated that she hadn't told him that she loved him like she had before. Surely, she still loved him. Gray wasn't the type of woman to flip-flop on her feelings.

Dwelling on what she had or hadn't said was ridiculous. He was self-aware enough to admit that he'd never told her anything. No grand declarations. Only that she was his, and he was hers.

The room he'd be staying in for the week was very nice. He couldn't be bothered with any of it, though, wondering how Gray and Imogen's day had gone. Throwing his bags on the bed, he pulled his phone out to see what messages had been missed.

His eyes widened when he saw that he'd been unblocked from his friends' old group text, Devils & Angels. He hadn't been mad when they'd deleted him from the group. He'd hurt one of them and didn't fix it, so he was a casualty and deservedly so.

He grinned, reading through some of the older messages before he got to the current ones. Daniel telling Gray to lay off Murphy's crab cakes or she would blow up made him laugh out loud. Ciar's dad would enjoy hearing that.

Thinking about his father, Ciar needed to make things right between them. They'd gotten in a million rows over the years, both of them hardheaded, but never more than a few hours passed before they squelched whatever issue had caused the disagreement.

Their last argument had been different, though, and they knew it. His dad had gone too far, or perhaps not far enough if Ciar were to hold more accountability for his actions.

Regardless of who was right or wrong, Ciar should have reached out to his father before now. Especially when he found out Gray was carrying his child, which still blew his mind, but in the best way possible.

His dad would know about the baby by now since he was the one who'd taken Tina to Ciar's home from the hospital. He decided to give him a call even though his dad and Uncle Cormac would be gearing up for the pub's dinner hour. He needed to start smoothing things over before we went to sleep for a few more hours. Ciaran Murphy's subdued voice answered on the second ring.

"Son."

"Gray's pregnant." Ciar sighed at himself. His father already knew.

"Came as quite a shock," his dad replied evenly.

"I only found out," Ciar defended.

"Gray told me. Makes sense now why I've not seen her around."

His dad was going to make him work for it, then. "I should have called before now."

A beat of silence passed before he said anything. "I should have too. You know, Ciar, I would never break your trust. It's only that I see your fears running you ragged, and it's almost impossible not to speak up."

Ciar gritted his teeth at the reminder of what was coming his way. In a week's time, he would be spilling every one of his fears on Gray.

Shaking that disquieting thought from his brain, he focused on his dad again. "I understand. I overreacted." He gritted his teeth against the feeling of being scolded as a child and cataloging his bad behavior.

"I pushed," his dad reluctantly admitted. "So, a boy, huh?"

Ciar huffed a laugh at his father, the argument over and back to normal. "Imogen will have a little brother."

"You and Gray?"

"I'm not letting her go again."

He and his dad spoke for another five minutes until his Uncle Cormac hollered at his brother, "Get your ass off the phone and help me."

As soon as he hung up with his dad, he stripped out of his clothes and lay down to call Gray. It was strange to feel exhausted and euphoric at the same time. She was back in his life and allowed him to call her.

She'd allowed him into her life and body again.

She picked up immediately. "How are my girls doing?" he asked.

"If you mean Imogen and Tina, they're doing great."

"I did not mean Tina, and you know it," he growled back. "I miss you." That was a huge understatement. He was desperate to be by her side again.

He heard her sigh and then, "I miss you too. You picked a good week to be gone from Imogen, though. Tina and I think the little stinker has three teeth coming in, and she is grouchy, but we've ordered all the binkies and chewies that can be frozen so she can gnaw on them for relief. Tina thinks that'll be enough."

"Tina thinks? I hope she's being respectful of your opinions. She was warned not to pull any of her bullshit on you. I swear, Gray, if she makes you feel uncomfortable, I'll find a new nanny. I left you in charge of our home and Imogen." He would hate firing Tina, because he'd come to, if not appreciate, then certainly respect, her no-nonsense manner.

Gray was quick to defend the woman. "Tina and I have come to an understanding. You don't need to worry yourself over that."

In other words, Gray wanted him to stay in his lane and out of theirs. He grinned. That was not a problem.

"How's our boy?" He was still strangled with guilt that he hadn't been by Gray's side from the beginning.

Her warm chuckle made him smile in return. "A shit like his father. Kicks me nonstop, and most of them are aimed at my bladder."

"He'll be a rugby star. Just you wait and see," he announced proudly. "Our fathers would be pleased with that."

"Oh, they'd be pleased until the time comes for the poor boy to choose between Scotland and Ireland."

"Surely, no choice." It wasn't quite a question, but...

"Exactly. Scotland."

Ciar winced. "We've a few years before that fight comes about at least," he said, half teasing. His son would definitely play for Ireland.

"Mom, Grandma, and the Byrne sisters were here today."

Ciar could hear the hesitancy in her voice, almost like she still wasn't sure if he wanted her to change things even though he's already assured her he did. "You do know that it's our house, Gray, right? I bought the building for us. I want you to change everything until it suits you."

She hesitated before answering. "Things have changed since then."

"Goddammit, Gray. It is ours. Ours," he repeated. "It's where we'll raise our family. I want you to make your mark on every surface. I want you to walk through every space and know it's yours.

"I warned you more than once that now that I have you there, I'm never going to let you walk away, so you might as well decorate it the way you want. Please."

Christ, he mentally swore. She was driving him crazy. He didn't deserve promises of commitment, but he damn well wanted them.

"I thought you lo—" he cut himself off. "I thought you cared for me."

"Don't turn this on me, Ciar. You know I care for you, but you lied to me for months. You hurt me, and you weren't there for me when I needed you. Just because you say you will make it right when you get home doesn't guarantee that you will. You know that." And the final nail in his coffin. "I know that."

There was nothing to say, but, "I won't let you down again."

forty-six

GRAY

"WHAT DO YOU THINK, TINA?" Gray was leaning against Imogen's door, watching the older woman turn this way and that from her wheelchair, taking in the room's new look.

If someone had asked her a few months ago whether she and Tina would be friendly with one another, Gray would have snorted in disbelief. Luckily for them, and Imogen as well, the two women realized they quite liked one another.

Gray had found that most of the nanny's bluster was a cover-up for her loneliness. She had no family left. Her husband had left her over thirty years ago, and her only son had passed away during a military exercise in Lebanon, where he'd been stationed.

He passed fifteen years ago and was buried in a small, rural cemetery outside Dublin, where Tina had lived and worked most of her life. Soon after his passing, she decided to sell everything and become a nanny.

Tina admitted that she'd been unkind to Gray initially

because she was afraid that Gray would decide to get a different nanny if she and Ciar reconciled.

When Gray explained that it would never happen because not only did Imogen love her nanny, but Imogen's little brother would need Tina's love and care as well, Tina had clamped her lips tight and simply nodded, but her shoulders relaxed and pink tinged her soft cheeks.

Her mom, Grandma Mary, Raven, River, Rowan, Bébhinn, and Mags all adopted Tina as a beloved family member, and together, they'd made Ciar's two-story building into a home.

Tina clasped her hands under her chin, taking in the changes of Imogen's suite. "It's lovely, Gray. Lovely," she repeated. "You and your mom and friends have created something special. Truly."

"And your rooms? Will they work?" When Rowan found out Tina's favorite color was yellow, which was the youngest Byrne sister's favorite color as well, she took over the nanny suite and transformed the white walled monastery feel of Tina's space into a warm, sumptuous sanctuary.

"You shouldn't have," she tsked, "but it's lovely."

"Ciar wanted you to love your rooms so much that you never want to leave."

"Outrageous boy," Tina muttered, even though she was clearly pleased Ciar had thought of her.

"Your son's suite is quite handsome. That Mary is something to behold."

Gray snorted at the description of her beloved grandma. "Grandma Mary is an opinionated wrecking ball, and no one gets in her way if they know what's good for them," she laughed.

There hadn't been a lot of work to do in the living areas except to add more furniture and art. Bébhinn, Mags, Raven, and River had taken over the kitchen and living rooms upstairs and down while Gray and her mother focused on the primary suite.

Gray still felt uneasy about working on the intimate space when things between her and Ciar were far from finalized, but she admitted to herself that she loved making the bedroom her own.

She was getting antsy about his arrival, which was already a week overdue. Ciar's deal with his Japanese client hit some snags, and he'd had to stay several more days to iron everything out.

At least she'd had Imogen, school, and the house project to keep her busy. Otherwise, she might have driven herself insane, wondering what revelations would be spilling from Ciar's mouth.

He was due back late that night, and though she was ridiculously excited to see him, she couldn't help but wonder if she could handle whatever news he'd been hiding from her. Handling and accepting were two very different animals.

Though he denied cheating, it was the only thing that made any sense. Why keep Imogen a secret? Clearly, she was conceived before he and Gray got together. Was his secret worse than cheating?

That thought shook her confidence and made her uneasy. Shaking off the unhelpful thoughts, she grinned at Tina. "Auntie Mags and Imogen will be back from visiting Daniel and Jonathan in thirty minutes. That's just enough time for you and me to make loaded ice cream sundaes for the two of us. What do you say?"

Tina laughed, her eyes twinkling. "I say you're a woman with grand ideas."

Gray woke up on the couch where she'd attempted to wait up for Ciar, only to find him naked and stretched out over her on the sofa, pulling her tank below her breasts.

"Ciar," she moaned as he sucked one of her nipples into his hot mouth, "we're in the living room."

"In our fucking house, baby. We can do anything we want wherever we want. Stop worrying and let me love your body. If Tina uses the lift, we'll hear. Now, get naked," he demanded.

Gray knew she should insist on them speaking first, but he'd been gone so long, and she'd missed him. She definitely missed his touch, so she caved and wiggled out of her clothes.

"But we talk after," she insisted.

His only response was to hum against the skin between her breasts before kissing and licking his way to the baby bump, lightly running his fingertips over the swell. He whispered sweet words to their son as he feathered kisses.

He lifted his eyes to meet hers, and Gray would swear she saw love staring back. Was it for her or their son?

As though he read her thoughts, he said, "You are everything to me, Gray."

Ciar shifted to his knees and gently grasped her knees and spread them wide until she was completely open to him. His tattooed hands dragged down her inner thighs until they framed her sex causing her breath to hiccup with need.

He ran one thumb over her seam and groaned. "So wet for me already, baby."

When he lifted her ass and replaced his thumb with his mouth, Gray couldn't stop the drawn-out, "Ahh."

What started as slow licks and laps of his tongue turned into frenzied sucking, his tongue imitating the sex act with deep penetration until her orgasm screamed through her body.

With little will of her own, her hips bucked repeatedly

against his mouth until the strongest of the pulses subsided, and his mouth gentled on her sensitive flesh.

Ciar gave one last gentle kiss to the inside of her thigh and then sat up, clasping her hips and sliding her ass up his thighs until his hardened length rubbed between her legs causing full body shivers.

Gray watched him through slitted eyes, her lids heavy from the sating orgasm. He seemed enthralled with her body, his eyes raking her up and down, lingering first on her breasts, then her belly, and finally fastening to her core.

She fisted his sex and slowly pumped. "This is one of the only places on your body that isn't tattooed."

He chuckled and groaned at the same time. "I considered it once when I was a teenager, even though the thought of having to get my dick hard for the tattooer to place the stencil wasn't appealing."

"No way. I didn't know that," she admitted. "I'm glad it isn't tattooed, then."

Ciar was now rocking his hips while encouraging her to tighten her grip. "I've been told," he grunted, "that the lack of color makes it look bigger."

"Not that I give a shit what past lovers have told you, but I don't think you need an illusion to appear big." He grinned like the cat that got the cream.

"You gotta stop that, Gray," he said while gently grasping her wrist and pulling her hand from him.

Gray frowned at losing her toy, but when he began to circle the thickened head of his sex up and down her seam, spreading their arousal across the apex of her thighs, she forgot about everything except what more pleasure his body was about to give her own.

"Stop teasing me, Ciar." She was so needy, had she been pre-pregnancy limber, she would have shoved him to his back and taken what she wanted. As it was, baby boy made defying gravity from her back tricky.

"But I like teasing you," he grinned, his dimples making his already handsome face irresistible.

Before she could demand action, he positioned himself at her opening and slowly slid in, the fullness he created was always a shock, making her bite her lower lip and whimper. The pleasure-pain of the stretch was beautifully perfect.

"Christ, Gray," he growled between clenched teeth. "I can't get enough of you. I think about filling you up a million times a day."

He bent over her chest to kiss her, a hint of desperation flavoring his tongue. "I'll never not need you," he admitted against her mouth.

Neither of them spoke another word. Moans and panting and slaps of skin on skin echoed in the silent living room. He played her body perfectly, wringing another orgasm from her. She felt the pulsing tug deep inside trigger Ciar's release.

They spent another half an hour touching and kissing softly, coming down from the intensity of their shared passion until he stood and gathered her into his arms and carried her to their bedroom and ensuite bathroom, where they showered. They smiled at each other whenever their eyes met.

She followed him into the bedroom and lay down after he threw back the bedding. Her nerves were starting to spark, knowing that this was the moment she'd been waiting months for.

The truth. Finally.

When he remained silent, Gray placed a hand on his arm. "Ciar," Gray hesitated, chastising herself for her timidity in demanding what she needed. "I need you to explain the last several months. I need to know why you ghosted me but named your daughter after me. I need to know a lot of things, and you damn well owe me the answers.”

Had she not been skin to skin, she might have missed the tensing of his muscles at her questions. But she did feel it, and her heart sank.

“I’m exhausted, baby. We have the rest of our lives to talk. Just let me hold you in my arms while we sleep.”

And there it was. He wanted her but refused honesty. She fought the tears that wanted to fall as she turned on her side and allowed him to wrap his front around her back.

She could feel the hope that she’d been carrying close to her heart since their semi-reconciliation break and shatter.

forty-seven

CIAR

Ciar,

I've gone home to Scotland.

You promised me answers the moment you set foot back in Dublin.

You didn't deliver.

You've been screwing with my feelings from our first kiss until our last. I can't keep being disappointed.

We've been friends for years, and I'm beginning to think that you've only ever been interested in friends with benefits.

Unfortunately for you, or fortunately where Imogen and your son are concerned, you got two of your "friends" pregnant, and now you must feel cornered.

Consider yourself uncornered by me.

I no longer hold any expectations. I lost all hope of a true partnership between us the moment you shut me down last night.

I get it. Finally.

I'll keep you informed of every appointment and where I choose to give birth, but that is where our interactions will end.

I am asking you to allow me to spend some time with Imogen when I come to town. I believe Tina would be amenable to meeting.

Do not fear that I will malign you to my family, our friends, or the children. Like I've said, we're friends. You never offered me more than that.

It was my silly heart and assumptions that got us here.

I offered you my heart more than once, and you handed it right back each time.

Goodbye, Ciar.

Gray

forty-eight

JOSEPHINE

JOSEPHINE SIGHED as she read over the messages in her friends' group chat. Gray had shown up unexpectedly two weeks ago, giving only a vague reason as to why she'd left Dublin and, more importantly, her baby's father.

Thomas was beside himself. He had not been a Ciar fan since he found out his daughter was pregnant. Truthfully, he hadn't been a fan since the night they'd seen him on a date, and Gray had cried.

Thomas was protective of his children at the best of times, but he'd never witnessed a man making Gray emotional, and it enraged him. As Gray's mother, Jo was more aware of a young woman's emotional ups and downs and knew that, with enough time, the situation might work itself out.

Which it had, just not for long. Having her daughter pregnant and alone wasn't making Josephine happy either. After their house decorating and watching Gray fall in love with Ciar's daughter, Imogen, she had believed that things between the two were finally healing, if not healed.

But here they were, living with their teenage son and an adult daughter who refused to answer a single question about where she planned to live once her baby was born. They didn't even know if she planned on giving birth in Inverness or Dublin.

There was a fully outfitted baby's room waiting at Ciar's while Gray had nothing of her own and refused Jo's overtures to buy her a home close to theirs and make it ready for the upcoming birth.

Rowan: Bébhinn is worried. Gray refuses to tell any of her friends what happened when Ciar got home from Japan, except that they had a "different opinion on what a relationship consisted of."

River: What does that even mean? Does he want some sort of open relationship? Christ, Jo, surely the boy isn't that foolish. Jonathan swears that Ciar isn't saying.

Catriona: No matter what has happened or is happening between those two, Gray needs to make some decisions about her future. Even one decision!

Aileen: Margaret told me to back off, and not as kindly as that sounds. She said that Gray needs support and zero questions.

Catriona: Blair is still in Wales, but she agrees. She told me to give Gray space. The baby was coming with or without Gray being in a relationship with the baby's father.

Josephine: She isn't wrong about that.

Raven: Daniel has been very quiet. If Ciar has opened up with him, he isn't saying. I think you should let it ride for now, Jo. Give her support and space. Let her soak up the comfort and safety of her family home without expectations.

Rowan: I agree. She will confide in you when the time is right. Bébhinn said that they speak every day. Gray isn't cutting anyone off, which is a good sign. She just needs a place to settle.

River: And if it comes to it, and she goes into labor without a baby blanket to her name, Great-grandma O'Connor will move heaven and earth to outfit her newest grandchild before he so much as sneezes.

Josephine: You guys are right. I'll love her only. No pushing.

forty-nine

GRAY

"LOCHLANN!" Gray screamed from her parents' kitchen. "So help me God, if you leave dirty dishes in the sink one more damn time, I will strangle you while you sleep."

Dramatic? Yes. Did she care? No.

"Christ have mercy, Jo," her father barked from his office, "do something with your children before I kick them both out."

An empty threat, but still, Gray felt a modicum of remorse and embarrassment over her childish behavior, even if her brother was a little shit.

She'd left Dublin two months ago. Left Ciar two months ago, specifically. Her son would be born in a few weeks, which didn't improve her attitude. Sure, she was beyond excited to meet her wee son, but she was equally downtrodden.

Ciar hadn't come for her. He hadn't sat her down and explained. Anything. He didn't text her or tell her he missed her beyond measure, like heroes did in the movies. He didn't sweep her off her feet and force her back to Dublin.

He didn't give her declarations of love. Or even declarations of like.

She wanted her child more than anything she'd ever wanted, but the unknown of "them" cut off her joy like a rusted valve.

She was stuck.

She had to move forward because babies could only grow so long in their mother, but her emotions were in stasis. She was exhausted from pretending.

Every day, she pretended, and her family knew it.

Lochlann sauntered in without a care in the world, smirking at his older sister. Gray didn't say a word, even though her teeth were so clenched, she had to be taking years off their life.

In his ever-deepening voice, gravelly like their father's, he passed the sink holding his late-night snack dishes and casually mentioned, "My God, you blew up overnight."

She felt her jaw unhinge and drop. Her cheeks flushed, too, because he wasn't wrong. She had gotten impossibly huge, and it did seem like it had happened overnight. *Still.* "You...you," she stuttered. "I pray someday you say that same thing to your wife when she's expecting and witness the wrath of a woman wronged."

"At least I'd be there to watch the mother of my child become a beached whale," he snapped back.

And then, as if the siblings had choreographed expressions of horror, time froze. Loch's eyes rounded, his hands were thrown high, whether to grasp her in apology or hold back her rage was anyone's guess.

"Gray," Lochlann gasped. Her name was a plea for forgiveness and regret.

Gray blinked rapidly to hold the tears that wanted to come at bay. Should her brother have brought up her relationship, or lack thereof? No. Was he within his rights to bring up the relationship elephant in the room? Yes.

She didn't want to cry—mainly because she was damn tired of crying—since tears from any woman, young, old, family, or friend distressed the men in her family.

As if the hint of her tears filtered into her dad's study, thunderous footsteps pounded down the hallway, coming their way fast. Lochlann and Gray looked at each other with renewed dread, especially when they heard their mom's lighter steps and exasperated, "Thomas."

"Start washing the dishes," she hissed, shoving him into the farmhouse sink while simultaneously picking up her cup of tea and scrolling through her emails.

When their parents rounded the corner, Gray hoped they saw their children relaxing and enjoying one another's company.

Her father filled the doorway, his chest pumping with who knows what overprotective things that fathers' chests pumped with. Wrath? Fury? Love.

Their dad stood still and looked between his daughter and son as he placed his giant paws on the kitchen counter. Gray smiled and sipped her tea, avoiding eye contact.

"Son."

That one word had Lochlann's shoulders tensing as he vigorously scrubbed a frying pan. "Why does your sister look like she's been crying?"

Defense. Defense. Defense.

"Way to make things weird, Dad. I'm always crying."

"Lochlann." Bone meet dog.

Her brother slowly turned and met their father's scowl. Thomas MacGregor didn't raise a wuss.

"I purposefully said something to hurt her feelings about the prick that got her pregnant," her brother admitted.

Gray sighed and closed her eyes briefly, wondering how she'd found herself in such a ridiculous situation. She was about to open her mouth to diffuse the tension when her dad asked, "Why?"

Lochlann's fists clenched at his sides, and his fair complexion reddened. "I shouldn't have. I know that. Christ," he swore, "but I'm pissed because my sister, whom I love more than anything, is hurting, and she's forbidden us to find the prick who's left her alone and pregnant, and I'm furious," he roared the last, shocking herself and their parents alike.

"I'm here now. Have at me."

Oh God. Ciar.

SIX WEEKS AFTER GRAY LEFT

CIAR

CIAR STOOD UNMOVING in his kitchen, leaning against a counter, a bottle of unopened vodka, a sentinel to his despair.

For the second time since Gray snuck out of his bed and his life, he'd stalked her as she went to her doctor's appointments. She was good about letting him know when her appointments were and how she and their son were faring.

After her appointments, she would meet Tina and Imogen at Gray's old townhouse. Tina was still on crutches, so Mags would pick the two of them up. He stood outside then too.

Gray was clear, through text, because she wouldn't speak to him over the phone, that his presence was not wanted.

He knew why. The night he'd come home from Tokyo, he panicked. He'd had every intention of putting it all out there, but after they had sex and he was so overwhelmed with how grateful he was to have her back and to be having a child with her, he froze.

The thought of coming clean, of losing her, of her looking at him differently...yeah, a coward.

There was no help for it now, though. Time was running out, and if there was a chance of fixing this, of her staying even after he came clean, he had to take it.

So, he did something that he never thought he'd ever do in a million years. He opened his phone and called his dad, who answered on the first ring.

"Do you know how to find Aunt Alya?"

It took another two weeks to track down his aunt and then another week to make the arrangements for her to fly to Dublin. When they'd finally spoken on the phone, Alya had burst into tears when he told her his name. She hadn't seen him since his mother's funeral when he was eight.

As a child, Alya had been the one bright spot in his miserable childhood and why Imogen's middle name honored the woman.

Operation "Get Gray Back" started with facing his past.

Alya and her thirteen-year-old twin daughters, Dunya and Dasha, descended on his Dublin doorstep in all their Slavic glory. He was thankful to still be fluent in Russian.

The three women spoke English, but their accents were heavy, which left his sheltered Irish father exasperated more often than not and cursing himself for not learning the language. Despite the language barrier, his father and Alya were bulwarks when it came to supporting Ciar in his desire to win back Gray.

His father fully supported Ciar facing his fears. Finally. Three times during their flight to Inverness, his dad had patted his son's knee, something he hadn't done since he was a child.

Ciar imagined the soothing gesture was meant as much for the older man as it was for him.

His dad insisted on traveling with him. He had known Gray's parents since before she was born and had said, "Thomas MacGregor is a good man, but you won't be facing that grumpy bastard without me by your side."

Ciar appreciated the sentiment, though it wasn't MacGregor he was worried about seeing. Now that they were standing outside Gray's front door, his nerves kicked up sevenfold.

"You've got this, boy," his father encouraged at his shoulder.

Ciar raised his finger to ring the bell when he heard shouting coming from inside, along with Gray's voice. Concerned, he tried the door and found it unlocked and, without further thought, let himself in.

No one noticed Ciar's entrance because a younger, red-faced, and clearly furious version of Thomas held the occupant's attention. Unfortunately, Ciar heard the tail end of Gray's brother's rant. "…and she's forbidden us to find the prick who's left her alone and pregnant, and I'm furious."

Ciar didn't blame him. The boy should be pissed. They all should be. "I'm here now. Have at me." Three sets of stunned MacGregor eyes turned his way. "The door was unlocked, and I heard shouting," he shrugged, the beginnings of embarrassment tightening his shoulders.

"My front door is never unlocked," MacGregor growled, crossing his arms over his massive chest. "I added your face to the biometric scanner, assuming you would eventually pull your head out of your ass."

Well, that was unexpected and left him momentarily speechless. Not ready to deal with MacGregor's wrath quite yet, he finally allowed himself to take in Gray, who stood silently beside her brother. Her face was blank of emotion.

She wore yoga pants and a soft-looking t-shirt stretched thin over a belly that had to be twice the size since the last time he'd seen her from a distance.

"Gray." He said her name softly, a plea, a prayer. He took a step toward her, but Lochlann stepped in front of his sister, blocking his view. Not that she stayed there. She squeezed around her much larger brother and elbowed his side. Gray clasped her brother's hand and whispered something that only her brother could hear. Lochlann frowned but relaxed his stance.

"Why the hell are you here?" MacGregor asked, ratcheting up the tension.

Now it was Josephine's turn to step around her husband and elbow his side. She walked to Ciar and his father, bypassing him with a stern look, before gathering his father into a hug.

"Ciaran Murphy, what a surprise. It's so good to see you." Josephine said warmly.

Ciar's dad's cheeks pinkened, but he nodded to Josephine and Thomas. "I appreciate you opening your home for my son and me."

"Like you gave us a choice," MacGregor muttered. A sharp look from his wife had him biting off anything else he might have wanted to say.

Josephine glanced toward her daughter and raised her brows in question, but Gray remained stubbornly silent.

"Please come in and take a seat," Jo indicated the large kitchen table, "and I'll get everyone a drink."

Ciar swallowed hard. This meeting had already gone off the rails, but he sat as instructed while trying to get Gray to look at him.

She was having none of it. Fear that he'd come too late flooded him.

He accepted his glass of ice water. Josephine must have

thought the tension radiating from the assembled bodies didn't need any alcohol.

His dad patted his knee under the table, and damn if it didn't almost bring tears to his eyes. This was the moment. He couldn't take the coward's way another time, or he would lose everything.

He would lose Gray, and he couldn't allow that.

Gray's mom settled between her scowling husband and son and fiddled with her own water, which he suspected was vodka. *Amen, Josephine MacGregor.*

As the silence ratcheted up in its intensity, Ciar slowly scooted his chair back and stood, gaining everyone's attention, including Gray's. Taking a deep breath, he asked, "Gray, might I speak to you privately?"

fifty-one

GRAY

GRAY'S BODY might be stiffly sitting in a chair, but on the inside, she was a quivering, emotional mess. Ciar had finally come, and though she'd told herself he was too late, that he'd left her hurting too long, her heart pounded in relief at seeing him again.

She was aware that he stalked her movements when she went to Dublin for checkups, just like she knew that if she didn't wish to see him, she could have switched to a doctor in Inverness. In fact, she had told her mother that she would ask her doctor to recommend someone for the last few weeks of her pregnancy.

But here he was, wanting to speak to her. Regardless of how upset she was with him, she and their son needed to hear whatever he had to say. For closure, if nothing else. Gray would also hear him out for Imogen's sake. She loved Ciar's daughter, and it destroyed her to hand the baby back to Tina and walk away.

She finally looked at Ciar, really looked at him standing before her family. He was nervous, though only she probably knew it since he was keeping his face as expressionless as possible. His father kept nervously glancing up at his son. Ciaran knew too.

She was about to stand and take him somewhere private when her dad said, "You want to speak to Gray privately, do you, after running around on my daughter for months?"

Her mother tried to intervene, but he was having none of it. "Whatever you have to say at this late date, boy, can be said in front of her family."

Gray found her voice at that. "Dad. Enough. I'll speak to him." She was about to rise, not as easily as it used to be, when Ciar stopped her.

"Stay where you are, Gray. Your father's right. I've hurt you, and your family deserves to know why."

"Ciar. No," his father demanded before standing and placing a hand on his son's shoulder.

Gray was taken aback. Something felt wrong. Whatever Ciar had been hiding for months surely wouldn't make his father react that way.

Ciar patted his father's hand. "Sit, Dad, please. It's the only way."

More worried than ever, Gray stood. "Ciar, no matter what this is," she paused and gave a halfhearted wave between him and his father, "you don't owe my family your privacy."

"The hell he doesn't," her brother growled. "Whatever he has to say must be bad, and you'll need your family if he hurts you again."

Ciar nodded at Lochlann, then her mom and dad. "Sit, Dad, and you too, Gray. Please."

Once they were settled, Ciar cleared his throat and took a sip of his water. Gray felt tears prick her eyes, and he hadn't even started.

"This is difficult for me to speak on, so bear with me, please.

I don't deserve any more chances from you, Gray, and my fear is that once I've finished, you'll ask me to leave you alone for good, but if there is even a small chance that you can forgive me, I'm willing."

He was only looking at her, speaking to her as if no one else was in the room. She could only nod, affirming that she would listen.

"I'm not quite sure where to begin. I've practiced," he said, wiping his hands down his shirt and clearing his throat again, clearly uncomfortable.

Gray didn't know at this point if she or Ciar was struggling more. She glanced at her mother, who shrugged and winced.

"I was eight when I went to live with Dad," he began and then shook his head, cursing under his breath. "No, I won't start there. I'll begin with Imogen. She isn't my daughter."

At Gray's gasp, Ciar corrected with, "I mean, she is my daughter, completely and totally mine. I adopted her. Imogen's mother gave up her rights."

Gray's head was spinning until she had to lay both her hands on the smooth wooden top of the table to steady herself.

"Christ. I'm doing this all wrong," Ciar swore again.

"Take a deep breath, son. You're doing just fine," Ciaran said firmly, nodding at his son to continue.

"Before Gray and I...before we made a go of things, I slept with a client's wife in London. She and her husband have an open relationship. He's a very old, extremely wealthy man, and Marie is only in her late thirties.

"They're Russian, and I admit that I enjoyed speaking to Marie in my native tongue after we concluded business. She asked me to join her in her hotel suite for sex, and I did."

Lochlann choked, and her mom scolded, "Ciar, there are children present." To which Gray's red-faced brother replied, "I'm not a child anymore, Mom, Jesus." Her father patted his wife's hand, "He knows about such things, babe, and has since he was thirteen. Remember, I told you."

"Without my consent," her mom growled, "and clearly you didn't stop with the birds and the bees. The absolute hell is that about, Thomas?"

Gray's dad grasped her mother's waist and sat her back in her chair, saying, "Might we discuss this later?"

Her mom clenched her teeth but nodded once, sitting back down, not before she looked at Ciar and said, "Keep it PG, or you'll leave this house limping and not because I kicked your shin."

If nothing else, some of the room's tension dissipated. "Of course," Ciar said solemnly. "Anyway, Marie and I spent the evening...together. The first time I heard that she was pregnant was the day after we got back from Colorado."

He was back to speaking only to Gray, and she felt her face flush with the beginning of anger and jealousy.

"Marie's husband had called my boss, Anders, and told him that I'd gotten his wife pregnant, and either I fixed the situation or we would lose them as a client. Anders and I made millions off Marie's husband, but that's not why I stepped up. Wait," he smacked one of his fists into the opposite palm, "I'm jumping ahead again.

"Marie had told Anders that I was definitely the father, but I knew that was unlikely because I used...took precautions," he amended, glancing her mother's direction.

"Jesus, Mom, way to make this conversation more awkward," her brother groused. "Do you think that I've no clue as to how a baby got in my sister's belly?"

Her mom blushed fiercely, giving her father a stern look, to which he leaned over and kissed her. She sighed when he sat back and shrugged, conceding the battle to her husband for now.

Witnessing the exchange, Ciar scrubbed his face briefly, probably trying not to grin before continuing with his story.

"I set up a lunch meeting with Marie. After we discussed the situation, she finally admitted that me being the father was unlikely. She'd hooked up with some good-looking, blond playboy passing through London at an exclusive sex club two weeks after our encounter. Apologies, Josephine," he broke eye contact with Gray to dip his head toward her mom.

"I did a DNA test. I was not Imogen's birth father. Marie was…what she was, but she did care for her child, just not enough to go against her husband or the lifestyle that she enjoyed. She said that she would give up all her rights if I adopted her baby.

"Her husband offered several million pounds for the child's care if I adopted her, which I accepted in Imogen's name, but that isn't why I did it.

"If I hadn't claimed Imogen, if I hadn't given her my name, Marie would have given her over to an adoption agency with no guarantee of her safety. That was," he closed his eyes and winced, before continuing with, "not something I could live with."

Gray was moved by Ciar's conviction, but she was even more confused by his secrecy. Surely, he would have known Gray would have understood. She couldn't help but ask, "Why didn't you just tell me? You had to know I would love Imogen. I do love your daughter. You didn't even give me a chance. You left me rejected and alone for months."

"I knew you would ask me why I felt compelled to adopt a child from a woman that I only had the shallowest connection with, and I didn't want to tell you."

"But you said it was because you didn't want to chance Imogen going to an unworthy home. How would I not have agreed to that?" Gray insisted. Ciar glanced quickly at his father before focusing back on her, making Gray wary of his answer. Again, she knew there was something she wasn't understanding.

"That's the other part of the story, or the beginning of it, I suppose. Dad hooked up with my mother one night after meeting her at a pub. She was Russian. Anna Morozova. Dad didn't know I was the result." Ciar turned to his father and grasped his father's shoulder, probably in comfort.

"Mama was a drug addict. She worked odd jobs and left me alone in whatever shared flat or hostel she could afford that week. I liked the hostels the best because I could raid the trash bins for food more easily than in flat complexes. She made enough money for her drugs with very little left for things like food or clothing for her son."

Gray's stomach cramped, not liking the turn in Ciar's recounting. This was not a happy ending story.

"I didn't go to school, and mama couldn't afford a television or books, so I was pretty ignorant when I was finally given to Dad."

Ciaran slammed his palm against the tabletop, shaking the glasses of water. "You were never ignorant. Never say such a thing again," he demanded.

Ciar sighed but nodded his agreement. "I was uneducated," he amended, "but there were a few neighbors that would let me sit in the hallway outside their flats and watch their televisions when I was older, and we had enough money for a real place to stay.

"I only spoke Russian, but I did pick up some English from whatever was playing. I also dug out old newspapers from bins on the street and would trace the letters. When Mama was sober, or soberer, she taught me to read and write, but only in Russian.

"I can't be sure, but Mama got worse when I was around four. We moved constantly, sleeping in alleys or under bridges.

"But things changed. Some of Mama's friends took a liking to me."

Gray felt bile rise in her throat. "No," she whispered, but Ciar didn't hear her, deep in his thoughts.

"Her boyfriends, which I realize now were her customers," he said, his jaw clenching at the omission, "offered her money or drugs if they could spend time with her son. She only told me she loved me before she left me with them. Her love meant pain. I learned that quick enough."

Gray stood so fast that the heavy wooden chair flipped backwards, crashing into the floor. "No, Ciar. Stop. You don't have to." Her hands covered her mouth in horror. Her eyes begged him to stop.

"It's okay, Gray. I need you to know who I am and how I became...me. From almost four years old to eight, Mama gave me to her friends to abuse for drugs. They never spoke Russian, so Mama's words were the only ones that I could understand.

"I love you, she would say before leaving me with a stranger, and while they hurt me, she would take the money and go get high."

Gray and her mother were sobbing quietly at this point. Ciaran, her father, and brother were stone-faced and furious.

"One night, I think it was my eighth birthday, because Mama filched a cookie from a Dublin open market and gave it to me and said, "Happy eighth birthday, Gavriil." I remember my body hurt everywhere. My privates were," he leaned his head back briefly, "sore, and my eyes were swollen, my lips split.

"I remember being so thankful for that stolen cookie, though. I'd seen birthday parties on television, the wrapped presents and the cake and candles. That cookie was as close as I ever got to what I thought a party must be like. I imagined it was like opening a present. I never ate it, just stuffed it in my pocket to take out and look at.

"It was late, and Mama was taking me down busy streets toward one lined with pubs. The music was playing loudly in a few of them. I remember the beat of drums felt heavy against my bony chest.

"Mama stopped outside a pub that was busier than the rest. Through the glass I could see people drinking and dancing and laughing. I couldn't remember ever laughing like that. Maybe when I was really little.

"Before I turned four.

"Mama kneeled on the pavement outside the packed pub—I know now that it was Murphy's, Dad's—and she used a diaper pin to attach a note to the collar of my stained t-shirt. I remember being so ashamed of how dirty I was.

"She kissed my cheek and told me that she loved me. She told me to go inside, that my father was waiting for me. She said she couldn't take care of me anymore.

"The note had my name, Gavriil Morozova, and that I was Ciaran Murphy's son. A patron found me wandering through the lively crowd and took me to the kitchen, where my dad was working at the time."

Gray watched as Ciaran stood and clasped Ciar's hands to his chest. "The best night of my fucking life, boy."

"Mine too. I didn't understand a word you said to me, but I instinctively knew you were good. Safe. Dad took me in, even though he didn't know if Mama's claims that he was my father were true. He asked one of his Russian customers to translate, so I knew that Dad wanted to take me to a hospital. That's when," he hesitated, "Dad found out about the abuse."

Gray forced herself not to wail and scream from the pain beating against her chest. If Ciar was brave enough to speak of his abuse, she'd damn well be brave enough to listen.

"He had a DNA test done that proved he was my biological father, though he said he would have kept me regardless."

"Damn right, I would have," Ciaran cut in.

Ciar smiled at his father before turning back to Gray. "I never saw my mother again. Police showed up not long after I moved in with Dad to say that Anna Morozova was dead. She was found in someone's basement with a needle still in her arm. Dad had already spoken to the hospital staff, the police, and a solicitor, so they knew where I was.

"Dad got me tutors to teach me English and everything else I didn't have a clue about. He got me medical care and counselors—though I suppose they never were able to absolve me of my shame, of feeling emasculated. Less than. Dad gave me a new first name, Ciar, because it was part of his own name, and Gavriil became my middle name.

"I met Daniel and Jonathan when I turned nine, when Dad gave me my first birthday party. They were a few years younger than me, but they became my first friends." He looked over his shoulder and grinned at his father.

"You and those wee O'Faolain shits snuck some Guinness, and you puked your damn guts all over the floor."

Gray smiled softly. Ciaran still sounded pissed.

"I met you, Gray, and Mags, Blair, and Bébhinn when you were but little things. But you grew up, and I wanted you to be mine. I think I hesitated because I knew it would eventually come to this. My biggest fear has always been losing you, and even without telling you my history, I managed to do just that.

"I was too much of a coward to tell you about Imogen and why I wouldn't, or couldn't, walk away. What if she were given to someone like my mother or the men she sold me to?

"I pictured myself telling you a million or more times why I adopted Imogen, but the words would freeze each time. How could you want a man who had begun his life in such a dirty, filthy way?"

Gray refused to stay seated another second and went to Ciar, hugging him tightly, their son settled between them. He sighed above her head, cupping her head and gently bringing her cheek to rest against his chest.

"I named her Imogen because it was your middle name, and my dream was that you would adopt her and become her real mother. Imogen's middle name is Alya, the name of my Mama's younger sister.

"Alya visited Mama and me a few times, and those were the brightest moments of my childhood. She knew her sister had issues, but she didn't know about the abuse or that I wasn't in school. Because of finances, she wasn't able to come in those last years.

"I tracked Alya down, and she and her twin daughters came to Dublin and are staying with Dad. It was, I suppose, not healing exactly, but it was nice to hear stories of Mama before the drugs."

Gray asked the only thing she could manage. "You thought I wouldn't want you if I knew about your childhood?" Her voice was thick with tears and disbelief.

"Dad made me do therapy for years, but that feeling like I'm dirty, unworthy—it's a hard thing to let go of. You didn't sign up for all my baggage, or Imogen, or any of it. It was easier to let you hate me for a deserter than to risk the truth."

"I would never have turned my back on you. I wouldn't then, and I won't now. You're all I've ever wanted. I'm wrecked that you had to go through so many horrible things, Ciar. I thought you were strong before, but now I'm humbled at how truly formidable you are." She leaned her head back and kissed him softly.

"Do you believe me?" Gray asked.

Ciar chuckled. "I don't think it's quite hit me yet that I finally told you and you're in my arms again."

Her family stood, and Gray's dad interrupted, asking, "Do you love my daughter, Murphy?"

Her dad's eyes were red-rimmed with emotion, but he honored Ciar by not treating him like he was broken. Thomas MacGregor spoke in a growling voice, and his eyes never wavered from Ciar's.

"According to Jo, you've never told her. Seems strange when you claim to want to be a family with her."

Gray felt the breath leave her body in one long exhale and felt her body stiffen against Ciar's body. She tried to move out of his arms, but they tightened insistently.

"Please stay, Gray," Ciar said, his voice roughened.

He'd been through it today, had opened up to her and her family about the deepest scars on his heart, she didn't want him put on the spot about her.

"Dad, enough, please."

"It's okay, baby," he whispered in her ear. "He has every right to ask after what I've put you through."

Ciar loosened his arms enough to take her hands and hold them above her belly. "I do know what love is, I suppose, so I can't use that as an excuse. I love Dad, and he loves me. If it comes to it, I would say I love our friends, though two weeks ago I would have said I only cared for them deeply.

"That was the bullshit I tried with you. I think," he stopped and closed his eyes and shook his head before continuing, "I think Mama broke something in me for years where I couldn't bear to hear the words spoken to me, let alone repeat them. But I wanted them. I know that.

"I love you meant pain and abandonment. You've said those words to me before, and I let you down. I never wanted you to leave me, so I didn't acknowledge them.

"In my bid to become a better man for you, and a father for our children, I realized that I had to take a chance that you do, in fact, love me as I love you. I hope you still love me, anyway," he added sheepishly.

"I've loved you since I was sixteen, you jackass. Glad to see you're finally catching up."

"I love you, and," he pulled their joined hands to kiss her knuckles, "I came prepared in case you didn't run."

Gray watched with increasing disbelief as he produced a ring from his pocket and shoved it in her face. Gray had to use his wrist to move it back far enough to see it properly. He blushed adorably and apologized.

"Sorry, I'm nervous. Your father got your mother gray diamonds, and I wanted to do the same."

Gray gasped as she realized that it was a simple yet stunning thin white gold band with gray diamonds surrounding it. "An eternity band," she breathed.

"Yes, because that's how long I'll love you. Will you marry me, Gray Imogen MacGregor?" He quickly added, "I would have asked your father for permission, but I knew the stubborn bastard wouldn't give it unless he saw for himself what you mean to me."

Gray and Ciar both looked toward her father, who shook his head and pulled her mother tight to his side. "I hoped you would deserve my daughter, and you do. I'm proud to have you in our family."

Ciar looked at Gray again. "Well?"

She was still reeling from Ciar's story and feeling extraordinarily lucky to love and be loved by such a strong man. "Of course, yes." She bit her lip to stop more tears from falling. "You've made me so happy," she whispered as he slipped the ring on her finger.

"I want to get married next week. You've always told your

friends that you wanted something simple with a grand reception. Let's get married before our son—"

"Colm Gavriil," she interrupted. She'd been tossing Colm around for weeks, but when she heard Ciar's original name, his Russian name, she knew.

Ciar's jaw clenched, but he nodded agreement. "Let's get married before Colm Gavriil Murphy arrives, and then your mom and Grandma Mary can plan a reception."

"Perfect," she practically squealed. He took her into his arms and gave her the sweetest kiss, not nearly long or deep enough, but considering their audience, perfect.

The kiss was everyone's cue to move. Animated congratulations and hugging, and kissing commenced. Ciaran hugged her and welcomed her to his family, saying he couldn't wait to call her a Murphy.

Perhaps one of the most poignant moments came when Lochlann approached Ciar, and instead of extending a hand to shake like Gray thought he intended, her brother wrapped his arms around her fiancé and squeezed him tight.

"I'm sorry I judged you wrongly," Loch said, his voice hoarse with emotion. "I'll be proud to call you my brother."

That sweet moment brought tears to her and her mom's eyes once more. Then Ciaran took Ciar by the shoulders and asked him how he was feeling. "Do you feel lighter for it, son?"

Gray watched Ciar's face closely. He nodded after a moment. "I feel lighter. Probably more than I ever have. I hated lying and keeping things from you, Gray."

Gray took his hand and made sure she had his complete attention. "You had every right to keep those things from me. Now that I know, now that I understand why you made certain decisions and why you struggled with being honest, there is complete forgiveness, Ciar. You are mine, and I am yours, and the sooner we are married, the sooner I can adopt Imogen."

Tears threatened Gray once again at the thought of being that sweet girl's mother.

"And in not so many years from now, our son will make us so proud playing for the Irish Rugby Union."

There was a beat of silence before Ciar's words registered. Ciaran whooped a cheer. Her dad...did not.

"Over my dead body, Murphy. Lochlann," her dad swung his gaze to his smirking son, "call Uncle Colly and Laith. This needs to be settled here and now."

"Neanderthals," her mom grumbled.

fifty-two

THOMAS MACGREGOR

IT WAS a hard thing for a man to watch his daughter grow up and marry, for them to trust another man besides their father—and this was his second time. Mirren, his oldest child, had been happily married for several years with a son of her own, and now Gray.

Gray was the mirror of her mother in appearance and her drive in work, but she'd always been just that little bit more reserved than her friends. She preferred to weather storms alone.

Like him.

He'd been crushed and trying desperately to hide it for months as he watched Gray's smile become forced, and the spark that was his daughter, diminish. She'd been hurting, and neither he nor Josephine could help her. He'd been satisfied knowing she could move home, that she'd known he'd wanted her to move home, and finally she had even though she was sad about it.

He'd almost given up hope on the Murphy boy. Josephine

told him that Ciar was a loving father to his daughter and that she still hoped he would make things right with Gray.

And he had. Ciar Murphy had pulled himself apart and bled out his most hurtful wounds in front of them to prove his love for Gray. Thomas didn't believe he could respect another man more.

It had been a sacrifice, and one Thomas would never take for granted.

He was standing in Dublin's grand City Hall next to Josephine and their son, and Ciaran and Cormac Murphy, watching Gray and Ciar exchange vows. Mirren and her husband, Finn, and their son were in the United States for a science competition that his grandson was competing in, and couldn't make it home in time.

Gray and Ciar decided they only wanted immediate family. No friends and no fuss.

The couple would celebrate with their large family and friend group after their son was born. Bébhinn O'Faolain—damn, but he missed her father, Hugh—and her mother, Rowan, were trying to talk Gray and Ciar into doing a double reception after Bébhinn and Dagr Griffiths' wedding.

If he had to wager, the Byrne sisters, Raven, River, and Rowan, who were best friends with his own wife, would get their way. He was happy to do anything that pleased the O'Faolains. That family still suffered from the loss of their patriarch, and if his daughter was happy with the arrangement, he was happy.

When the Registrar pronounced the couple wed, Thomas felt his eyes burn with unshed tears. Ciar gave Gray a soft, thankfully short kiss before the newlyweds turned to look at their family with wide grins.

Josephine's hand tightened in his grip and grinned at him, tears flowing freely from her beautiful gray eyes. Thomas remembered knowing that he was the luckiest man alive when she tied herself to him. He still felt that way.

He stepped forward and shook Ciar's hand and slapped him on the back before drawing Gray into a tight hug, kissing her head, and gently swiping away one of her happy tears.

"I'm married, Dad," she sighed.

"So I see," he replied gruffly, glancing at her husband before returning his focus. "You couldn't have chosen better."

Before she could pull out of his arms to hug her mother and brother, he added, "It's hard to let you go."

Gray gave him a strange look. "Why would you ever let me go, Dad? I never plan on letting you go."

The women in his life never ceased to surprise him. He could only nod at Gray's announcement as she was pulled into her mother's arms.

Family was a wonder. It was tears and laughter, heartbreak and healing, and everything in between.

fifty-three

CIAR

ANDERS' solicitor stood silently by the large center island in his and Gray's kitchen. He was the same man who had overseen Ciar's adoption of Imogen. Now, he was handing a pen to his wife—he got a thrill each time he thought of Gray as his wife— to sign her adoption papers.

No matter what it cost, Gray was adamant that she wanted to adopt Imogen before their son was born. It was a good thing because their family didn't think Gray would make it another week, let alone almost three.

Gray's brother called her huge every time he saw her, to which Gray pretended to be offended. Ciar didn't have any siblings, so who was he to judge? In reality, she looked like she had a flesh-colored basketball over her lower stomach.

Her friends said she only looked about six months gone. He'd only been around one pregnant woman before, and Marie was shorter than Gray and had gotten much rounder.

Today was merely a formality. No one could deny that Gray

was Imogen's mother with or without the court's consent. She loved their baby girl fiercely.

Gray was reading over the document, but must have felt his eyes on her, because she glanced his way, the pen hovering over the page. He knew what she saw. Need, lust, want, love. What she couldn't see was that Ciar planned to strip her bare and stand her naked before the tall living room windows and take her from behind while her breath fogged up the glass the minute they were alone.

Gray blushed, and she bit her lip as she returned to the document. Satisfied, she signed her name and pushed the papers across the counter.

"Congratulations, Mrs. Murphy," the solicitor offered while repacking his bag. "I'll get this filed with the court immediately."

Ciar rounded the counter to walk the man out, but when Gray started to follow, he whispered in her ear as he passed. "No. I'll go. I want you naked and standing by that bank of windows before I get back."

"Ciar—"

She began to protest, still modest about her body. He was having none of that. "I need you," he growled. "Do what I say, baby."

Ciar gritted his teeth when Mr. Lenton became chatty all of a sudden, deciding right then was the perfect moment to discuss some business contracts he'd be filing soon for one of Ciar's clients.

Picturing Gray naked with sunlight highlighting her perfect body, he jumped in when Lenton paused to take a breath. "Email me when you get back to your office, and I'll look them over." One more handshake and a nudge out the door, and finally, he had Gray to himself.

Tina and Imogen were visiting his dad and Aunt Alya at

Murphy's Pub. He glanced at his watch and smiled. They had one hour until mommy-daddy duty resumed, and he planned on using every minute.

He fully expected to round the corner and find Gray still standing in the kitchen, but his eyes were drawn to the stunning woman standing in the waning sunbeams at the window, back turned toward him.

His mouth went dry, and his dick went hard at the vision. Her beautiful back was partially covered by the golden waves of her hair, and her perfect ass and long legs brought saliva rushing back to his mouth.

She heard him approach and slowly turned. He stopped two steps before her. "You are so beautiful, Gray. So beautiful, you take my breath." She only blinked, her eyes hooded. Lucky for him, pregnancy made his wife insatiable, but he was up to the challenge of satisfying her needs.

He grinned, slowly stripping out of his clothes, revealing his body to her voracious stare until he was as naked as she was. Stepping closer, he lightly traced her lips, which parted on a gasp, then dragged a fingertip down her chin to her throat. Her collarbones were delicate and lovely, so he traced those too.

Her breasts were heavier and fuller since pregnancy, mouthwateringly so. He dipped his finger down the center of her chest, brushing against the sides of her breasts, drawing circles around each globe but staying just outside her areolas.

Soon, Gray's nipples were stiff peaks, and her breaths were coming in short pants. "Ciar," she begged.

Usually, he would draw out the anticipation, but his need was hers tenfold. He flicked and rolled one peak while laving the other with his hot tongue. Gray grasped his head and held him in place, moaning and begging for more. Her hips were bucking, and she'd found purchase for her center against his thigh that he'd pressed between her legs.

As Ciar sucked and played at her chest, he backed his leg away and slipped his fingers over her sex, gauging how ready she was, whether she could take him. He was hard and leaking, and so turned on his eyes could barely focus.

He sighed in pleasure. His fingers found her hot and wet as he moved them up her channel. She immediately squeezed, rocking and pumping herself over them.

"More, Ciar. Please," she begged.

He pulled from her and watched her eyes dilate as he sucked his fingers into his mouth, licking them clean.

"Turn around and place your hands on the glass. Legs wide." The sun was setting, but there was still an orange glow highlighting Gray's shape as she turned and got into position.

Ciar gave her ass one sharp slap. She yelped but lengthened her arms enough to push her ass further in the air. "You have no idea how crazy your body makes me."

He stepped close enough until she could feel his length against her spine. Gray moaned and shimmied her back, rubbing against him like a cat begging to be petted.

Taking himself in hand, he leaned back enough to position his sex between her legs, rubbing its head up and down her slick seam.

"Can't wait," he breathed against her neck.

"Thank God," was her husky reply.

Finally, he allowed himself to line up at the very center of her heat and push. "Fuck me," he groaned, "nothing better than this, baby."

He slid shallowly in and out until her body was primed and ready to take all of him. He pumped slowly, wanting to make it last, but eventually Gray pushed back, meeting his thrusts with thrusts of her own.

He could feel her body start to quiver and reached one hand to her front, pressing his palm firmly to her mound and rubbing back and forth until her orgasm broke and her walls started pulsing tightly around him.

He couldn't withstand the onslaught and, with a roar, came furiously, joining her in euphoria.

"I love you," he panted above her.

fifty-four

GRAY

GRAY AND CIAR decided to walk the few blocks to Gray Eyes that evening. They were meeting their friends for dinner to celebrate Imogen's final adoption.

They were running late. Initially, because Tina and Imogen had gotten home and their daughter insisted on lots of love and attention. Not that she and Ciar wanted or even tried to resist.

By the time Imogen had finished her dinner and got ready for bed, they'd barely managed showers for themselves before heading out, which led to the second reason they were running late.

Heat suffused her cheeks when she remembered Ciar getting into the shower with her. He'd already been fully hard.

"I need you again," he'd groaned while stroking his length.

Those four words were all she'd needed to hear to capitulate and open her body. Her need for him was as fierce and driving as his own. She couldn't even blame it on hormones. She'd always wanted Ciar desperately.

He'd sat on the large teak bench and pulled her slippery

body onto his lap until she straddled him, her belly pressing against his erection.

Ciar had touched her then, every slow stroke of his hands up and down her back, her stomach and breasts, ass and thighs, left her moaning and compliant. Her husband was as meticulously thorough at sex as he was in every aspect of his life.

His tattooed hands contrasted with her smooth, white skin, and had Gray leaning into his body, arching her back for more. When he gripped her hips and lifted her above his sex, she might have shouted at how good it felt when he let her body slide down him. She'd been helpless to do anything but take what he offered.

After climaxes ripped through their bodies, Gray had bent her head and whispered in Russian, "You are my heart. Forever."

Ciar tightened his arm around her shoulders as Gray Eyes came into view, clearly also thinking about their shower. "I can't believe you never told me you spoke Russian."

Gray snorted in amusement. In his shock, he'd stood in the shower, keeping them connected as he stared in disbelief.

"And let you know how obsessed I was with you. No thanks. Plus," she admitted, rolling her eyes, "I'm nowhere near as good as you and your Aunt Alya, of course."

"The hell you aren't," he disagreed. "That old Russian woman has you speaking like a native."

While they dressed, she'd told him how she'd come to learn Russian while he begged her to keep speaking in the language.

Before they reached the front door of the pub, she placed a hand on his chest and stopped them. "You mentioned that part of the reason you spent the evening with Marie was that you enjoyed the nostalgia of conversing with someone in your mother tongue.

"I know you have more bad memories of your childhood

than any one person should have to endure, but," she had to swallow her tears so they wouldn't fall, "I want you to know that you can speak to me in Russian any time you feel like it."

He wrapped his arms around her waist and cleared his throat. "I would like that. Thank you for this, Gray."

"I also thought we might teach our children."

He leaned in to kiss her cheeks. "I'm the luckiest man in the world. Truly. You've given me everything."

"Well, you've given me your heart and two children. I'm feeling pretty damn lucky myself. Now," she started, moving them toward the doorman, "we'd better get inside before our friends ask us why we're late."

Ciar smirked. "The guys won't need to ask. No man looks this relaxed unless they've just finished coming inside a woman."

"Men are animals."

Dinner was loud and obnoxious and completely amazing. Even Blair made it since she was back in town from Wales to meet with her professors.

Many of the staff remembered Gray from their training and were excited to see the owner in house. If Gray didn't have such an upset stomach, the night would be perfect.

She surreptitiously massaged her belly under the table in an attempt to alleviate some of the discomfort, to no avail. She didn't tell Ciar she wasn't feeling great because he would immediately put an end to the evening, and since their group nights out were becoming less frequent, she didn't want to ruin the fun. Her stomachache was likely just gas—nothing ruins romance faster than talking about trapped farts with your partner.

Blair caught Gray's attention and asked her if she was feeling okay. Conversation died immediately, all eyes now focused on Gray. Blair flinched and mouthed, "Sorry."

"Gray?" Ciar turned in his chair and began running his hands all over her body.

Was he looking for an open wound? Gray brushed his hands off, assuring him she was fine. Mags piped up, stating, "I think you've had your hands on Gray enough this evening already, Ciar. You know sex can bring on labor, right?"

"Shut up, Mags," Gray said, throwing a napkin at her friend. "I'm weeks away. Also, I don't recall you being in our home earlier, Miss Know-It-All."

"I didn't need to be there, Mrs. Prude," Mags smirked. "Everyone at this table with a wiener was all but high-fiving your husband. Dagr even went in for knuckles, for crying out loud."

"Oh my God, Dagr," Bébhinn elbowed her fiancé, who only laughed.

Gray turned to Ciar, who was sitting back in his chair, looking smug. She shook her head but couldn't help the smile that stretched her cheeks. "I'll never understand men."

"You understood me just fine earlier. Twice," he chuckled and leaned to the side to miss her batting him in the chest.

Gray laughed and relaxed back into her chair only to have the worst cramp of the night squeeze her entire belly. She couldn't hold back the moan as she bent over the contracted mound.

"Oh shit," she heard one of the guys swear.

Ciar was on his knees and in her face instantly. His hands were shaking when he clasped her forearms. "Gray. Baby. Christ, Gray. Is it time?"

The pain eased, and she was able to sit straight again. "I

doubt it. Honestly." Even if she was beginning to suspect the discomfort wasn't trapped gas after all.

Mags stood and walked to her side of the table, giving orders as she went. "Daniel, call your mom and have her call Josephine. Just in case this isn't a false alarm, she'll want to be here. Jonathan, call an Uber. When the car gets here, you and Daniel ride with Ciar and Gray to the hospital."

When Mags stood next to Ciar, she placed a hand on his shoulder. "Get a grip, Ciar. It's probably not the real thing."

Except Gray's body appeared to disagree with her assessment, and another pain ripped through her abdomen, forcing another moan from her.

"Forget what I said. Carry your wife to the front, you moron. How long for the car?" Mags barked at Jonathan.

"Two minutes."

"Dagr," Bébhinn started, standing now too, "call an Uber for us. You, me, Mags, and Blair can go to Gray's and grab her hospital bag. We'll also need to let Tina know."

Gray's pain eased enough for her to say, "Tina and I decided that she and Imogen would come to the hospital after the birth, but she will want you to let her know. Thank you, guys."

Ciar was still frozen at her feet. He looked stunned. "Ciar," she gently urged. "The car will be here."

"I'm sorry, Gray. Christ. Did I do this?"

Her badass husband was near tears, and she just about melted then at how much she loved him. "Your penis is magical, babe," Gray assured, patting his cheek. "Best you don't let your ego inflate more than it has, or we won't fit in the hospital room."

"Right!" Her head spun as Ciar jumped to his feet, then lifted her in his arms and rushed to the entrance, amid clapping and whistles from the patrons.

The car ride wasn't the funnest experience Gray had ever

participated in. Her contractions—she'd finally admitted they were, in fact, contractions and not gas—were riding her hard.

"Ninety seconds," Jonathan shouted, unnecessarily loud in the small car.

"Why do you keep barking out fucking numbers like an idiot?" Daniel complained.

"Mom told me to track Gray's contractions and report in. Our dads would kick my ass if I disappointed the Holy Trinity," Jonathan quipped.

In between contractions, Gray was able to snort her amusement. Sometimes, the Byrne sisters were referred to as the Holy Trinity. Never out of disrespect to the Church, but in reference to how the O'Faolain men worshipped the sisters.

Well, not Rowan anymore. "Damn it," Gray whispered. Now wasn't the time to think of Hugh O'Faolain's passing.

Gray kissed Ciar, who was holding her across his lap and looking close to tears. "I love you, Ciar. Your son clearly set a different due date for himself. Stop worrying."

His response was to clench his jaw and use the shirt at his shoulder to pat aggressively at his eyes.

"For me, Ciar. You're the strongest man I know, and I need that strength for myself now. Tell me you love me and that you have this."

Ciar tipped his head back and took a deep breath. His arms banded tighter around her body just as another contraction took her. As she moaned, he leaned close. "I love you, and we definitely have this."

fifty-five

CIAR

"WE DID GOOD." Ciar could barely choke the words out as he watched the love of his life cradle their newborn son against her chest.

She'd been so brave, from Gray Eyes to the delivery room, his wife was the most fearless woman he'd ever known.

Labor progressed quickly, and from their admittance to delivery, only twenty minutes had passed.

"Three weeks early and eight pounds two ounces," Gray said, staring at their son's face.

Colm Gavriil.

"Turns out, my penis is magic. Three more weeks and your lady parts would have really been in trouble."

"Asshole," she muttered, tipping her chin up so that he could kiss her. "If I so much as hear any stories about the birth of our son and your bits and bobs—you'll suffer, Murphy."

Ciar chuckled, but soon enough, he felt tears stinging his eyes. "We have a family, Gray. We made this family."

A year ago...well, a year ago, he was still hiding behind his trauma. Now, he was proud to call himself a father. A husband.

Gray's eyes started leaking tears over their son's forehead. She bit her lip, wiping the evidence from the head of their baby. "I'm so proud of you, Ciar. I don't think there are enough days in a year to tell you how proud I am of you, of being your wife, the mother of your children."

He traced Gray's jawline and then Colm's, more precious than gold. He prayed Anna Morozova was at peace, that she no longer lived by regrets but spent her afterlife protecting children, as she couldn't do for her own son.

His life restarted with his father's first hug, but his life truly began when he held one woman in his arms.

"Gray."

fifty-six

THE RECEPTION OF MR. & MRS. DAGR GRIFFITHS AND MR. & MRS. CIAR MURPHY

MAGS

IT WAS A GORGEOUS, sunny day at Three Wolves Distillery, but even the property's rolling green hills, lush lawns, and sumptuous flowers paled in comparison to watching one of her best friends get married. Mags could still feel one or two stray tears trying to fall. She took a moment to gather her composure, leaning against her friend and cousin, Blair, while surreptitiously dabbing at her eyes.

The priest had done a lovely job. The ceremony was short and sweet at Bébhinn and Dagr's request. All the guests present sighed in relief. Having a dreadfully long Catholic wedding shortened into a compact study of love and commitment— many prayers were granted.

Blair nudged Mags' side and signed, "Bébhinn has to be the most beautiful bride, and look at Gray, strutting around with two children in her arms, looking like a supermodel instead of a woman who was only pregnant weeks ago."

Mags sighed, watching Bébhinn and Gray grinning and

laughing easily with family and friends. Dagr and Ciar rarely took their gazes from their wives.

"I know we're young, but do you ever feel like we're being left behind?" Blair asked, leaning more heavily against Mags' side.

This, coming from one of the smartest humans in the world, had Mags shaking her head in exasperation. "Stop being dumb. Our time will come when it's supposed to and clearly when you and I are both in the middle of making ourselves famous, now isn't the time."

Chuckling, they straightened. Best friend duties wouldn't wait for pity parties, even short ones. Curling her arm through Blair's, she made sure her friend was looking at her so Mags didn't have to sign. An unfortunate side effect of so many of their friends and family knowing BSL was that it was way too easy for them to be nosy.

"Let's go find some hot guys to hang off of and rile our dads up. Well, your dad, anyway, mine is way too chill, thank God." She would rather be dragged over hot coals before admitting that her dad wasn't who she hoped to piss off.

Blair grinned. Her inner naughty sprite didn't come out to play often, but when it did, Mags was all for making the most of it.

"I noticed Dagr invited a few of his friends from London—a few very hot friends from London," she added and winked.

"Let the games begin," Mags chuckled.

Mags was careful not to allow her smile to slip. She'd been given devastating news the night before, and pretending like her world wasn't imploding was paramount to survival at this point.

Mags and Blair laughed and danced, ate, and consumed Three Wolves in all its versatile glory.

They each found handsome arm candy. The men in their

families reacted in their usual overprotective ways. Blair seemed to be in the same "zero shits" state of mind that was Mags' mantra because they enjoyed the hell out of the attention while ignoring the frowners.

There had been a moment, a brief moment, where the man whose attention she hoped to catch had looked furious. It might have been a trick of the light, hopeful disillusionment, but there did seem to be a moment when her group strolled close to his.

Mags had been laughing at a joke by the man whose arm she was holding—she would have sworn rage crossed his otherwise unflappable face.

Good. She hoped he choked on his feelings because God knew that she'd done nothing but swallow hurt for years.

Shaking her head, Mags reminded herself that she had more vital wounds to compress. Playtime was over, and at twenty years old, it was time to put aside childish hopes and whimsy.

Goodbye, Jonathan.

also by anne gregor

Irish Wolves Legacy

Irish Goodbye

Irish Breath

The Scottish Lions

Josephine

Catriona

Mirren

The Irish Wolves Trilogy

Raven

River

Rowan

Anne Gregor has a Master of Arts in History with a Civil War emphasis. For her thesis, she focused on Irish immigrants working the transcontinental railroad across America, specifically those who settled in Oklahoma amongst Native Americans. A love for research turned into a love for fictional writing, and soon, every old document Anne studied became the premise for a novel. Though Oklahoma remains near and dear to her heart as she lives on Grand Lake O' the Cherokees, she enjoys traveling the world with her characters. **Anne is the author of three contemporary romance series, The Irish Wolves, The Scottish Lions, and Irish Wolves Legacy.**

A small press bound by the belief that every voice matters.

Sign up for our newsletter to learn about new releases and more.
https://oliver-heberbooks.com/subscribe/

Follow us on social media:

facebook.com/oliverheberbooks

instagram.com/oliverheberbooks

amazon.com/oliverheberbooks

youtube.com/@OliverHeberBooksPublisher